THE AUT...

Raymond Williams was born in 1921 in the Welsh border village of Pandy, and was educated at the village school, at Abergavenny Grammar School, and at Trinity College, Cambridge. After serving in the war as an anti-tank captain, he became an adult education tutor in the Oxford University Delegacy for Extra-Mural Studies. In 1947 he was an editor of *Politics and Letters,* and in the 1960s was general editor of the *New Thinker's Library.* He was elected Fellow of Jesus College, Cambridge, in 1961 and was later appointed University Professor of Drama.

His books include *Culture and Society* (1958), *The Long Revolution* (1961) and its sequel *Towards 2000* (1983); *Communications* (1962) and *Television: Technology and Cultural Form* (1974); *Drama in Performance* (1954), *Modern Tragedy* (1966) and *Drama from Ibsen to Brecht* (1968); *The English Novel from Dickens to Lawrence* (1970), *Orwell* (1971) and *The Country and the City* (1973); *Politics and Letters* (interviews) (1979) and *Problems in Materialism and Culture* (selected essays) (1980); and four novels – the Welsh trilogy of *Border Country* (1960), *Second Generation* (1964) and *The Fight for Manod* (1979), and *The Volunteers* (1978). He is now at work on two more novels, *Loyalties* and *People of the Black Mountains.*

Raymond Williams was married in 1942, has three children, and divides his time between Saffron Walden, near Cambridge, and Wales.

THE FIGHT FOR MANOD

Raymond Williams

THE HOGARTH PRESS

LONDON

Published in 1988 by
The Hogarth Press
30 Bedford Square, London WC1B 3RP

First published in Great Britain by Chatto & Windus 1979
Hogarth edition offset from original Chatto edition
Copyright © Raymond Williams 1979

All rights reserved. No part of this publication may be reproduced, stored in a
retrieval system, or transmitted in any form, or by any means, electronic,
mechanical, photocopying, recording or otherwise, without the prior
permission of the publisher.

British Library Cataloguing in Publication Data

Williams, Raymond
The fight for Manod.
I. Title
823'.914 [F]   PR6073.14329
ISBN 0-7012-0809-0

Printed in Great Britain by
Cox & Wyman Ltd
Reading, Berkshire

I

1. THE telephone rang, with a conventional urgency. He lifted it abruptly, still looking at his work.

'Price.'

He had learned the convention.

But then a girl's voice, light, uninquiring.

'Is that Dr Price?'

'Yes, speaking.'

'Dr Matthew Price?'

'Yes.'

'Hold on, please, I've a call for you.'

He looked back to the desk, to his unfinished calculation. But he went on holding the receiver. There was the sound of a room at the other end of the line: a background of unknown voices, a typewriter, another phone ringing. He heard that phone being answered, somewhere within that unknown and continuing life.

'Yes?'

'Your call for Dr Price.'

'Who was it called him?'

'It was from your extension. Dr Matthew Price.'

'Hold on. I'll find out.'

Footsteps away from that phone. Then a voice at some distance, moving away across the room.

'There's a call for a Dr Price. Do you know who it is?'

'Dr Lane, I think.'

'Well, ask him, Joan, will you?'

A longer pause, with other voices in the background. A distant door slammed. He looked again at his work. He would not be kept from it. He put back the receiver.

It was several minutes before it rang again.

'Dr Price?'

'Yes.'

'We were cut off.'

'No. I hung up.'

'I see. Well, I'm sorry. But we have Dr Lane for you now.'

A man's voice cut through.

'Lane here.'

'Price.'

After the exchange of identities, the next convention: an adjustment of the voice, a quick move up the register, an injection and projection of engaging human speech.

'Dr Price, this is Robert Lane. We've not met, I'm afraid, but . . .'

'Robert Lane?'

'Yes, I used to be at Oxford.'

'I know. I've read your books.'

A sudden heavy breath, surprisingly loud on the line.

'You remind me, Dr Price, of my past. I've moved out of all that. Well temporarily, anyway. I'm at the Department of the Environment. Since our good government got in again.'

'I didn't know that. I'm sorry.'

'I'm not asking you to agree to the good government. There are several opinions on that. But I called you, particularly, because a problem's come up and I'd value your advice. Can I tell you about it? If I'm not interrupting you? And then we might meet, if you're at all interested.'

'I don't know. Yes.'

'Well, does the name of Manod mean anything to you?'

'Manod?'

'In the Afren valley. Welsh border country. Your part of the world, am I right?'

'Yes, I know that Manod, of course. It's about forty miles from where I grew up.'

'I was sure you'd know it. Up here, of course, it's not primarily a place. It's a name, a codesign, perhaps even a symbol.'

'I don't understand.'

'You don't remember the Manod development?'

'The city, you mean? But that was . . .'

'Yes, I know. It's eleven years, now, since it was first announced. When there was a whole choice, you remember, of new worlds. On paper.'

'It seemed a very serious idea.'

'You think so? I'm glad. Because it's been in and out of every department, council, committee, pigeonhole, until for all of us here it's not a city but a chaos.'

'Yes.'

'Well either way. I meant administratively. Like most other new worlds it's just a debris of yellowing paper.'

'I assumed that had happened. I read the opposition.'

8

'Did they convince you at all?'

'They made some real points. Though mainly about the past. But in any case . . .'

'I know. It could never have been easy. It reached a kind of deadlock, just from its own difficulties. Then for years it simply got lost: a change of Minister and then a change of Government. Like you, I expect, we all supposed it was forgotten. Just another new world indefinitely postponed.'

'Due to lack of interest, tomorrow has been cancelled.'

'Exactly. It's what they will say of us eventually. But now here's the strange thing. It would take too long to explain on the phone, but the point is that Manod's come up again, actively, by a rather unusual route. And since I have to give some advice, well—may I put it frankly?—I feel the need for a different mind. Somebody who's not been in on it yet who would know what it's about. I mean really about.'

'I see.'

'It seems very arbitrary, but the more I looked at it, the more I pencilled in your name. There are problems of course, and we'd have to discuss them. But if you were interested enough to come and have a talk about it. Or if only to tell me why you are not interested.'

'I see. Yes. But you don't have to ask me if I'm interested in Manod. It isn't a matter of choice.'

2. He stood on the island, looking along the street of the Ministries.

Buildings opaque from the street that are blind to the street. In the centre of the street stone men, cast men, metal horses. Stone helmeted features running with grime. An upraised stone arm, leading an empty charge. Power in stone.

A girl was waiting in the lobby for the visitor to arrive. A man of fifty-eight: you can only ask.

'Dr Price?'

'Yes.'

'I'm Joan Reynolds. Dr Lane asked me to look out for you. I'll take you along to his office.'

A man of fifty-eight. Tall, heavy-boned, with thinning dark hair. An old rough dark coat, like a porter's. A deep, broken voice, perhaps Welsh. A hard, set face, almost carved. Then the sudden break to mobility.

'It must be difficult for you. Recognizing people.'

'I suppose so. We get used to it. It's in the new block. We go up and over the bridge.'

'This is only the public face then? This opaque stone front?'

Beyond the wide staircase and the long narrow corridor a bridge spanned the yard to the new building: a lighted glass tower, glittering and dazzling.

'The new block is much more convenient. And warmer. But people lose their way to it. We have to come across.'

'Do you mind that?'

'No, not really.'

'When I was first rung up I heard someone speaking to you. In this office I didn't know there was a succession of voices and then I heard someone say: "Well ask him, Joan, will you?"'

'It's the switchboard. They're always . . .'

But then suddenly she laughed.

3. Robert Lane got up and shook hands. He said friend, friendliness, all over his short stocky body. You weren't bound to believe all he said.

Very thick greying hair. Soft pink clear skin. But fatigue in the eyes: grey and shrinking. Intelligent features seeming to come and go in a face blurred with overweight.

'We should have met before, Dr Price. I don't know why we haven't.'

Matthew took the hand and sat where he was put, in the leather chair by the window, with the wide view out over the miles of the city. Robert Lane stood over him, his voice like a hand on his shoulder.

'Your book impressed me very much, Dr Price. I believe I wrote and told you.'

'Yes, I remember. Thank you.'

'You didn't reply.'

'No. I'm sorry. I was nervous of patronage.'

Lane moved and sat at his desk.

'It took a long time, I expect?'

'Yes, very long. I keep being reminded it's the only thing I've done.'

'It took a long time because it had to be lived.'

Beyond the window there was a railway terminus: sidings, engine sheds, glass roofs over the platforms. Matthew looked at the signal-boxes: long rectangular brick buildings: each ten times

bigger than the little box in Glynmawr. Beyond the terminus the
land rose to what had once been a hill. The grey streets climbed,
brick and slate. There was a haze over them, under the wide sky.
Lights were coming on, in irregular patterns. In the fading day-
light a tower block was slowly losing its mass and becoming a
column of light.

'Just because it was a book on population movement it wasn't
only,' Lane said, 'the statistics. You had the statistics but you
turned them back into people.'

'I tried to.'

'We should have met before, at the beginning of this scheme.
It's not the same, of course, but it's the kind of thing you described. A human movement. The flow of actual men and their
families into the mining valleys. And now in Manod another
movement, a planned movement, into valleys as empty as those
valleys were before the coalrush started.'

'The planning now making the difference?'

'Making some of the difference. And the rest of it, Matthew,
we have to get clear.'

He stopped and lit his pipe. He looked intently at Matthew
through the thin screen of smoke.

'In a job like this . . .'

The pipe had gone out. He laid it impatiently aside.

'One doesn't get cynical, Matthew. It may look like that from
outside. But there's still a kind of numbness: a hard rut of hopes
deferred. A project begins with some clear human content. If we
had real power we would simply order it. But we can only
negotiate, through the long overlapping meetings. It becomes
more actual than any general social vision. But past a certain
point only the plan is real. Nothing directly human attaches to
it.'

Matthew shifted.

'You said, on the phone, you'd consulted almost everyone. But
that can't be true. In all the councils and committees, what, two
or three hundred people?'

'Representing,' Lane began, and then broke off and smiled.

'You're making what you think is a point against me.'

'Yes, that in that valley alone there are several thousand
people.'

'I took the point. But then that was just the reasoning that led
me to you.'

'To add one to three hundred?'

Lane smiled and re-lit his pipe.

'Yes, I wanted this stubbornness. But let me go over it. Manod started, I suppose, in the early sixties. The idea of new towns, and of regional development. These came together in several places and among them mid-Wales. The people there need it, they have to leave their homes to get jobs and even so there is chronically high unemployment. At the same time, in what used to be cities, now great sprawling and jammed conurbations, life is simply breaking down, will break down altogether in a measurable period, unless there is relief, moving work and homes to a better environment. So it seemed to fit, as an initial idea. It was the human need of many thousands of people, but they couldn't solve it individually. It could only be solved by some social decision, indeed by a planned and conscious development.'

On the hill beyond the terminus there was now only the network of lights. Far away, to the horizon, only the lines of the streets were visible, past the high lighted towers. Lane turned and looked where Matthew was looking.

'You're seeing Manod, perhaps?'

'I was wondering, yes.'

'No, whatever it may be it won't be like this. This is just layer after layer of muddle, money and dirt.'

'It looks very conscious to me.'

'But if so a past consciousness. Not of our own life and time. Anyway, as I was saying, Manod emerged. By the middle sixties it seemed easy to plan. A general idea got a local name. Along that valley, from Nantlais to Pontafren, we would build a new city. No smaller development would really stand up. Nantlais and Pontafren had asked for development, but just limited expansion, for their local needs. What could be done in either or both would be simply marginal. No significant body of work would be brought there, and without the work there is no real point. So a planning unit went down there. It was their report that was published. May I show you? I've got the map.'

They got up and went across to the facing wall. Lane lighted the map on the high glass screen.

'Begin at each end of the valley. Nantlais and Pontefren would expand to their limits: say twenty thousand in each. Then along the Afren, in a linked development, would be seven other centres. Manod's in the middle, that's how it gave its name. And because the Afren floods, and because in any case we don't want a ribbon along the banks of the river, the centres are set back on the higher

12

ground: hill-towns really, except St Dyfrog, which has a different role. Each of the centres would go up to ten thousand. Between each, as you see, at least four or five miles of quite open country, which would go on being farmed. So what you get, as a whole, is a city of a hundred, a hundred-and-twenty thousand people, but a city of small towns, a city of villages almost. A city settling into its country.'

'The descriptions are difficult.'

'Yes, of course, because it's so new. There isn't, anywhere, a city like this. But there could be, that's clear. All the detailed work has been done and costed, and there's no real doubt that it's viable.'

'Work, communications, roads, schools?'

Lane moved away from the map.

'If you go on with this, Matthew, you'll have more than enough of the details. It's about ten feet thick, just the technical studies. But they'll impress you, I guarantee that. Some very able people came in to work on it. The transport and communication technology is right at the frontier. The work–housing relation is also very advanced. If it ever gets built, and who knows about that, it will be one of the first human settlements, anywhere in the world, to have been conceived, from the beginning, in post-industrial terms and with a post-electronic technology. And then just think of it Matthew: a working city, an advanced working city, in that kind of country. With the river, the mountains, it would be a marvellous place.'

'But then the politics start.'

'You're right. The politics start.'

They moved back to their chairs by the window. Matthew was silent for some time.

'You say if I go on with it. Go on with what exactly?'

'Well, let me be frank. A year ago, when I came back here, I'd have said it was dead, stone-dead. The general situation, the shortage of money and so on, but also a kind of deadlock in the idea itself. A political deadlock, of course. What the local people still want is nothing so grand. They want small local developments, improving but not altering the kinds of place they've got used to. But then even for that they need money, and to get the money, frankly, means having to fit in with what other people want, which is planned dispersal on a big enough scale to make the investment economic. At the two extremes that's the basic problem: two quite different views of what needs to be done.'

'Yes.'

13

'The political papers are twenty feet thick. If you go on you can read them, though it's a lot to ask.'

'Go on with what? You still haven't explained.'

'I said I thought it was dead. And I had, God knows, enough other things to do. But now most unexpectedly Manod has come up again, and come up in what are called around here very powerful quarters. I'm not really at liberty to give you all the details, and I may not myself know them all. But I can assure you of this. It has come really alive again: suddenly, urgently alive. This happens all the time, in what they call the political process.'

'And you have to give an opinion?'

'Well, somebody has to. And the real trouble is, everything's happening at once. So that however alive and urgent it may be, nobody at all wants that formal process again. It would be another twenty feet thick and it would reach the same deadlock. And in the end, it's quite right, the government will have to decide. The information is all there; that isn't what's wanted.'

'It could be published perhaps? Get a general response?'

'Thirty feet thick?'

'The essential issues.'

'That will be done, of course. But not quite yet. My advice so far has been much more simple. That we should turn it back, from paper, to the human issue it began as.'

Matthew stayed silent.

'I wasn't flattering you, Matthew, when I described your book. I was trying to define just what you had done: to make a history human and yet still a history. And what I want with Manod, what I'm asking you to do, is to come to this fresh, to make it human again, to help us see it again as it is.'

'Going through the files?'

'Yes, you'd have, I'm afraid, to do that. But what I'm suggesting is a different inquiry: a lived inquiry. That you should go to Manod. That you should live there as long as you need—it could be anything up to a year. That you would go informed; you'd have every access. But that you would go as yourself. To the place, to the people. That you would live the problem. And then that you'd come back and tell us.'

'The three hundred and first.'

'Yes, perhaps, but having made the journey. Having come out of that country and now going back to it. Taking with you, in yourself, the two worlds you belong in. The two Manods.'

4. 'Did you get through the files?'

'I had a first look through.'

'You have my sympathy. Still at least you came back.'

'Yes.'

It was the middle of the morning, a week later. Matthew found Lane more harassed, less mannered, than at their first meeting. He had made his offer, and as part of that had encouraged discussion. But now, clearly, he wanted a simple reply.

'And have you made up your mind?'

'It's as you said. It's complicated. Very deeply complicated.'

Lane nodded understandingly. At the same time he looked at his watch.

'I'll be straight with you, Matthew. I could have chosen, couldn't I, a much easier man?'

'I don't know.'

'I do. They come in great numbers. They depend on us for work.'

'Perhaps a mutual dependence.'

'I was given authority to appoint two consultants. I've asked you and Peter Owen. Do you know Peter Owen?'

'He wrote *Industrial Estate*.'

'That's enough in itself. It's a marvellous book. And it's this problem exactly, from the other way of seeing it, in the existing cities and factories. So I've asked him, though the people I have to deal with, the permanent people, didn't like the idea at all.'

'The idea of consultants?'

'Oh no, that's quite normal. And they have, by the way, no objection whatever to you. It was a popular nomination. But Peter, well—his book was very open and angry. And then of course he got six months in prison, after a Vietnam riot. He has no job, no real status.'

'But he used to be your pupil.'

'He left that. He went to work on an assembly line.'

He looked again at his watch.

'So I don't have to stress it, Matthew. I'm not asking yesmen.'

'You're still doing the asking. Someone said yes to that.'

Lane got up and stood by the window. The outside light was reflected in the clear pink skin of his face.

'All right, you see me here in a government office. At some cost to yourself you've avoided the usual rackets. But when you look at me you say that's where rackets start.'

Matthew didn't reply. Lane raised his hand and pointed.

'I could tell you what made me come here. The work's much harder than Oxford. And I'm a democrat, a radical. I hate the guts of this system. But I learned one thing, that the only way to defeat a bureaucracy is to get inside the bureaucracy. To fight officials in offices. Committee men in committees. Not avoiding where they're entrenched, but going directly in on them. It's the only way if we're to get anything done.'

'Look, I'm not examining you. I'm not your inquisitor.'

'You have that effect. No, I'm sorry, I didn't mean that. I mean you tend to dominate, without doing or saying very much.'

'An idea, that's all.'

Lane sat again at his desk. He pulled his papers towards him but did not look down at them.

'With you, Matthew, I'm thinking about Manod. I'm asking you to think about it. You may see me as managing men and opinions. But it isn't that. I'm just pushing at inertia. You must know what we're up against. The old drift, the old dirt, of the industrial revolution. The new drift, the new indifference, brittleness, of this stage of capitalism. This frantic southeast, the London–Birmingham axis. And beyond it, its counterpart, the emptying country, the men without work, the communities dying.'

'Of course.'

'Somebody will make decisions, you can be sure of that. And it's to help towards good decisions that I'm inviting you to go.'

'Yes. And I must give you an answer. But first, if I may, a few practical questions.'

'That's what I'm here for.'

He bustled his papers. The movement brought his watch into view again.

'Well, first, I'd be allowed to say why I'd come there. I mean the people there, if they wanted, would know who I was and what I was doing.'

'Of course. No problem. That's entirely up to you.'

'I could only go if it was perfectly open.'

'Perfectly open. With the one limitation, of course, that some of the documents have to be kept confidential.'

'Which documents?'

'They're already classified. Minutes of some of the meetings. Some of the technical studies. But mainly, of course, the detailed land requirement studies. We have to sit on those to prevent speculation: people buying up the land.'

'The particular areas, you mean?'

'Yes.'

'But you've got them marked on the map.'

'Not on the public map. The outline of the centres has been published, but no usable details of just where they'd be.'

Matthew looked across at the high glass screen. The map was not lighted and he could see only a vague blur.

'Right. Then my own situation. I'd need leave of absence. I don't know if I could get it.'

Lane smiled.

'You're too modest, Matthew. Anyway let me tell you. After our first talk I rang your Principal. I explained, of course, that it was all still provisional, but he was very reasonable. If you want to go, you have a year's consultancy secondment. Even if you don't stay the full year.'

'I see.'

The phone rang and Lane answered it. Matthew hardly noticed. He had caught the familiar smell of a world of arrangements beyond him; of things happening, planned, brought about, without people even being told. He stared through the window at the railway yard, the office tower, the streets climbing the hill. By narrowing his eyes he could see the window and the city beyond it as a framed picture. It reminded him of the map on the opposite wall.

Lane put down the phone. He was now especially abrupt.

'Is there anything else then? I mean anything immediate?'

'Well yes. Two things. But they're difficult.'

'Shall we try?'

'You said the scheme had come up again by an unusual route. You said there were details—presumably details inside the government, inside your department—you weren't able to tell me.'

'Yes, and I'm sorry, but it's how these things happen. I didn't invent the system.'

'Of course. But you're asking me to give a year of my life. Its general importance is obvious: a year for that is nothing. But I want one assurance: that it isn't merely some political manoeuvre, with no serious intentions. That it isn't a political kite, on some other wind.'

Lane looked at him sharply, and hesitated.

'An assurance, that is,' Matthew said, 'that I shan't from the beginning be simply wasting people's time.'

Lane was still watching him. The grey eyes were very tired.

'Matthew, no. How can I possibly give you an assurance like that? It's not a thing that can be said, in any real world.'

'You mean it *is* a manoeuvre.'

'It may be. I don't know. So far as I'm concerned I can assure you that it's not.'

'But then . . .'

'No, Matthew. This is where I stick. You can take my word, an honest word but no more than my own, in a system so shifting, so complex, that to ask for more is a moral fantasy. A moralist's fantasy.'

Matthew got up, slowly. Lane's voice seemed to follow him.

'In any real activity there are so many motives. To abstain because of that would mean doing nothing at all.'

Matthew remained very still. He was standing awkwardly: the stiff heavy figure struggling to cancel movement. His eyes were very dark and withdrawn.

Lane spoke quietly.

'Your Principal said that you had not been well.'

Matthew didn't answer.

'I was very sorry to hear it. It was heart trouble, wasn't it?'

'Yes.'

'Well a year in the country, a year of a different kind of life.'

Matthew seemed not to be listening. When he spoke he went back to Lane's earlier point.

'I accept what you say about the assurance I asked for. And in the way you put it I'll take your personal word.'

'Good. That's settled, then.'

Lane got up as he spoke. He picked up a file.

'There was the second question.'

'Yes?' Lane said quickly.

He now openly looked at his watch.

'The difficulty, you say, is the two ideas of development: what mid-Wales needs but then what others need and will pay for.'

'Of course.'

'Then why ask me to go to Manod? To go only there? Shouldn't I go, also, where there's this other need?'

'But Matthew, you can go where you like. It's entirely up to you.'

'Maybe, but the dangers are obvious. The most likely outcome is not a city at all, but just the old overspill. An industrial estate

18

dumped down in mid-Wales. And then we would be looking at Manod just to see on what terms it could happen.'

'We've been through this, Matthew. And again I'd remind you of the people I've asked to advise us: you and Peter Owen. Overspill, dumping, an industrial estate: none of these, surely, would get past either of you.'

'Maybe, but we'd not be deciding.'

'Well you must accept that, surely. You'd be the first to say you have no right to decide. But advice, clarification, at a critical moment . . .'

'I've accepted that. All I'm saying, really, is that the problem, the need, has to be looked at both ways round: from both kinds of place.'

'Of course. Absolutely. And now you really must excuse me. I have a meeting I'm late for.'

Matthew stood aside. Lane walked towards the door.

'Peter's in Sweden, did I tell you, until early November? But he's said that then he'll get straight on to it. He'll come and see you first.'

'All right, I'll expect him.'

Lane touched Matthew's arm.

'What I wanted, from the start, was you both working on it. Different generations, different experiences, but wouldn't you say the same interests, the same values?'

'So far as I know, yes.'

Lane opened the door. The file he was carrying was prominent.

'The same language anyway, Matthew. Just as you and I have been able to talk.'

II

1. HE leaned to the pane and the screen of reflection dissolved. His eyes became used to what at first, past the curtain, was a cloud and cover of dark. He could see no stars and there was no visible moon, but he could begin to trace the skyline, far across the valley at Bryndu.

There was no sound, no light, across the whole of the valley. Yet slowly, as he looked from the window, the shape of the country seemed to come out of the darkness. He could see first the trees, along the line of the lane: the heavy black of the yew, the lower dark mound of the holly. In the faint bleaching mono-chrome of this light before dawn the trees were solid outlines: in their familiar shapes but without depth, as if they were metal cutouts. He could begin to see now the tower of the church, on its low mound, and the flat pyramid of the bellhouse: lines without detail. Every latent shape seemed to wait, to hesitate, before at last coming through as itself. The line of the lane was a loose grey shadow, slowly gathering direction. The wall from the school was a darker shadow, with what seemed below it a movement: a gathering of shadow into the humps of bramble and elder. He stared into the centre of each bush, looking for the familiar detail of twig and light, but there were only the same shapes, the patches of shadow. Every feature seemed not itself but the deepen-ing shadow of the disappearance of darkness.

It was only in knowing the country that he could see this far. When the first light came, and the colour seeped back, he would see the familiar country: the branches, the stones, the rooftiles, the great cleft of the watercourse. It would lie ordinary and quiet in the first minutes of the day: the mist of light out of sleep. But now there were only these growing outlines of shadow, in a world as yet without detail, without colour. He felt a certain awe, a certain coldness, as he continued to watch. What he saw in this country, which he believed he knew, was very deeply unfamiliar, a waiting strangeness, as if it was not yet known what world would come out of these shadows, what new world, that begins every day.

2. Manod stands on a plateau, almost hidden from below by its sheltering trees. Behind it, to the north, stretch the empty miles of Waunfawr, where the sheep graze on the springy turf, among the windswept acres of gorse and heather and whin. Below the village, to the west, is the steep winding valley of the Dowy, with a narrow road running north between loose stone walls to Llancadog. To the west again, beyond the Dowy, rise the successive long whaleback ridges, Frith and Cefn and Daren, and below them scattered meadows and pastures cleared to a thousand feet.

The Afren is broad, a slow brown water, below Manod. Where the tumbling Dowy, still breaking into white over its litter of stones, flows into the Afren, just two miles down from Manod, stand the village and old railway station of St Dyfrog. This is halfway along the great curve of the valley between the market towns of Pontafren and Nantlais. The broad river, the road into central Wales and the now closed and weedgrown line of the railway follow each other, crossing and recrossing, along the length of the valley. At St Dyfrog they run close, within a hundred yards.

Manod is still in many ways remote. It is reached by a loop of road, which runs from the narrow Llancadog road by the Dowy, up over the plateau, and then down again to the main valley road to Nantlais. From this loop road there is a further loop. Coming up from the Dowy, the ways divide by the old low timbered inn, the Evening Star. The road runs on along the edge of the plateau, through earth banks and high hedges of hazel and thorn. To the left, towards Waunfawr, runs the lane along which most of Manod is built, from Pentre Court, the farm near the entrance, past the school and the church and the other houses, past the mountain track to Pentwyn, to rejoin the loop of road half a mile farther on. The lane is poorly metalled and is torn near the entrance by the tractor from Pentre.

Few people now call the farm Pentre Court. The Vaughans who live there, Gwen and Ivor, have never done so. Its age and dignity are qualified by its ninety acres. The farmhouse is long and low, built in the local sandstone, a soft reddish brown, almost pink after rain. The roof is tiled, with spreading patches of orange lichen. High stone chimneys rise at each end of the ridge. The eight front windows are surprisingly large, each with twenty-four small panes; the bars, now, a gleaming white. There is a long barn along the lane, in the same stone as the house, and beyond it, from the yard, a large black wooden shed. Behind the house, and rising to more than twice its height, is a colony of larches, protecting the house and the yard.

Across the lane from the farm, and a little farther up, is the late nineteenth-century school and schoolhouse, grey and sharp-gabled, with a high classroom window set above the level of a look into the playground. The school has been closed for the last six years; the children go down to St Dyfrog. The former teacher, Mrs Jennings, a widow who came to the school in her thirties, still lives, retired, in the schoolhouse. The school itself is unoccupied but is used occasionally for parish meetings, whist drives and as a polling station. Across the lane from the playground, where the spear-headed railings are peeling with rust, are the Pentre cottages, which used to belong to the farm: bare and whitewashed, with slated roofs and white picket fences on the lane. Mrs Lewis whose husband used to work at Pentre lives in the west cottage. The other was empty for three years until the Prices rented it. A few yards up the lane, on the school side, there is the rough ivied wall of the churchyard, marked at its ends by a fine dark holly and with bramble and elder growing under it, along the wide grass verge. Beyond the wall are the lichened greystoned graves, under a tall heavy yew. The low tower of the church is at the western end, built into a mound which was a pre-Christian earthwork. It is capped by a wooden pyramid bell-house, its walls and timbers finished in black and white. The short nave and chancel were built in the fifteenth century, in the local stone, but this is now much greyer, its dust held in the thin rough claws of its ivy, than the warm reddish stone of the farm. There has been no vicar in Manod since the early nineteen-forties. The church is used, with four others, by the vicar of St Dyfrog, but notice has been posted that within the year it will be permanently closed. The fine eighteenth-century vicarage, considerably larger than the church, was bought from the patron family, Mortimer of Llancadog, by a St Dyfrog builder and agent, John Dance. He lives with his wife Juliet in this house beyond the churchyard, opening to the loop of road. They have the best view in Manod, on a southern slope to the sun, looking down directly into the green valley of the Afren and beyond it to Bryndu and the twin dark peaks of the Brothers.

Along the lane again, on the same side as the farm, is a low spreading redbrick bungalow, in a garden of paved paths and lawns, with rows of standard roses and a clump of pampas grass

22

by the ornamental wrought-iron gate. It is described as Long View, on a varnished and deckled wood sign with antique lettering. But it is generally known in Manod as The Bungalow. It was built by John Dance in the mid-fifties, for George Powell, a Birmingham ironmonger. Powell's wife, Dilys, was a Parry from Pentwyn, the small isolated farm two miles up on Waunfawr. It was built for their retirement, but they are still working, and it is lived in now by their daughter Mary Pearson, who moved from Birmingham after divorcing her husband. Her only friends in the village (though she will, undertake, on introduction, a little skilled dressmaking) are John and Juliet Dance, at the Old Vicarage.

There is open ground past the bungalow, and then the last houses. Fronheulog is a pair of square semi-detached villas, built in 1910 by John Dance's grandfather. They are in the local stone but with decorative timbered gables and facings of hard yellow brick around the windows and doors. Two pensioners live in them. Will Rees is a retired signalman from St Dyfrog. He was retired early, when the line was closed, and his wife died in the same year. His son has been away for more than twenty years, working in an engineering factory in West Bromwich. Mrs Celyn, next door, is nearly ninety, and is confined to the house. The square villas, with their two elderly inhabitants, stand facing the lane behind a yellow brick wall that is surmounted, at the gates, by stocky brick pillars capped with red pottery figures that might be acorns or pineapples. There is a Virginia creeper over the front of the houses, with a shadowed space cut into it, over Mrs Celyn's window, for the old board of the shop and post office.

Twenty yards farther on is the last house, in the corner of the track running up to Pentwyn. It is in white roughcast, with a high redbrick chimney. It has an angled ironwork porch at the central front door. It is called Cae Glas, and Trevor Jenkins lives there, with his wife Modlen. They are in their late twenties. Trevor is the youngest son of the farming family at the Bedwen, a mile below on the Llancadog road. He worked as a platelayer from St Dyfrog and then Nantlais, until the line was closed. He works now for his elder brother, Gethin, who lives alone at the Bedwen. Trevor has two acres behind the house, where he breeds ponies and pheasants. The house is bare and damp, without shelter from the winds.

From Pentre to Cae Glas, along the loop of lane past the church, is the centre of Manod. But for three miles, west, north and east, it is still Manod, with scattered farms and cottages, along the network of roads, lanes and tracks. These bring it, in the seventies, to fifty-eight inhabitants. A hundred years ago there were seventy-two. It is easily missed, from below, almost hidden by its trees. It is a place nobody comes to, without a specific reason.

3. Matthew opened the door from the boarded stairs. He looked across the living-room to the small curtained window. He went over and drew back the curtains and the pale morning light slowly gathered in the room, over the sharp scent of last night's fire. The heavy furniture kept its shadows. The only colour came from the blue-and-white pot in the window and the pointed crimson and green of its coleus. A large leaf had fallen and was lying, crimson, against the fresh white paint of the sill.

The lane outside was quiet. Each morning in Manod seemed to begin like this: a slow waiting for the day. It was now nearly two weeks since they had moved into the cottage. They had thought they were lucky to find one to rent, but three uninhabited years had left an impressed dampness and coldness which it would take weeks to drive out. The vacant years behind the blank windows seemed to eject their cold stillness as each door was opened. They had bought two tons of Welsh coal and three loads of ash blocks. They kept several fires going. But each morning it seemed, over the sharp smell of smoke, that they were back at the beginning, the damp cold still deep in the floors and the walls.

He cleared the living-room grate and relaid and lit the fire. He carried out the ash and spread it, carefully, on the path he was making down the back garden. The looser dust came up into his face. He stood and looked around. The October morning was cold and damp. The grass under the big old apple trees glistened with wet. On the high hawthorn hedge the damp air was distilled into clear small globes on each twig and thorn. The leaves were yellowing and just beginning to fall. He stood for some minutes, looking up the fields to Waunfawr and then across the Dowy valley to the misted spurs and slopes of the Frith, the Cefn and the Daren, past the sharp black edge of the shed-roof at Pentre. His talks with Robert Lane, and his reasons for coming here, seemed far back now, in a different world.

He went back in to the kitchen. Susan had come down and was cooking breakfast, on the calor-gas stove they had gone to

24

Pontafren to buy. He saw her thick yellow hair against the dark blue jersey. In the pan the bacon was spitting, and she moved to turn it.

'Is the fire going?'

'I lit it. I'll see.'

As he was crossing the kitchen there was a quick hard tap at the window. Susan looked round, startled, and then across at Matthew. He could hear, through the door from the living-room, the sharp cracks of the sticks in the rising fire.

The kitchen door opened.

'There, sorry, can I come in? Are you having your breakfast?' Modlen Jenkins, from Cae Glas, had been the first to help them, when they were moving in. She still came down often, to talk to Susan.

'Only I saw Mr Price in the garden, taking the ash out. So I knew you was up.'

Susan moved the pan from the heat.

'Come in, Modlen.'

'No, I won't disturb you. Only I wanted to ask Mr Price, are you going today to Nantlais?'

'You are, aren't you, Matthew?'

'Yes. I'm seeing Walters. I shall have to leave about ten.'

'Oh that's it then, thank goodness. Only Trevor said the van might be going but he's just come back says it isn't. And I want to get in if I can.'

'About ten then, Modlen.'

'Thank you very much. I won't keep you hanging around. Only if I'm lucky I'll get the twelve bus back to St Dyfrog, then I can walk up. Mind there used to be buses, right up here into Manod. Only they stopped them, years back. There wasn't the people.'

Modlen smiled. Often what she said had the ring of complaint, but while the apparent reproaches piled up she usually smiled. She seemed to appeal against the world but this never included the actual person in front of her. She was tall and very fair, her hair loose and unbrushed. Whenever she spoke her voice was loud and unchecked. It could have reached, now, far beyond the crowded kitchen.

'So I won't disturb you. I'll come down before ten. Only I hope you didn't mind me tapping the window.'

'No, of course not.'

'Only I always tap. Trevor says it's daft, with the door got a knocker. Only we've always, our family, tapped the window.'

'Yes, so did we,' Matthew said.

'That's right. Yes. Well see you about ten then.'

She closed the door. Susan finished frying the bacon. Matthew stood beside her with the plates. The move to Manod had come at a time when their life was in any case changing. Their two boys had finished university and had now finally left home. This breakfast on their own, just serving each other, was something they had slowly got used to, after the years with the boys, the hurried getting ready for their buses to school, the still regular family life of vacations. It took them back in some ways to the very first months of their marriage: alone and very conscious of each other; happy because they were hardly ever physically separated. But there was this other persistent, irrepressible feeling: that something vital had ended; that the way they had shaped their lives, with the boys to look after, was now suddenly gone. And then just as this was happening, a foreseen but unknown and fundamental adjustment, Matthew had had his heart attack: collapsing at a meeting, rushed to hospital, nursed slowly back, over what seemed endless weeks, to a strength which like his father he had previously taken for granted: a more than usual strength but now so deeply questioned.

'Only we've always, our family,' Susan said, echoing Modlen.

'Yes, not what Trevor does.'

'You remember we used to say: we did this at home; we had that at home. And then at some point, with the boys . . .'

'Yes when they said home, about what was still to us a place where we happened to be living. And as they said home I suppose we did. The others faded.'

'And how long now will they go on saying it?'

'Till they're through the same stage. Making their own settlements.'

'I just wish they were here more often,' Susan said. 'I miss them all the time. Though I'm glad they're doing what they want.'

'Will Jack ever write, do you suppose? Harry never seems to.'

'He's been able to ring up. But he can't here.'

'I've asked again about the phone. It'll take some time.'

'When they were still at university I said I'd get them some field-service cards. I am/am not well. I have/have not changed my shirt. I have found/lost some friends.'

'I am/am not occupying the administration offices.'

Susan laughed. They held to each other, standing with their plates in the cold kitchen. In all the years of bringing up the boys

26

they had wanted no other life but could have done with a week off, a month off: the freedom others talked about. The war had come in their late adolescence. It had imposed inescapable conditions in their first adult years. Thus they had never known a situation which seemed common in others: gaps of time to fill as you wanted; most journeys easy to make. Yet now that they had this condition which others called freedom they knew it, first, as an absence. To live in and for a family, but then to come out beyond it, was to see, in new ways, the emptiness and indifference of their immediate society. While the boys were with them they had avoided the usual alternatives: the casual company of meetings and parties; the routine small-talk of careers, personalities, exhibitions and distractions. So it was now the right time to come somewhere different: to feel the change of Manod in their own change. But they were still nervous of it, almost as if they were marrying again: knowing each other so well but more physically alone than for twenty years.

'We'll have to live it through,' Matthew said, 'learn a new kind of waiting. And this is the right place, for a part of it anyway.'

'Because it's a general experience?'

'Well it happens everywhere but here more completely. The history of this place is that the young go away.'

4. As he was backing the car, Modlen came running down the lane, her overcoat unbuttoned and flapping behind her.

'No hurry, Modlen,' he leaned out and shouted.

'You coming?' Modlen shouted, breathlessly, to Susan.

'No, I don't need anything. And I've got the back bedroom to clear. The last lot of cardboard boxes.'

'Wait till I come back, love. I'll give you a hand.'

Matthew opened the door and Modlen got in. He waved to Susan and drove down the lane. Just short of Pentre he jammed on his brakes, as a tractor came suddenly out of the yard. Ivor Vaughan shouted down to them.

'Want a tow then this morning?'

'No, I stopped for you.'

'I thought you might have my trouble. I've been fighting this bugger best part of an hour.'

'It's the old damp,' Modlen shouted. 'Go on, Ivor, you want to look after her better. Keep her wrapped up nights.'

Ivor looked at them irritably.

27

'I'll pull on in,' he said.

Matthew eased past as the tractor heaved to the verge. Its wheels cut deeply into the soft bright grass. He drove carefully down the lane, which was very steep where it joined the road by the pub. It was again steep and blind, through high banks, down the road to the turn from Llancadog. And where the two roads joined it was so very steep—the roads built at quite different levels and only joined, unexpectedly, in the last few yards—that he slowed and stopped, to listen beyond the blind corner.

'You're right to watch out,' Modlen said. 'We call this bit the Wall of Death. Only I keep telling Trevor, he rides that bike down here like a madman. He'll be through the bloody fence and into the river.'

'Not quite the river, it's a hundred yards.'

'Then more likely hang himself on the wire.'

Beyond the loose wire fence, where a stretch of stone wall had been broken, a field sloped sharply, rough with thistles and mole-humps, to the alders along the line of the river. On the far side of the hidden Dowy was the fine high slope of the Frith, the mist clearing now above the yellowing bracken. As the road ran down there was a long green pasture: the last field of Pentre. In there, on the map, the new houses began, running back up to Manod on the long southern slope: the first eight hundred houses, in curved rising terraces.

'Trevor was asking, Mr Price, this idea of a town. The new town.'

'They're still arguing about it.'

'Will it be round here then?'

'Well along the Afren, that's the general idea. That is if it ever gets built.'

'Only I hope it's round here. Like we need it at Manod, bring a bit of life.'

She shifted her bag on her knees. He glanced across at her as the pitch straightened.

'You want it to come then?'

'We want more people anyhow. And some work for us here.'

At the bottom of the pitch was the main valley road: left for Pontafren, right for Nantlais; St Dyfrog just beyond. They were out of the trees and could see across the valley: its green breadth surprising after the close steep country behind them. It was four miles across to the long dark ridge of Bryndu, but they could see the white road climbing to the Saint's Pass, through the forestry

28

plantation. Farther west, in the distance, above Nantlais, were the twin blue peaks of the Brothers.

'There are some against it,' Matthew said.

'Aye, all the ones are all right already.'

'Would you want this a town though? A really big town? Most of the country built over.'

'Of course. Certainly. Whatever's wrong with that? I like towns.'

He could increase his speed a little along the main road. The old railway came close on its deserted embankment and shut out the view to the south. The road turned continually, twining with the railway, now under, now over. The longest straight was about thirty yards. It was only in summer, with the coaches and caravans and the tourist cars, that there was any real traffic, but then for some weeks, and at weekends especially, it was very crowded and dangerous.

On the right, all the way, were the high spurs and ridges of the Frith, the Cefn and the Daren. Matthew looked up, whenever he could, at their surprising shapes: the long folds, the sudden scarps, the deep watercourses, the edges of rockfall. Sheep and ponies were high along all the main slopes: a sign of settled weather it was always said. It was so much its own country: solid, remote, self-contained. The road climbed towards the Daren and crossed a transverse ridge. From the top they looked down to Nantlais, just two miles below them. The town seemed always dark grey, as if drying from the rain. Along the valley the stone had changed, from the warm russet of Manod and St Dyfrog to this cold blackish grey. The compactness of the town was surprising. Where most towns now spread along the radial roads, Nantlais was confined, with a sudden clear break between country and town. There had been no development outwards, and little building of any kind, in the last sixty years. From the top of the ridge the history of the town stood out very sharply, as if on a slide. A dark grey outline, on a screen of glass.

'You're going back on the bus?'

'Yes, the twelve to the corner.'

'I'll be later than that.'

'Don't you worry.'

They crossed the old stone bridge to the main street, with the tall grey clocktower and the stone pillared market at the end. The town was very quiet. He could park anywhere. He stopped under the clocktower. Modlen got out quickly, as if there was no time to

29

waste. She turned, smiling, and thanked him. He watched her hurry away down the almost empty street, her bag swinging and bumping her loose coat. When she was out of sight he took out his keys. He sat looking down at their tight hard bunch in his hand.

5. The deeply glowing brass plate, in which years of polishing had absorbed and overlaid even the blemishes of wear, announced Parry and Parry, Solicitors. Screwed in the dark stone above it was a smaller plate of grey plastic, with neat white lettering: District Planning Officer. Matthew climbed the dark stairs to the top floor, which Parry and Parry had been surprised and delighted to let.

Bryn Walters was waiting for him, at a big mahogany desk, with his back to the two high windows over the quiet street.

'Mr Matthew Price? Yes, yes. Come on in and sit down.'

Matthew stared, covertly, at the surprising face. The forehead was sharply receding, under the jet black hair. The eyes were deepset, under the very large eyebrows. The mouth was tight and thin, under the long nose: a nutcracker mouth.

'That's right,' Walters said, 'I've got a letter here somewhere, asks me to give Mr Matthew Price any necessary help.'

The voice was sharp and sibilant: a calculated sound.

'Only I didn't altogether understand it.'

'Really?' Matthew asked.

'Oh don't worry, boy, don't worry. It's not unusual. You could say, in fact, it would be unusual if I did, the letters most people write.'

'Yes.'

'But then fortunately, very fortunately, I got a telephone call. From Dr Robert Lane. From London.'

'Yes, he said he'd write.'

'Did he now? Did he? That's a very gifted man, wouldn't you say, Mr Price? An unusually gifted man?'

'Yes, of course, he's very able.'

'Able. Exactly. That's a word I haven't heard used in a long time. But yes, as you say. A very able man.'

He stared down at the papers on his desk, with a surprising concentration of attention. Then he looked up with a sudden interest, as if he had solved some problem.

'You'll have a cup of tea, Mr Price?'

'Well yes, thank you.'

30

Walters got up from his desk, moving very quickly and smoothly as if avoiding obstacles. He opened the door to the outer office.

'Nesta, two cups of tea if you would. Mr Price, sugar?'

'No. No, thanks.'

Walters came back to his desk. He looked closely at Matthew as he passed.

'They tell me you come from Glynmawr, Mr Price.'

'Yes, originally.'

'Originally. Exactly. I was talking the other day to a man I know in Gwenton. He said he remembered you when you were both at grammar school.'

'Really? Who was that?'

'John Evans. Price-Evans. He's a solicitor, well his father was, he's just carried on the firm. Like they say, practising.'

'I remember him, yes.'

Walters knotted his knuckles and again stared down at his papers.

'He said Will Price actually.'

Matthew looked across at him. The deepset eyes were very fixed and intent.

'I was called Will at home and then of course at school. But my registered name is Matthew.'

'People call you Matthew then now? Your official name, you might say? Dr Lane called you Matthew.'

'Yes, almost everyone does.'

'You call yourself Matthew?'

There was a flick of the finger, as if pointing and identifying.

'Yes. Matthew.'

'All right. Very good. Matthew it is then. But I'm glad you come from Glynmawr.'

'Yes.'

'He's an able man, as you say. A very able man. It makes a difference, wouldn't you say, having men like that near the top? Near the top of the system is what I mean to say.'

'Well I suppose it makes a difference. If they're not just window-dressing. I have no idea how much power they have.'

'Exactly. Exactly. Though enough power, at least, to have you come down here.'

'He probably explained,' Matthew said, and then caught his breath.

'Yes, it wasn't quite clear from the letter. But he did explain it: that you're an official consultant.'

31

'That sounds very formal.'

'It is. It is formal. I've got the letter here. Any necessary help.'

Matthew waited, looking across the broad desk.

'Will that be difficult to give, would you say?' he eventually asked.

'No, no, boy. Not at all. No trouble at all.'

The secretary, Nesta, brought in the tray of tea. As they took their cups Walters still watched him carefully.

'Do you think they'll do well this season?' he asked, suddenly.

Matthew smiled and waited.

'You still follow the rugby, of course?'

'Yes. Yes indeed. I think they'll do well.'

'Of course. Naturally. Well that's all right then.'

There was another silence, another long scrutiny of the papers.

'A very gifted man,' Walters said suddenly, as if lifting a phrase from the file in front of him.

'Robert Lane?'

'Robert Lane. It's like a title, isn't it? Like having a title. A famous name on a book.'

'It's important anyway. His books are important.'

'Yes, I read the big one soon after it came out. I've been meaning to read it again. The title fascinated me: *Social Method*. Of course in work like my own . . .'

'Yes?'

'I see social method in the raw. It cuts down my time for books.'

He again stared intently.

'The rawer the practice,' Matthew said, 'the more need for theory.'

'Of course, of course. A very gifted man.'

Matthew put back his cup. The tea was sweet and scalding hot. Walters leaned forward and smiled. With the light behind him the face seemed reduced to two or three sharp lines.

'Only there's practice and practice, wouldn't you say, Matthew?'

'Sure.'

'And in this case, for example?'

'You mean Manod? The city.'

'Exactly.'

He leaned back, smiling broadly. It was as if some game had been completed, the decisive move made.

32

'You don't mind me bringing it up?' Matthew said. 'It was, after all, why I came.'

'No, don't get stiff, boy. Not you.'

'I'm sorry.'

'You've been away too long, is the trouble with you. You don't fight back. You fit in.'

'Well anyway I don't need the approach work. Just tell me.'

Walters laughed. He got up and stood by the window. Over the dark slate roofs, on the other side of the street, they could see the spurs running back towards Manod. Walters turned.

'You said the city. That means, already, you've made up your mind.'

'No it doesn't.'

'About the city it does. Because look from where I am, with my social method. For twenty years we've been asking, begging, for some help with development. More jobs and then more housing; like keeping our railway open and improving the trunk road. Nantlais and Pontafren would have grown steadily. And the road and railway would have brought in more holidaymakers. We had a plan for a sports centre up on Lake Teilo—climbing, water-skiing, boats. Two or three grants for hotels. And then the basics of course: better subsidies on hill sheep and cattle, and for ploughing and reclaiming steep land. A whole balanced programme that would really help us.'

'I know. I've seen all the files.'

'Files, Matthew? What sort of social method is that? But if you've seen them you'll know we didn't just ask, we begged. When they closed our railway we all campaigned. And all we got was the donkey's handshake. Go away, little men, you've got your hills to die in. You're not even, remember, a parliamentary constituency, your whole damn county only makes a poor half; there's not a single vote in the lot of it. So again we go up to London, we beg them. And they turn to *their* social method. Terribly sorry, old boy, have a drink. When's your train to Cardiff? Pity you can't go all the way, that's closed now, isn't it?'

'But Manod was meant to be the change from that.'

'Was it? You really think so?'

'It's how Lane put it to me.'

'Aye. Social method. You want to watch them, mun. They can wring your neck like they're doing you a favour.'

Matthew pushed back his chair.

33

'I've been watching,' he said.

'No but those practical things, those things we needed, they threw straight back at us. Go away, get lost, we've got a busy modern country to run. Then after years of that, more years than you can think—my girl started infant school and took her A levels just through one of those bloody committees—after all that they say "Ah yes, mid-Wales region. You asked for a crust of bread. Right then, tomorrow, twelve sharp, you're getting forcibly fed the whole bloody loaf. And no arguing mind: either the whole loaf or not a single crust to keep you alive".'

'Is that how you all see it?'

Walters smiled. There was a ring of white in the deepset eyes.

'You can ask, of course. With any necessary help. But what do you expect us to think? No help at all, even deliberately letting the whole area run down, and then out of the blue, full of pretty pictures, an entire new city right down to the design of the lamp-posts. Like there's never been so creative, so imaginative, so daring an idea. And shall I tell you why? Because they had to get us to that state, depressed and desperate, before they could do what they really wanted: come in on our land to solve the problems of Birmingham. When they'd pushed us low enough we couldn't, they reckoned, afford to say no.'

'But you have said no. You're saying no now.'

Walters nodded. He sat again at his desk. He looked across at Matthew with a frank curiosity.

'Well it all seemed dead. Dead and mouldering, like all their other fancy talk.'

'It seems to have come up again.'

'Yes. It seems so. Robert Lane tells us so. And now another man from London: an official consultant. Sounding local opinion, putting this and that point of view.'

'Taking this and that point of view.'

'It's what they all say. It's the social method. Except that this consultant is Will Price from Glynmawr. Did he know that? Lane?'

'Yes he knew where I came from.'

'Exactly. Exactly. Social method again. A man from the area, a man will get on with them.'

'Talk them round, you mean?'

Walters opened his mouth, and then laughed.

'We'll see, boy, we'll see.'

'Yes, I hope so. Because I came here to learn. I've no commitment past that.'

'Uncommitted?'

'Yes. On this.'

'It's good to hear you say that. If you're serious, Will.'

'I shall try to be serious at listening.'

'Aye, so I notice. Very watchful, very quiet.'

Matthew got up, and Bryn Walters quickly followed him. They began to make arrangements for their first detailed work. At the door, shaking hands, Bryn smiled and said:

'Any necessary help. You can rely on that.'

6. Where the road climbed over the ridge from the Daren, Matthew stopped the car and switched off the engine. With Nantlais behind him, he could see far out along the curve of the valley, past St Dyfrog and Manod towards Pontafren. The weather had changed during the day, the misty stillness giving way to strong winds and high clouds from the west. The afternoon sun lighted the whole valley. The great river, from this height, was a silver line. Far away to the south, beyond Bryndu, he could see the long ridges and scarps of the Black Mountains, moulded by the light into unfamiliar shapes. On the far horizon he could just make out the high plateau above the Kestul, and below that, hidden, was his own village, Glynmawr.

He got out of the car, and the wind ripped at his coat. It was cold but he turned his face to the wind, closing his eyes. It was many years since he had felt this chilling pressure on his face. At first it was only a general force from outside but then it pressed unevenly in continual variations, as if moulding the flesh to the bone. He stood for some minutes, as if surrendered to the wind. Then he swung away, feeling a sudden spring through his body. He walked up from the road to an outcrop of rock under a mountain ash. Most of the berries had already gone from the tree, and the wind along the ridge was ripping away whole twigs of fading leaves. But what was most remarkable, as he stood on the rock and looked into the tree, was that on its windward side it was shaped into a dense smooth concave of small growing twigs: as trim and apparently unnatural a shape as if it had been clipped.

He felt the wind hard on his back. A long passivity, the hard set of experience, seemed to be moving and breaking into a new

35

activity. On the phone, in the street, in the office with Lane or the different office with Walters, he had been at a distance. The identity of others had been sharply present but he had been like a watcher, lonely and silent: an occasional voice from an oblique consciousness, a life deeply withdrawn and held back; the detail of human contact just barely dealt with, in a few learned responses, but behind this a different and preoccupying dimension, as if he were hearing and seeing only sound and light.

The Kestrel, the watcher. He remembered now, as from a different existence, the boy on the mountain, looking down at Glynmawr, seeing the history of his country in the shapes of the land. He saw the meeting of valleys, and England blue in the distance. On the high ground to the east were the Norman castles, and the disputed land in their shadow. On the limestone scarp to the south was the line of the ironmasters, the different frontier: on the near side the valleys still green and wooded, on the far side blackened with collieries and slagheaps and grey huddled terraces. That history had been clear, at the moment of going away. A defining history, which he had managed to write, and which in turn had become his profession.

Yet within that history a more involving life: not sculpted beyond him in the shapes of the land but a pressure, a shaping, a long movement and settling and unsettling of ground, behind the watching eyes. He saw his father standing at the window of the signalbox. He saw Morgan Rosser's van along the narrow country road, which had now been straightened and widened, making a long clear run for the lorries. Glynmawr station, now, was not only closed but flattened, obliterated: the platforms and waiting rooms bulldozed down into hard core. Morgan Rosser's factory, local food and local work—'a bit of country quality'—had lasted twenty years as a branch of a large corporation and then been closed as uneconomic; it was now a tyre depot. None of it felt like change; it felt like cancellation. Yet within all these movements there were still particular lives. They had a lasting closeness, though their bodies had died. In himself, still, in this other valley, he could feel his father's experience. There was a connecting, unnerving persistence, in movement and voice. He saw the hard watching face, with the prominent cheekbones and the broad heavy jaw. He saw the wide mouth with the ugly irregular teeth. He felt the heavy solidity of the body, and then the surprising smallness and delicacy of the hands and feet. There was a curious stillness in the features and there was distance and withdrawal in
36

the very deep blue eyes. The rough breaking voice was reluctant, involved, inarticulate.

Harry Price sat watching, and his eyes lost focus. Harry Price stood listening, reaching silently, obscurely, for his words. In the office by the tower block, which became a column of light. In the street of the offices, the stone helmeted features, the upraised stone arm. In the quiet office above the empty streets of Nantlais. In the car, in the wind, in the outcrop of rock under the scoured mountain ash. In this other valley.

Matthew knew the separation. In his own middle age, after his own first collapse, there was still a long mourning through all the reaches of his body. So much change had come, so much time and distance from that remembered death, that he could at any moment get up and leave that heavy body sitting there, move away and talk to others in an altered, accommodating voice. But under pressure, always, this particular consciousness came back: a heavy possession, self-possession beyond the ordinary self: the immediate detail just barely dealt with, as if hearing and seeing only sound and light.

The wind was now piercingly cold. He looked down and saw the valley: St Dyfrog, Manod, Llanerch, Pontafren. The long silver curve of the Afren was like a line on glass, an outline on glass. He must take this future seriously because the past was honoured and loved. But was this why he had come here, within the meanings of generation? In all the years between he had worked on the past. That learning was now a habit, to make a single experience common. But where there has been past life there is no problem in finding substance; that kind of attention has a natural hold. To work on the present and on the future is a different kind of attention: at once alert and hesitant, intent and open. He could close his eyes and then open them on the city in the valley. The grey cluster of works at St Dyfrog. At Llanerch and Manod, at Bronydd and Fforest and Parc-y-Meirch and the Cwm, terraces of houses, central white towers. Circles of white light at the road intersections. The traffic, the sound, of a hundred thousand people.

But then this was a city seen from the mountain: lines on glass, an outline on glass; the immediate detail just barely dealt with. For there was no route in the senses from the thousands of details, the working papers of the city, to this green valley where they might eventually be realized, these fields in which thousands would build and move. Clusters, communications, densities,

37

neighbourhoods: these were scrawls and projections, lines on glass, over the known places, the embedded lives, the long valued words in all their moving rhythms.

But then any future must be like this: abstract, angular, a blank manufactured page. It stretches far away from the intricate present, from the checks and inhibitions, the persistent man-oeuvres. It is easy to reject it for the warmth, the heaviness, of a known past: a green past, in which lives have been lived and completed, in which remembered men and women, overheard silent voices, are more actual and more convincing than this unfinished everyday living or this projection and outline of a future. Seen from above, from the height of the Kestrel, from this ridge below the Daren, it must be like this, always. It is history past and future, an extended landscape, until you get up and move.

He turned and walked back to the car. The wind tore at him again and he shielded his face. He got into the car, holding the tight bunch of keys. It was suddenly quiet again: a closed familiar-ity. After the spread of light, the particular day.

7. It was late afternoon when he got back to Manod. A green Jaguar was parked at the gate of the cottage. There was the sound of voices, from around the back door. He hurried through, under the high hawthorn hedge. Susan was standing with John Dance, who had rented them the cottage. He had his yard in St Dyfrog, his office in Pontafren and lived in Manod, in the Old Vicarage. Susan looked at Matthew and smiled.

'Mr Dance came round to see if we were all right.'

'And found a problem, Mr Price, as you see,' Dance said. Will Rees, from Fronheulog, the retired signalman, was bending with a stick over the drain from the kitchen. Susan explained to Matthew:

'Mr Rees came down with some vegetables for us and he found me out here trying to clear the drain.'

John Dance smiled. He was small and active, with a sunburned bald head and a strongly growing blond moustache. He narrowed his eyes as he looked at Matthew.

'I was just telling Mrs Price. If there are any jobs you've only to give me a ring.'

Will Rees was still bent over the drain, pushing upwards with the stick.

'Mr Rees just offered, out of kindness,' Susan said.

'Of course, of course, Mrs Price. I know how it is. And between ourselves, some of the men I have to employ, it's a toss-up which way gets you the real amateur.'

Will Rees was pushing harder. He had got right down on his knees.

'This isn't London, you know,' Dance said.

'No, it isn't,' Susan agreed.

Dance switched his attention to Matthew.

'Down here, Mr Price, we have to take what we can get. And some of it's rubbish, I don't mind telling you. A lot of the bright ones, see, like yourself, cleared off out as soon as they could. Though we try to do our best.'

'There's not enough training, anywhere, in building.'

'Agreed. Definitely. But before you can train them you've got to have something to train. A bit up here, I mean.'

He patted his bald skull, affectionately. As Matthew watched him there was a sudden gush of soapy water from the stubby black pipe. Susan moved back quickly to avoid being splashed but John Dance went closer and leaned down over it, watching the flow with great interest. There was a rush of drain-grey liquid, with the curd and scum of used soap and scraps of food and other debris tumbling inside it.

'Where does it go next?' Matthew asked.

'Ah now that, Mr Price . . .'

Dance had straightened up and was smiling, as the flow stopped.

' . . . that is a secret between us and our ancestors. We get to know, occasionally, when we dig it all up. But otherwise no, we have to leave it to history and to nature.'

Matthew was watching Will Rees, who was pulling the sleeves of his grey cardigan back down to his thin wrists. He noticed that he was avoiding looking at Dance.

'Thank you, Will,' Matthew said.

'That's all right, mun. No trouble. Just a bit of a blockage.'

Susan went into the kitchen. Will Rees followed her, to get his jacket and basket. Dance turned towards Matthew and walked a few steps down the garden, lowering his voice.

'Of course, Mr Price, when the scheme comes . . .'

'The scheme?'

'Any new estate will have proper main drainage. And it's normal practice, for any developer, to let the local people in on the estate services. Water, sewerage, even as far as roads. It's good public relations, to put it no higher. Keeping the local people sweet.'

Matthew looked back at the kitchen window. Susan was at the sink. Dance walked farther down the garden, his voice still pitched low.

'Like you take my father and me. Jobbing builders we were, in St Dyfrog. A house here and there, an extension, a garage, a bit of a cesspit in a garden, a tank and piping for water. It's all we used to do, a bit here a bit there. And I saw no future in that.'

'It's always hard to get maintenance done.'

'Oh, I've kept up that. Naturally. Though there's no money in it, scraping and patching or putting up a bit of gutter. All housing see, now, is changing. It's proper modern development, from the ground up. Proper planning, proper services, proper modern materials.'

'Even then it isn't easy. Things still go wrong.'

'Well yes, they do. And the local people are the first to resent it, that's been my experience. They've got used as they are to any old rubbish: damp walls, bad drains, old rotting dark passages. But put them in a new place and have a door warp a bit, or the central heating get an airlock, they're like the risen gentry, calling their tradesmen to book.'

'They'll have paid a good deal. They expect a difference.'

'Yes but that's it, mun. They want it much better but they don't want it different. Not different enough for it to be properly done.'

'Well we're all like that, I suppose.'

'Of course. Granted. But you take this new estate . . .'

'I really don't know which estate you mean.'

John Dance smiled. He touched his nose.

'I know, Mr Price. You're a professional man. Like everyone else you have your job to think of. And I'm not trying to push it. Good Lord, no.'

'You said estate, that's all.'

'Look it's pretty well known up and down the valley. Some very influential people are interested.'

'In the new city, do you mean?'

'Ah well, city, now. That's just an idea.'

'It's what was proposed.'

'Aye, back in the sixties, and you know what happened. Governments, Mr Price, never understand the first thing about people. An empty valley, backward farming, old sub-standard housing. It must have looked easy but it's what I was saying. You've got to offer them something, let them in on what you're doing. Because if you don't the whole lot starts up: meetings, petitions, the preservation of rural Wales.'

'And there's another way? Which would let them in on it?'

'Not on their city, no. That's why it folded up.'

'But there'd be other development if the city didn't happen?'

'Well of course. It stands to reason. The place is wide open.'

'For what then, exactly?'

'For something with advantage to the people already here. That's the only development ever really happens. The rest's just talk in the papers.'

'Estates, you said?'

'Exactly.'

He turned at the end of the ash path. He looked back at the cottages.

'Anyway you're comfortable here, Mr Price?'

'Well, we're getting comfortable.'

'That's good. That's good.'

They walked through to the lane. Dance was moving to his car when there was a noise behind them. They looked up towards Fronheulog and Cae Glas. A horse and rider were coming down fast. As Matthew watched, he found the urgency of the gallop startling. Soft turf was flying on the wide green verge by the church.

'Gwenny,' Dance said.

Matthew was still watching the extraordinary gallop. The horse was a tall roan stallion, very powerful. Gwen Vaughan of Pentre looked across at them and shouted. She reined in suddenly, swerving across the lane. She brought the stallion to a stop just beyond the green Jaguar. Then she smiled, looking down. She was in her late thirties, with cropped black hair, dark eyes and a very pale skin. Her clothes were rough and mudstained: brown jacket and breeches, high boots and a black jersey. Matthew looked up at her, his attention caught by the strain of the face. The lips were still working from the urgency of the ride. Across the cheeks and temples there were disfiguring spots and patches of reddened skin.

'I've been up Pentwyn,' Gwen said, looking over their heads. Her voice was surprisingly soft and light: the shy voice of a girl.

'I thought it was life and death, Gwenny,' John Dance said, smiling.

'It usually is when I ride Cavalier.'

The voice was still quiet, but open and friendly. Though she was nearly forty, Gwen still spoke, to strangers, like a child brought into the room. It was difficult, watching her, to connect the voice with the deeply strained face and the very dull, cautious eyes. Matthew was looking intently at her, and she caught his look and was at once embarrassed. Her face coloured, making the disfiguring blotches stand out more angrily. He looked quickly away, ashamed to have disturbed her.

'Well I must get on,' Gwen said. She leaned, slowly, over the stallion's neck, and he moved at once, in a controlled walk. They watched her ride slowly down the lane and turn into Pentre.

III

1. VAUGHANS had lived in Pentre for a hundred and thirty years. Few other families in the neighbourhood had been settled for so long. From the registers and graveyards in Manod and St Dyfrog it is easy to trace a persistence of families, on this land where the Dowy flows into the Afren. To anyone growing up here, the history of the farming families is close and intricate; it seems to form, in itself, a whole past. But on these small tenant farms, as until the late nineteen-forties they had nearly all been, the actual history is different. Many of the families have lasted, though many have disappeared and the remembered past has closed over their heads. Of those who have survived, nearly all have moved, often, within the district, from farm to farm. People say the Vaughans have been lucky to have stayed in Pentre for so long. But you could also say that they have not been lucky enough: the bigger and more fertile farms, around Pontafren and to the border with England, have been beyond their reach. Several times indeed they have come near to having to leave Pentre, for some smaller farm in the rougher land back towards the mountains. Their ninety acres at Pentre are little enough, but much of it is good pasture and with grazing rights back on Waunfawr they have kept their place.

Indeed their only decisive move was as far as they knew back, when Emlyn Vaughan, son of a Llancadog labourer, had built up a carrier's business, then at forty sold out and leased a small mountain farm on the northern slopes of the Cefn, moving on from that to bigger holdings at the Cwm and by Nantlais until finally, in his sixties, he had come to Pentre. Since then, unusually, there had been always a son to inherit, and many of the other sons had, through the generations, been set up in farms of their own, in different parts of the county, while most of the daughters had married the sons of other local farmers. Over the generations other families had emigrated, to England, to North America, to Australia; others had ended, without children; others again had left the land and gone to work in the cities. But while there was a living from this marginal land the Vaughans, for the most part, had stayed in the county. It was not from such families that the

43

blood of this country had drained away. Those who had gone and were still in their hundreds going to the towns and the cities were the families without land, the labourers and the craftsmen. Most of the farming families had stayed, and in every succeeding generation this was more and more their country.

In the late nineteen forties, after the prosperity of the war years, life had been easier at Pentre than anyone could remember. In 1948 the estate of the Mortimer family, of Llancadog Hall, was broken up and sold to meet death duties. Thomas Vaughan, to his great delight, was then able to buy Pentre, with only a small bank loan which he quickly repaid. His children still remembered that sense of achievement. They kept an article from a London magazine about the history of the Mortimers and the sadness of their estate being broken up: 'an ancient and honourable tradition of landowning has ended in the brutal materialism of a postwar England intent on destroying its past.' It looked very different from Pentre, where the Mortimers had been disliked and at times hated, though usually with some formal and necessary respect. Thomas Vaughan used to say that the Mortimers were keen on Wales because it gave them enough income to go away and become English. The last two Mortimers, in the history of the estate, had been a Liberal cabinet minister and the director of a Birmingham rubber company and seventeen of its subsidiaries and associates. An ancient and honourable tradition of landowning, Thomas Vaughan told his children, was now just beginning: now in 1948, when Pentre was owned by the family that for a hundred and ten years had been working it.

Yet the change, in practice, was not all that great. Better times and the end of rent gave a considerably higher annual income. But Thomas had five children, and it was as much as he could do, even in these better times, to provide for them all, with the cost of land rising. The eldest, Gwen, did not marry. At twenty-one she was engaged to Gethin Jenkins, at the adjoining Bedwen Farm, but she broke the engagement, a month before the date of the marriage. The next, Gwilym, married and was settled on a small farm south of Pontafren, on a heavy mortgage. The next again, Lewis, did not get a farm until just before his father's death, when some money came into the family through his mother. He now farmed, still a bachelor, on thirty-eight acres on the northern slopes of the Cefn, not far from the first holding that old Emlyn Vaughan had leased, six generations back. There was then no more capital in the family, but the fourth child, Mary, married an

English stock dealer and went to live in Devon. That left only two at home: Gwen, unmarried, running the house after the death of her mother; and Ivor, seventeen years younger, the baby of the family. When old Thomas died, Pentre came to Ivor, but with adjustments of money to the other four. So the youngest at Pentre was the luckiest, though in the course of the settlement, to meet the claims of the others, a large mortgage had to be raised on the farm, and Gwen still had a nineteen hundred pound share in it. The struggle for independence, which had once seemed only a struggle against the Mortimers, had to start all over again. It was normal, in the district, for the youngest son to inherit the family farm, with money adjustments to the others. But this actual settlement was tense, and the surviving family were still at odds about its justice. Gwilym and Lewis kept away from Manod as much as they could. The farm they had grown up on was very much better than the farms they now had, though if all were sold up they would be roughly even. Mary had taken her share of the money and now only rarely came back. And in Pentre itself the situation was strange. Mrs Vaughan had been forty-three when Ivor was born, and after his birth had been only rarely well. Much of Ivor's bringing-up had been done by Gwen. When their mother died Gwen was twenty-four and Ivor seven. It did not seem so strange until their father also died and the other three had gone away. But now it was Ivor's farm, with Gwen as its housekeeper: Gwen at thirty-nine, and the boy she had brought up now a man of twenty-two: self-confident and assertive and looking to marry to start a family of his own.

2. Gwen laid Ivor's supper, in the big kitchen. He was singing in the bathroom that had been built on to the end of the old wash-house soon after they had bought Pentre. There was another small bathroom upstairs, but they needed a place where the men could come straight in from the yard. Since she had been running the house Gwen had made it more comfortable but also much stricter in its division from the yard and the outbuildings. Ivor was well used to her rules about the house and made no objection to them.

She looked across the yard to the high larches. They had turned to a fine pale gold along the curved branches, and a pink-ness in the wood was beginning to show through. They were Japanese larches, her father had said. That seemed very strange.

45

Ivor had parked the tractor, as always, on just the curve he had driven in. If he would only put it away under cover, there wouldn't be the cursing delay of getting it to start every morning. At first she had gone out, each evening, and driven it on into the barn, but lately he had shouted whenever she went to touch it and so now she left it alone: let him learn the hard way. The big tyres were coated with red mud and bracken. He had begun ploughing the last steep field by Waunfawr, where they were slowly re-claiming what had been rough hill for centuries, though within their boundary. At the beginning of the clearance they had dis-covered, deep under the gorse and the bracken, old stone and earth banks of tiny square fields and enclosures. They had no way of knowing how far back these had been made, but there were several half-filled small pits and in one place a litter of stones as if some building had once been there. It was a hard clearance, reworking the land over successive years of ploughing and root-crops, but they got a grant for it and to Ivor that was decisive. Indeed he was readier to give time to the fight with the hill—the continual fight against bracken and bramble and thorn and gorse—than to any of the rest of the farm. He was like a boy, Gwen said, still doing rough jobs at the edge of the work, taking all the central management for granted. Even the good pasture, stretching down to the Dowy, was getting badly infested with thistles and nettles and foxgloves. She had offered to plough the bracken herself, but Ivor had refused: the slope, he said, was too dangerous for a woman, and she had no patience, going at it like a gallop.

This afternoon she had made the excuse of riding her stallion up to Pentwyn so that she could watch from a distance and see that Ivor was all right. She couldn't give up the habit of years in which she had been bound to look after him: the child, the boy, the young man. Most things she had done for him she had still to do, but now often indirectly, deviously, and with a tact she found difficult.

'I saw you riding up Pentwyn, Gwenny.'

'Did you?'

He had come through the washhouse still carrying his towel. He was drying his arms as he looked across at her.

'See any of the people?' he asked.

'Where?'

'Well, Pentwyn, of course.'

'I saw Mrs Parry.'

46

Ivor threw the towel on the table. He was looking across at her with a boyish defiance. For the past year he had been going out with Megan Parry, the daughter at Pentwyn. Megan was eighteen, small and dark and pretty: a child's prettiness, it seemed to Gwen. She looked at him irritably.

'Better eat your food now before it gets cold.'

'All right, girl. Don't fret.'

He had taken to calling her 'girl', as his father used to call his mother, especially in teasing. She had always been Gwenny until their father had died and he had come into the farm.

'Sit down, boy. Come on,' Gwen said, impatiently.

He went to the table and began eating. Gwen picked up the towel and took it back to the bathroom. When she came in again he stopped and looked round at her.

'Where's your food then, girl?'

'I ate before. I didn't want much.'

'On a diet, is it?'

'No, it isn't. And mind your own business.'

For years now she had been careful about her food. She had been to the doctor about her skin trouble when it had got much worse after her father died. Her complexion had never been good since she was a girl of sixteen, but she had got used to it: 'nobody ever sees me up here.' The doctor had wanted her to go on to a specialist but she had not gone. Yet she had followed his other advice, cutting down on fats and on acid foods. This had had no effect. She was used now, whenever she looked in the mirror, to seeing her face past this screen of minor disfigurement. If she leaned back, just a bit, into the beginning of shadow, she could see the face she still distantly remembered, her real face.

Ivor finished his food and stood up, gently rubbing his stomach. He had put on a lot of weight in the last year, though he had always been heavy. His big shoulders had been the first thing Gwen had noticed when she went into her mother's bedroom to see the new baby.

'I'll go on up and change,' he said, still rubbing his stomach.

'You going out then?'

'Aye, look around.'

'Will you be taking the truck?'

'Aye I expect so.'

'That back tyre's down again.'

'I'll give it some air.'

He was smiling now, looking across in a friendly challenge. She didn't want to look at him. She turned away to the stove.

'You want to watch that track in the dark,' she said.

'What track's that?'

'You know very well.'

'The one you was galloping down?'

'You don't take proper care. You'll be sorry one of these days.'

'Still on I'll have an accident? You worry about me too much, girl.'

'I've had to,' Gwen said.

He went quietly upstairs but after a few minutes he was moving noisily about, whistling and singing. When he came down he was wearing his best dark suit. His face was a bright healthy pink and he smelled of aftershave lotion. He took the keys of the truck and went through to the yard door.

'Don't be late now, Ivor.'

'What do you reckon's late?'

'You know very well.'

'So long as you don't wait up, girl.'

'Don't you worry about me.'

He went out and started the truck. He drove straight out, without looking at the tyre. Gwen moved to call after him but then forced herself to stop. It was no use any more. He must do whatever he wanted. It wasn't her fault that she had a mother's anxiety for him. She hadn't chosen to bring him up, it had just been left to her. And she couldn't, suddenly, just switch it off: not without some change. And for her, anyway, there was no sign of that.

She washed up and tidied the kitchen, and laid the table for breakfast. Then she went to the parlour and put on the television. She watched the picture come clear but then got up impatiently and went to the window. She leaned closer to the glass, to see out beyond the reflection. She could see the pyramid of the bellhouse against the pale sky, and a light beyond it, from the other side of the valley. All her life had happened within these few hundred yards: this house, the school across the lane, the fields down to the road. It was so lonely and quiet, all the life now left to her, but what else could there be? She turned round half expecting that she would see her father sitting in the high leather chair by the fire. But there was only the empty room, the heavy furniture, the shadows beyond the door. The television was still going but she could take no notice of it. Across the empty room all she could see

48

in detail was the track to Pentwyn: the tyres wrenching in the lumpy ruts, the lights picking up the curve of the sheepwall and the loose stones by the gorse, the pull of the wheel at the bad corner where the stream flowed over. It was all full of risk. They were too young to marry, however you looked at it. How could a child like Megan run a house this size and the share of work on the farm? Yet it was going to happen, along that track. And when Megan came here, Gwen would have to go.

That's right, though, isn't it? That's the way life has to go. She looked across at the empty chair. She didn't need that absent voice. They would all say it was only fair to Megan: after they were married, Gwen couldn't stay on, still running the house. But then all she had got was her nineteen hundred pounds in the farm. Nineteen hundred on paper, because Ivor couldn't repay her, not without selling stock and that would be stupid. It would be years of saving before he could really afford to get married and pay Gwen off her money to help get a place of her own. Years of waiting, but he wasn't going to wait. A few months at most and they would open that door and come in and tell her: this is our farm, our house; we, Ivor and Megan, are the new family in Pentre.

Nineteen hundred pounds. And if she got it what could she do? It had been worth something once but now it was nothing. And a woman of forty, used only to running this house. No jobs in any case, not anywhere round here. She looked again at the empty chair by the fire. On the mantelpiece above it were the cups she had won as a girl. Her father had put them there proudly: what Thomas Vaughan's daughter had won at the shows. She went across to the cups and put her fingers up to touch them. Four from the best year, 58, when she had won Nantlais, Pontafren, Llancadog and then the County Open. Miss Gwendolen Vaughan, on Prince. In that Open, and in two of the others, she had beaten Sally Mortimer, who had gone on to national jumping. Tom Vaughan had wanted Gwen to go on to the big competitions but her mother was ill and she had the house to run. And if she had been free she wouldn't have much wanted it; there was a lot of showing off, in the big rings. Only the jumping mattered, the horse and the jumping, and she still had that. On Cavalier, now, she was better by a foot than she had been on Prince. Miss Gwendolen Vaughan. Gwenny Vaughan.

It was in that same year that she had given up Gethin. But he was the least of her losses, the way he'd turned out. And she'd

49

seen, even then, how mean he would be. Only that wasn't the main thing. She couldn't bear him touching her. It was just hard and cold, as if she was nothing. She'd worn dresses more often then. She and her mother had made them. It had all been taken for granted, just because they were of an age and had always known each other, and because their farms joined. But he had gone so hard and mean. Sour Gethin. Ugly Gethin. He had never much bothered, never bothered about her. She would have gone down to Bedwen and just been what he wanted, like stocking the farm. Whereas in Pentre she had the children, a family to look after. Much the happier life.

The news came up on the television. She didn't want to watch it; she went out to make coffee. After the news there was the show-jumping; it was all she was waiting for. She turned off the light and stretched out by the fire, in her father's chair. It was the horses she watched, not the riders. It was a ladies' competition but it all looked the same girl, really, under the big lights: the roll of hair under the cap, the black coat and white breeches. They came in on parade, like at a dance. But then it changed every time when the bell went: the leap of energy, the lean and strain of the jumping.

The programme was extended, for an extra jump-off. It was after eleven when it ended. She put on the light and looked down at her clothes: the black jersey, the rough fawn breeches, the mud-spattered stockings. She was going to wait up, whatever the time. But it passed so slowly, in the big empty house. She went out to the lane and looked up towards Pentwyn. It was very dark along the lane: only one light, from the Prices' cottage; keeping London hours. Beyond it was only the spreading darkness from Waunfawr. Back inside from the cold, she sat up very straight in her father's chair, trying to stop herself going to sleep. But she woke with a start when at last the truck came. It was twenty past twelve. She quickly picked up her things, put out the light and hurried upstairs. She didn't want to see Ivor tonight, now that she knew he was home.

3. It was heavy work in the raw autumn morning. Ivor was ploughing again, in the top field, after the usual row and fight with the tractor. He had to get the ploughing finished in the next few days, before the heaviest rains. Most of the sheep were still up on Waunfawr, though the grass was hardly growing now and they

must soon be brought down. Gwen, meanwhile, had to see to the cattle, in the flat meadows by the Llancadog road. She could look across from there to the Bedwen, where Gethin was out ploughing, on a field running up to the Frith. She altered the lines of the electric fences; since they had been strip-grazing they had almost doubled their herd. Then she walked back to the house and cleaned up and set the dinner going. Ivor always came in on the stroke of twelve. In this, at least, he exactly followed his father.

They hardly spoke during dinner, except for a brief argument again about the field next the house, from the larches to the backs of the Pentre cottages. It was a good field, but it was usually neglected. There were great spreading clumps of nettle, and the infesting thistle and foxglove had seeded again. Gwen had wanted Ivor to cut them down earlier, but she thought it was still worth spraying before the winter. Ivor refused; he could do nothing but the ploughing. If the field was a mess it was as much as anything her fault, with the geese making everything filthy. Gwen said that the field had begun to go down when he had started using the dingle in the far corner as a rubbish tip, and the trees he had cleared before tipping were still lying where he had dragged them, in the middle of the field, and the nettle and bramble were growing up through them. Yet it was a hopeless argument: there was too much to do and they had got used to their own ways of doing it. Every month, every day, they had to try to choose work with clear money at the end of it. Almost the only thing of which this was not true was the hedging, always due in September. Everyone in the district did the hedging to a very high standard; most of the field hedges were like garden hedges. Yet this too had clear economic reasons, in stock-raising country. The sheep and cattle still got out; even the best hedges had to be backed by pig-wire. But still the hedging was the best indicator of the priorities of the work. At least the hedges, almost everywhere, were in better condition than the fields they enclosed.

Ivor went back to the tractor and drove off again. He was on the last piece, the steep slope at the west end. Gwen waited until he had gone, then went out for Cavalier. She had to ride up to Waunfawr anyway, to look round the sheep. But she wanted, also, to steady her mind.

She rode slowly up the lane past the cottages and the church. The early afternoon was quiet and though she was used to this in Manod the silence now seemed to drive in on her. It was hanging in the air as if it were the only truth of the place. She could close

51

her eyes and remember children shouting along the lane: Gwilym and Lewis and Mary; May Lewis from the cottage; Johnny Rees from Fronheulog; the Celyn girls, Betty and Dilys, whom she hadn't seen for more than twenty years, since they had gone away to town jobs; they were married now. She pulled lightly on the rein to turn up by Cae Glas. Modlen was hanging out washing in the long back garden. Trevor had finished all his digging and the soil was fresh and bright in the long beds. Modlen called hello to her and she answered, but in the same moment she eased Cavalier to a trot and climbed from the narrow track to the short bitten grass among the gorse and bracken. She could feel the wind now on her back, and she was glad to let go.

It was a good ride up, until she saw Pentwyn ahead: the low grey house and the stone barn, huddled under high broken pines. The tracks divided, and on an impulse she turned for the house. She would talk to Mrs Parry, perhaps even to Megan. She couldn't go on, sitting alone, waiting for Ivor to tell her what was about to happen to her. Yet at the same time she was afraid that to say anything, to show her interest too openly, might only set in motion all that she most feared.

She found Mrs Parry alone, in the dark kitchen. She didn't know how to start what she had really come about, and for some time they talked about anything else. Mrs Parry was no more than fifty but she looked much older: small and lean, with a darkened skin under the wiry black hair. She had a basket of tabby kittens by the big wood fire; they would have to be got rid of, but not just yet.

'Ivor was up here again,' Gwen said, suddenly.

'Last night, yes,' Mrs Parry said quietly.

'He comes often now.'

'Well they like to see each other.'

Gwen was standing over the kittens, getting the warmth of the fire.

'Do they sit with you, in the kitchen?' she asked.

'Well sometimes, yes. Or other times in the room.'

The room was what at Pentre had become the parlour. Gwen's grandparents had still called that 'the room'. At Pentwyn it was the only room on the ground floor, apart from the kitchen and the washhouse.

Gwen stared down at the kittens. They were not pretty yet.

'You know, I expect, I've still got money in the farm. Ivor couldn't manage without it. He knows that.'

'Well yes, Gwen, I thought it would be. I remember your mother talking about it.'

'So till he gets that saved, he can't set up on his own.'

The words sounded hard, coming out like that. Gwen had meant them to be softer. Mrs Parry glanced at her, then pulled out a chair and sat at the scrubbed long table. Gwen turned with her back to the fire.

'I've talked to Megan,' Mrs Parry said. 'Only she won't listen to me. She says the young ones have got the right to fix their own lives.'

'Well they have,' Gwen said, looking down at the kittens.

'I waited eight years,' Mrs Parry said sadly. 'Till he could get this place. He was thirty-one, I was twenty-eight.'

'It's usual,' Gwen said.

'Megan's a good girl, but it's getting on her nerves. Her temper's got very bad, even with me, her own mother. I suppose we get in each other's way.'

'You've got more patience than I have,' Gwen said sharply.

Mrs Parry stared down at her hands on the table. It was some minutes before she spoke again. Her mind was following a line of its own.

'Ivor was saying the other night your father did wrong, selling the cottages to Dance. And now that new fellow's in the one, Mr Price. Ivor reckons Dance will knock the two into one, when Mrs Lewis passes on.'

'He might. I don't know.'

'Only Ivor was reckoning if you still had the cottages . . .'

'Well we haven't,' Gwen said.

Mrs Parry looked down again. In her face and body there was an unspeakable tiredness and sadness.

'They'll just have to learn to wait then. Like we had to.'

She was looking up at Gwen as she spoke, but then she jumped up, startled. She had heard a noise in the yard.

'Oh hullo, Gwen,' Megan said from the door.

'Hullo, Megan.'

'What brings you up here then?'

'I've been riding round the sheep.'

'Yes, we saw Cavalier. I went across to see Ivor. He's still on the tractor, up your top field.'

'Yes, I know.'

Megan went to the sink and washed her hands.

'I bet Mam hasn't offered you a cup of tea, Gwen.'

She was shaking the water from her fingers and blowing between her hands to dry them.

'It's too soon for tea,' Gwen said, watching her.

'No but would you like one?' Mrs Parry asked anxiously. 'It would only be a minute.'

'No, I must get back down. I oughtn't to have stopped.'

Megan came close to Gwen and crouched by the kittens. Her thick black hair went down over her face, brushing the edge of the basket. She put her fingers in among the kittens and played with them. Gwen stood away.

'Dad and Ivor was quarrelling about the sheep,' Megan said without looking up.

'What?'

'Dad said Ivor'd got more on Waunfawr than the agreement. He's had one row already, with Davies Maesyberan. He says the numbers was fixed at the meeting but now everyone else is going their own damn way.'

'Don't swear now, Megan,' Mrs Parry said quickly.

'We've kept to our number anyhow,' Gwen said.

'Well I'm only telling you what Dad said.'

'It's no use talking,' Mrs Parry said. 'It's for the men to settle between them.'

'Well that's what they was doing. Or trying to. Ivor and our Dad.'

She looked up at Gwen as she spoke. It seemed an innocent look but Gwen turned away from it. Megan smiled and went on playing with the kittens. She seemed happy in herself, and cut off from the two older women. Gwen nodded to Mrs Parry and left.

4. There is an old track, cart wide, the *rhiw*, across the southern scarp of Waunfawr. At its notched edge, on the outcrop of rock, is a burial mound, grass covered, rising out of the bracken. Around the heaped grave are several shallow depressions, each littered with old lichened stones lying loose and uneven in the cropped turf. Gwen let Cavalier pick his own way through. The wind was blowing hard in her face. She could see right down to St Dyfrog, very small and isolated in the broad valley. The sun was shining down there, briefly. She watched the line of the river change from brown to silver and then back to brown again. She could now hear the tractor, beyond the ridge, but she could still not see it. Most of the Pentre sheep, with the big crimson V on their sides,

54

were grazing across the intervening hillside. She could make her way down through them and get close to Ivor, or she could follow the *rhiw* towards the Bedwen and look back at him from a distance. She sat undecided, her mind still back in the kitchen at Pentwyn. Then the sound of the tractor stopped suddenly. It could be a trick of the wind, which was blowing in gusts and continually veering. But she went forward at once, making straight for the field. Every yard she went she urged the stallion more strongly. He responded fiercely and she held her breath.

She was past thinking now, except for the ride. He was going much faster than she usually risked along the narrow tracks through the bracken. She was bent very low, just over his neck. She could feel the cold of the wind through her cropped hair, striking down to the roots. She veered him right, twenty yards from the wall, and then set him hard at the gap by the dingle, where the wall had crumbled and there was a larch pole and wire to keep in the sheep. On the far side it was boggy but he was stretched, landing, and the water flew up and he was through and away. She turned for the track through the dingle, ducking low from the trees. Her eyes were half-closed, narrowed down to the track. As the wind still beat and whistled at her, she felt the long cold flow over her face and hands, that she knew from far back, as if her body was separate and she could ride and feel it.

Now she could see the stretch of the ploughed land below her. It was wet and dark red, with torn jagged fronds of fern in the furrows. The tractor hadn't started again. It was still just under the rise, on the steep slope. She followed the fence along, to the top of the rise. Then she reined sharply, almost afraid to look down.

The tractor was on its side, half turned away from her, one wheel still spinning slowly. She felt a scream in her throat but no sound came out. She swung Cavalier and jumped the fence, shouting at him as he jumped. She shouted again as he galloped down to the tractor, over the unploughed land. As he reached it she jumped down, seeing Ivor lying there. He had fallen almost clear but his left leg looked trapped. He was lying twisted over it.

'Ivor, Ivor.'

He was bleeding from his forehead but his eyes were open and he smiled as she came to him.

'Stay still, Ivor. Still.'

'Don't worry. I'm all right.'

She bent over him. She looked along his body to where the tractor lay on his leg. The blue edge of the engine cowling was lying across the leg, just below the knee. The leg had twisted as he jumped. There was oil seeping along the line of the leg. The smell of the stalled engine was acrid.

'How bad does it feel? By your knee?'

'I can't feel it at all, Gwen.'

'Turn your head just a bit. I can ease you round.'

She held him so as to get his arm more comfortable. His head was against her breasts. There was blood now on her jersey, but only thin blood, not important.

'I'll lay you back now, Ivor. I'm going to try to loose the leg.'

He didn't answer. He had begun shivering violently. Gwen gently lowered his head, to the wet grass. Then she stood and pulled off her coat and her heavy black jersey. She folded the jersey under his head and laid the coat over him. There was a sickly taste in her mouth and she shivered suddenly. Only then did she notice the bite of the wind through her thin blouse. She closed her eyes, to concentrate, then as quickly opened them. She looked at the tractor. The danger was that it would roll again. The hill got steeper just where it was lying, dropping down and away to the brook. He had been turning downhill and the weight had fallen outwards from the slope. It had bedded a little, in the soft earth, but any attempt to move it would be very dangerous. She crouched down over his leg, trying to see how far in it was trapped. It was only the cowling, as far in as she could see. She looked up at the bulk of the tractor above her.

'Lie very still now, Ivor.'

There was no answer. She touched the trapped leg, moving her fingers along the dark trouser that was stained with oil and with mud.

'Have you got a fag, Gwenny?'

'Never mind a fag now.'

'In my pocket, Gwenny.'

She turned, reluctantly, and felt in the pocket of his jacket. The lining was torn, and the matches had slipped through, but she got the two packets out, moving her fingers gently and slowly. She leaned in the shelter of his back to light a cigarette and when it was drawing put it round between his lips. He sucked at it, deeply.

Gwen turned away and kneeled where the leg was trapped. She touched the blue metal edge of the cowling and curled her fingers under one side of it, away from the leg. She dared not put pressure on it, in case the whole weight might slip.

56

She breathed deeply. She turned and looked down over the steep fields. A lorry was turning up to Manod from the Llancadog road. It had red sides, she noticed. It would be the brewery lorry, for the Evening Star. She pulled her attention back. She looked down towards the Bedwen.

'Ivor, listen. I've got to go and get help!'

'Is it trapped that bad?'

'No, not bad, but you've got to lie still. We'll need another tractor to move it. I'll go down for Gethin.'

'Aye, he'll be the nearest.'

'Don't talk. Just lie still. I'll be as quick as I can.' He smiled as she spoke down to him. She wanted to get out her handkerchief and wipe the blood from his forehead. It was gathering, as he was lying, in the dark eyebrow. But she must go for Gethin, without wasting a minute. She ran to Cavalier and rode fast down the fields to the road.

Gethin was still ploughing, in the narrow field up the Frith. As she rode up to him she shouted what had happened and he turned at once, heading his tractor for the road. Gwen rode to the Bedwen and phoned for more help: for a metal-cutter, from the garage at St Dyfrog, and for the doctor from Nantlais. She shook with impatience in the delays of the calls. She could work out how long any real help would take. As she rode back across the road she could see Gethin's yellow tractor climbing past the edge of the dingle to where Ivor was lying. She galloped after him, gaining ground, but he arrived before her. When she rode up and dismounted he was standing quite still, staring down at the point where Ivor's leg was trapped. She did not interrupt him. She stood close to him, waiting.

'We can't lift it, Gwen.'

'Can't we?'

'No, she'd slew, like as not, soon as I started to pull.'

'Then what?'

'Get the rope. We'll hold her. That first.'

He was still looking down, with an extraordinary concentration. His lean face was dark and bloodshot. He had not shaved, and Gwen saw how many of the bristles were grey. She had known Gethin all her life. The grey ugly stubble was cold and shocking.

She knelt beside Ivor. He was lying very still and his cheeks were pale and cold. The blood from the cut on his forehead had run down the side of his nose but it was missing his mouth, trickling away over the turn of the big upper lip.

'Gwen,' Gethin called.

'Yes.'

She got up and uncoiled the rope from the box on his tractor. She was starting to tie it to the towing bar but Gethin took it from her, roughly, and tied it himself. Then he climbed to his seat, reversed, and then drove very slowly up the slope until he was above the fallen tractor. He looked down and back. Gwen, following his look, could see how carefully he had chosen the position. The angle at which the holding rope would run was exactly related to the complicated slope and to the way that the tractor was lying. It was as if he could feel every inch of the ground.

'Gwen.'

'Yes.'

He lifted the rope and gave it to her to hold. Then he took the end and walked slowly in on the upper side. He stared in at it, then slid the end of the rope around the propeller shaft and up over the loose wheel. He kept his right hand still, holding the end of the rope. Moving only his left hand, rolling the rope along his fingers, he made it gradually tighter, avoiding any sharp movement. Then he quickly knotted a bowline and walked back up the rope, past Gwen, to his own tractor. He looked again and checked his brake. The fallen tractor was held.

Gwen went back to Ivor. Gethin came and looked down at them. Then he went down first on his knees and then on his stomach, lowering himself on the wet earth until his face and hands were only inches from where the cowling trapped the leg. Gently he tried to insert his fingers, along the line of the leg. Ivor cried out sharply and Gwen comforted him, holding his head. Gethin stood up, straddling Ivor, and bent to get a grip on the cowling. He was almost back on Gwen, as she crouched by Ivor's head. She felt him jerk and strain, as he tried to lift, but though he held the grip, fighting with his breath, he could not move the metal. He let go and went down again on his stomach, feeling beyond the cowling.

'Try and ease him back, Gwen, when I say.'

Gwen stood and bent, holding Ivor's shoulders. Gethin bent in front of her and she felt him jerk again, breathing out sharply.

'Ease the leg back, girl. Now.'

Gwen crawled under his straining body and gently, afraid of herself, tried to draw the leg towards her. She moved the fabric of the trouser but the leg was still trapped.

'No, leave it,' Gethin said sharply.

He stood away, stumbling slightly. Gwen drew herself back and looked at Ivor. His eyes were open and he was staring up at her. Tears were gathering at the lower lids of his eyes.

'It won't be long now, love,' she reassured him.

'Aye, stay with me, Gwenny.'

There was the sound of an engine down the field. It was the garage pickup, its engine screaming as it took the strain of the slithering four-wheel drive, up the steep wet slope. Gethin ran, waving, and directed him round an easier way. He jumped in and was talking to the driver as the pickup arrived.

Len Birch, who had come with the pickup, was younger than Ivor. He nodded to Gwen and walked easily across to look at the cowling. He and Gethin stood by it, and then Len fetched his cutter.

'Cut this first bit anyhow.'

Gwen bent over Ivor who had again closed his eyes. She heard the rasp and whine of the cutter against metal. It seemed to last several minutes but time had changed since that instant, up on the ridge, when she had heard the engine cut out. Gethin was bending again in front of her, his rough hands pulling at the cowling, below the cut. He managed to bend it upwards, his whole body straining. Then he was on his stomach again, reaching along the leg to the ankle. He drew his knife from his pocket and started cutting the top of the boot. When he had cut the leather two inches down he elbowed round and cut the loops of the laces. Then he pushed in his hand, palm up, rough fingers inside the boot.

'Ease him back, Gwen. Now.'

Ivor screamed and grabbed at Gwen. But suddenly the leg was free, although the boot was still trapped. They lifted him away a few paces, and set him down on his back. Gwen replaced her coat and jersey over his shaking body.

Gethin gave his orders.

'In the pickup back to the house. I'll ride with you, Len. Gwen you ride on now, be ready for us.'

'I want to see him into the truck.'

Gethin stared down at her. Her thin blouse was stained and she was grey with cold. The cropped hair was rough and disordered.

'You don't want to waste time,' Gethin said.

Gwen looked up at him. She seemed to isolate his face: the dark lean features, the bloodshot skin, the grey stubble. She could not connect this face with her idea of Gethin. It had seemed very different, just a few minutes back, when they had been so close to each other, in the struggle at the tractor.

'I'll see him into the truck.'

Gethin held her look. Then Ivor moved and cried and she reached down quickly for his hand. Gethin and Len bent and lifted him, and carried him to the back of the pickup. Gethin got in beside him and Len went round to the cab.

Gwen moved without thinking. She fetched Cavalier and rode fast for the house. The pickup was taking a safer route, lower down the slope and then across to the road. But she had barely time to remake his bed and to fetch extra blankets before the pickup arrived in the yard. Len and Gethin carried Ivor through the kitchen and up the old curving staircase. He did not move or speak, but some colour had come back to his face. They got him into the bed and Gwen laid the extra blankets around him. The blood was drying, along his nose and lip. She soaked a clean handkerchief and laid it over the cut on his forehead.

Len and Gethin went downstairs. Gwen stood watching Ivor and then, as he slept, went down to the kitchen to get hot water. The big kettle was already on, and Len was standing by the stove. Looking round she saw Gethin sitting at the head of the long table, watching her. As she noticed him, he smiled. He didn't often do that. He was sitting and waiting easily: the man of the house.

'When you make him some tea, Gwen.'

'Yes, what is it?'

'When you make him his tea, I'll have mine.'

5. Ivor was kept in the house. The doctor came and examined him. The leg was badly cut and bruised, and probably fractured. But the main danger was shock. Overnight, anyway, he should stay where he was. The doctor was talking to Gwen at the foot of the stairs when Gethin came up to them.

'He should be got in to hospital,' Gethin said.

'Tomorrow, Mr Jenkins. Let him rest tonight.'

'Are you trying to save yourself work?' Gethin asked.

The elderly doctor, Harold Bowen from Nantlais, knew Gwen and Gethin well.

'I've explained things to Miss Vaughan. I'll call again in the morning.'

Gethin would have gone on arguing but Gwen went with the

doctor to the door. Gethin went back and sat in the kitchen. Len was still there. He and Gethin had decided to go out later, to get the tractors back. They went on talking in the kitchen. Gwen gave them tea and cake. She served them quietly, hardly noticing. Her attention was elsewhere.

At last, by the evening, with the tractor towed down to the garage in St Dyfrog, and with everything done, Gwen was on her own, and sitting by Ivor's bed. He was sleeping, after a sedative. Gwen herself almost slept, under the pressure of feeling that was gathering now, at the end of the day.

There was a knock at the yard door. She hesitated, too tired to get up and look. It came again, very loud. She stood up and looked at herself in Ivor's wardrobe mirror. There were blood-stains on her blouse, and the breeches and stockings were coated with mud. But it was her eyes, deeply staring, that caught her attention. She was like a stranger, watching herself. The red blotches and spots of inflamed skin stood out, sharply, against her pallor.

She glanced back at Ivor and then went downstairs. She dragged through the kitchen to the yard door. It was Megan.

'Gwen. Is he bad?'

'He's sleeping now.'

'I only just heard. It's his leg, is it?'

'Yes. His left leg.'

'What, broken?'

'Bowen thinks so.'

Megan waited.

'Can I see him, Gwen?'

'What?'

'Can I see Ivor.'

'I told you. He's asleep.'

'I won't wake him. I just want to see him.'

Gwen stood aside. Megan looked nervously at her, but stepped in. Gwen led the way, moving slowly across the flagged kitchen and up the narrow back stairs. She opened the door of Ivor's bed-room and let Megan past her. Megan went quickly across to the side of the bed and bent to look down in his face. Gwen watched every movement, from the open door.

Megan looked round, her face catching the light. A gleam moved in her loose black hair. Gwen stood, watching. Megan turned back to the bed and kissed Ivor on the cheek. Then she drew away from him and followed Gwen back down to the kitchen.

There was a knock at the front door. Gwen went through and unbolted the heavy door, which was only rarely used. It was Susan Price.

'We just heard about Ivor. We saw Mr Jenkins. Is there anything we can do?'

'No, he's sleeping, thank you. There's nothing for the moment.'

'Can I bring you round a meal? Or help you sitting with him?'

'No, it's all right, Mrs Price. But thank you.'

'Well you know where we are. And I brought you this.'

She handed Gwen a bottle of red wine. Gwen took it, surprised.

'You'll come in?' she said.

'No, not now, thank you. Unless I can help.'

'I can manage,' Gwen said.

Susan went, and Gwen rebolted the heavy door. Megan was standing in the kitchen. Gwen put the bottle on the table and went across to the stove. She took no notice of Megan.

'She's from London, isn't she?'

'Who?'

'That Mrs Price?'

'Yes.'

'What they come here for?'

Gwen didn't answer. Megan looked around the kitchen.

'Can I take him anything?' she asked, trying to get Gwen to notice her. Gwen stood at the stove as if nothing had been said.

'Or help you now, Gwen? You're tired, you look tired. And I could get the supper. Or outside. Anything.'

'Gethin saw to the cattle. There's nothing more.'

'That was nice of Gethin.'

'He's seen to it all,' Gwen said.

She was speaking very quietly, as if to herself. When she noticed Megan it was as if she was surprised to find her still there.

'I feel like it happened to me,' Megan said.

'Yes,' Gwen said, but without attention.

'Only he said you was always warning him. That he'd have an accident. He said you worried too much, like he was still a child.'

Gwen looked at her, sharply, but then again turned away, as if reassured.

'I'm tired, Megan.'

'Yes, I know you're tired.'

'And I must get back up to Ivor.'

Megan hesitated. The colour rushed up into her face.

'He asked me to marry him, Gwen. And I said yes. He said he'd talk to you.'

'Well, he didn't.'

'Only now, with the accident . . .'

'I can manage, Megan. You heard me say.'

'But all the work of the farm. And him in bed to look after.'

'It's my living, Megan. I'm used to it. This is my home, remember.'

Megan drew in her breath and looked down at the table. She began to cry suddenly. She turned her face away.

'You'd better go home now,' Gwen said, without emphasis.

'I'll go,' Megan said, rubbing her sleeve across her face. 'I'll go. You don't want me here, Gwen. You don't want anybody. You want to keep him to yourself, you've always tried to. And you're set against me, though I've done nothing wrong to you.'

'Did I say you had?'

'He wants to get married. There's no wrong in that. You never got married yourself but Ivor wants to and I want to. And you'd just keep him here. Keep him like a kid so that you can go on as you are.'

'So that the farm can go on.'

'We could run the farm. I work, don't I? And it's *his* farm. It was his father left it to him.'

Gwen tried to turn away. She could feel the dull pulse of her tiredness.

'No, Megan, you don't understand. There isn't the money, not unless I stay.'

'He said that. But he said he could clear that off in a year.'

'He's got a broken leg.'

'Yes, *now*, yes. But it was the same before. You was still against it.'

Gwen went to the stove. She took a dish and ladled soup into it. 'I must go up and see to him.'

'Let me help you, Gwen. Please. I can't bear doing nothing.'

Gwen put the soup with bread and the wine on a tray. She walked across the kitchen in her stockinged feet. She felt the cold of the stones, as if from far outside her.

'There's nothing now, Megan. You heard me say. I can manage.'

IV

1. PETER touched the catch and the curtain sprang up. Beth, lying on her bed, saw the lights of the city moving beyond his head and shoulders. He was tense and thin, his head awkwardly angled as he strained to look out.

'You're sorry to be leaving it.'

'Yes, love, I am.'

'Damned Sweden you said, when we came.'

'It's still damned Sweden. As humane and affluent as capitalism can get, and still damned.'

'But you've enjoyed it.'

'Of course. Anyway a foreign capitalism is easier. You go as a consumer, or on some temporary job. It doesn't hit you where it hurts.'

'And a foreign socialism?'

'That hits you where it hurts. Because you know you don't belong to it. You're a foreigner and a dissenting comrade.'

'You'll find reasons for anything, Peter.'

He turned and laughed. The light was reflected, strangely, on his pale drawn face. Even after this summer, the best time she could remember, she still saw him, at moments, as unknown and far from her. He rubbed his hands back through his tallow hair, and turned again to the window.

'Come and look at the lights in the water.'

'All right. The last time.'

She pushed herself up from the lower bed. Her head was aching and she was afraid of being sick on the journey. It was still eight weeks before the baby was due but she had had a lot of sickness and this journey frightened her. Yet she was glad to be going home for the baby to be born.

They were three days late starting back. The night sleeper from Stockholm would get them to Copenhagen in the morning and make the connection to Esbjerg for the English boat. Then as soon as they landed they must get down to Wales, for Peter's job.

'It's beautiful, isn't it, the lights in the water?'

'Yes,' Beth whispered.

'You can see the city as it should be. How any city should be. A whole open centre of light.'

'An idea for Manod?'

'I've got no ideas about Manod. I told you, that whole scheme's a con.'

'Then why are we going there?'

'Because it's a salary. And because you can be near your mother for the baby.'

'No more? Honestly?'

'Well if we can show it's a con it will help to bust them.'

'Did you tell Lane that?'

'Robert Lane! Of course not. He's part of the con.'

He was still staring from the window. Beyond the floodlit City Hall there was an avenue of lights along a road and over a bridge. The pattern of lights seemed to move in several dimensions: within itself, as the train moved past it; in its reflections in the water; and in its varying distances as the line swung away.

'There's that bridge, look, Beth, where we got lost that night.'

'Is it?'

'We shouldn't have walked there. It's only for cars.'

'Yes.'

Her answer was so tired that he turned and looked at her.

'You're tired.'

'My head's splitting.'

'Go back to bed. We'll get a good night's sleep and then rest again on the boat.'

'I hope so, Peter.'

She pulled back and stretched out on the bed. In the tiny cabin every surface was close: an arranged, convenient, enclosed world, but pitching slightly all the time, over the noise of the wheels. As soon as they had got in Peter had shown her, excitedly, all the switches and racks and containers: an efficient small world. But now he was still pressed close to the glass, watching the last lights of the city.

Beth kicked off her shoes. It was very warm in the cabin; the window was beginning to steam over. Peter wiped it with his sleeve and then as it misted again snapped the curtain down. The noise of the wheels seemed louder suddenly.

'Does it upset you, going back?'

'No, Peter, it's only the journey.'

'Just forget you're travelling. This is as peaceful as anybody could want.'

'You've got a funny idea of being peaceful.'

'Yes, eighty miles an hour, in this box, going to bed as usual.'

'It's only the moving. It's like different rhythms inside me.'

'We didn't choose our time,' Peter said.

He lifted the curtain again, restlessly. He wiped the glass and looked out but all he could see now were the dim shapes of birch trees, running close along the line. He pulled the curtain down and began to undress.

'This is the right feeling, anyway, to take to that job. On the move between places.'

'I thought the point was to go somewhere.'

'Yes. Do you remember in Rome, that stone in the Forum from which all distances were measured? I stood and closed my eyes and thought of the long march to Britain: all that necessary distance, carrying a different world on your back.'

'That's a long time ago.'

'Yes, we move faster now.'

He finished undressing and climbed up the ladder to the top bunk. The train swayed over points and he had to clutch the rope handle. He squatted with his head near the metal ceiling.

'But if I know Matthew Price,' he said, laughing, 'he'll be sitting on a hill, watching the legions arrive.'

'Will he?'

'Yes, that's his position. He's very conscious of history but not at all that he's helping to make it.'

'I don't know. I've not met him.'

'I've only heard him lecture. But when he talks about the past you can hear his voice break. He's a man who has sat too long, watching the legions arrive.'

'I thought you approved of him.'

'Yes, very much. He knows what has happened. He seems to carry it about with him. But when the legions arrive in that valley . . .'

'What?'

'I don't know. You can't tell. I expect, really, he'll still be sitting and watching.'

Beth closed her eyes. She had started to undress but was still sitting holding her jersey.

'I know how he feels,' she said quietly.

'What?'

'It doesn't matter.'

There was a pause and then Peter leaned over from his bunk, staring in at her. She had to laugh as she saw his face upside down, its tense angularity comically emphasized.

'You're all right, though, aren't you?' he insisted.

'I'm in dispute,' Beth said. 'I'm idle. Management and labour have broken off negotiations.'

'You look all right. You look fine.'

Beth smiled. She dropped the jersey and held her bare shoulders, crossing her arms. Her usual high colour had intensified. Her long dark red hair hung over her face. Peter wriggled along his bunk and let his head and shoulders go farther down, offering to kiss her goodnight.

'Don't be daft, you'll fall out,' she protested, as he continued to come down.

'Controlled downward mobility,' said the upside-down face, breathing hard.

'You're impossible,' she said, and reached up and kissed him. There was an extraordinary rattle of noise as he scrambled back up. But then he went quiet almost at once. In a minute or two he would be sound asleep. It was usually like this. She lay down and pulled the blanket over her shoulders, putting out the main light. She lay, quite awake, listening to the beat of the wheels.

It had been so long, so very long, waiting for the life she had hoped for when she had married Peter. She had known from the beginning that there would be some waiting. When he had dropped his research and gone to work in the car factory she had kept on her job in the bank, in case he changed again. That was now seven years ago. He had worked on the assembly line for sixteen months, then left it to write his book. That, really, had been the worst time, the worst feeling time. He had the plan laid out, his material all ready, but then he found he could not write. Some rhythm, some adjustment, had changed, and he could only talk and plan.

Then, after six wasted months, which had taken all the money he had saved from his job, they had gone on what had seemed an ordinary demonstration, against the bombing in Vietnam, and when a policeman pushed him Peter had pushed him back. That was assault and a nine months sentence, of which he served six: a month in Wormwood Scrubs and five in an open prison in Somerset. He was thin and hard when he came out. It took two months doing nothing to get him settled again. And he had then said that he would not, after all, write the book about the factory.

He would get out his old thesis, submit it for a doctorate and become respectable again. That had lasted until he re-read the thesis and then in a burst of angry energy he had written the book: *Industrial Estate*. It took eighteen months to get it published, and through all that time Beth had supported him.

Well, she had promised him that, in the original decision. All her friends had blamed her. Even his friends blamed her, for making it easy for him, letting him go on postponing getting a regular job. And then, ironically, when the book was a success, getting wide recognition, it was the bad time for jobs and instead of something settled and permanent there was only this series of short-term jobs, taking them all over: Canada, Italy, Sweden; conferences, journalism; now this year in Wales. It was very much better than nothing but it was not what she wanted and what she had worked to secure: some life they could settle to, some place to grow into: a normal life.

Yet she could only complain to herself. She knew Peter too well, from all the years of growing up together in Goldsmith Street. He could fit in, very easily, with what other people wanted, accepting their kind of work and postponing his own. And she had seen what then happened to him, what kind of man he became. It was still a bitter memory: the man she had first come to know, in that way, when he was working with Robert Lane. He had been conforming, active, almost endlessly talking, but behind this all the time he had been on the run, hardly knowing why he ran: on the run from himself, from that adjusted person; building every postponement, every empty conformity, every stage of the flight, into an effective personality: meeting all his external commitments but incapable of love and bitterly hostile to all settled relationships. All his intelligence went into tricks of adjustment and of subtle explanation, but behind them all the time there was a racing, destructive, annihilating anger: a blind anger behind the accepting face.

Beth did not want him like that. She could not have him like that. She preferred, even now, any kind of unsettlement, any conscious disturbance or anger, to the recurrence, inside him, of that terrible flight. And she had come to understand why there was no easy way out. Seeing his time as he saw it, as a civilization and a society systematically repressive and false, there was a hard, bitter choice very early: to acquiesce or to oppose. No ordinary settlement had ever been possible. He would either fight that world in the open or, afraid to fight it or having taken its knocks, learn the means of pretence and disguise: despising all he joined, all he did, all he tacitly affirmed.

Others would say that he had settled, that he had learned the conforming contempt of his time: the durable habit of a particular generation. 'Nobody believes in this system; just millions operate it.' Or what he had said going to Sweden: 'to write a critique of industrial capitalism on a grant from a foundation sustained by industrial capitalism. And I'm glad to relieve them of the money.' Or of the offer from Robert Lane: 'a public relations con, but it's a year's salary and I'm good at public relations.' But Beth was in touch with the man behind this: the systematic opportunist, the man with no feeling, no connection, that had any meaning or hold. It was a hard judgment, but she had learned its truth in all her own deepest feelings; learned it, quite directly, in her body. This wasn't the active, vigorous, connecting man everyone else seemed to know. It was a dreadful nullity: a cancellation of everything. And while he did not fight he would inevitably be that. The driving anger was too fierce to be dissolved or to fade; it would either get expressed or destroy him.

And then because she had loved him, because she had always wanted to be with him, to keep his life going, she had known, years back, that there was no real choice. When he had fought she had lost him, as in those months in prison. When he had not fought he was even more lost to her, in the persistent flight that only she could feel and touch. And while this was so, though hoping against hope that the world might still change, she had settled to holding her own life back; taking disturbance, discomfort, the repeated and endless postponements, in whatever came their way.

The cabin was swaying, above the steady beat of the wheels. She breathed deeply and pushed herself up, to get aspirin from her bag by the window. As she stood by the bed she looked in at Peter. He was not asleep, as she had been assuming. He was still sitting up, staring silently, under the metal roof.

'Peter.'

It took him some moments to answer. Then he looked down at her. He seemed to be searching her face. She held a rung of the ladder and reached up to touch his hair.

'Is there room for two down below?' he said quickly, touching her hand.

'There's two down here already.'

'Yes or I wouldn't be perched up here.'

She went for the aspirin. As she came back she said:

'We shall stay there, love, shan't we?'

'What?'

'Stay the full year. In Wales.'

He stared at her again. Then his eyes changed focus.

'Well yes, I suppose so. If they don't kick me out.'

'They wouldn't do that.'

'That depends, doesn't it?'

'I want to stay, Peter. I want the year for the baby.'

'Well of course, love, don't worry.'

He leaned over and kissed her, on the edge of her hair.

'You still want the baby, don't you?' she said, feeling stupid.

'With you, Beth, any time.'

'No, Peter, the actual baby.'

'Well we've got it now, haven't we?'

Beth nodded and turned away.

'Lie down and get some sleep,' she said, as she got into her own bed. But she went on listening to the deep beat of the wheels, in the long journey home.

2. 'Petrol!'

Peter rang the bell again, loudly, as he shouted. A muffled voice answered, from the metal shed.

'Be with you in a minute.'

'Do you expect us to wait all day? Don't you believe in service? That's what's wrong with this country.'

Gwyn came from the shed, wiping his hands on a rag.

'Aye, I thought it was you two,' he said, smiling.

Peter banged on the side of the van.

'Non stop from Sweden and now we get to the land of our fathers there's nobody to serve us.'

'Come on in', Gwyn said. 'Myra's waiting.'

Beth got out of the van, stretched her legs, and went to kiss her stepfather. He was as lean and drawn as in the years in Goldsmith Street, working down in the car factory. But in other ways he had changed, since he had moved to Trawsfynydd. He was slower, easier, his clothes and movements looser.

'You must be tired, love,' he said.

'Yes, we had a gale on the boat.'

Gwyn took Beth's bags and walked through to the back door, with its benched porch. Peter drove the van round the single petrol pump and into the repairs shed. As he came out he looked up the fields at the dark ridge of Brynllwyd and the black rockfall from the Kestrel. The air was damp and mild: very soft on the skin.

'Peter, love, you coming in?'

'Myra.'

He hurried along the path to the door. Myra was standing with her arms out, waiting for him. She seemed hardly to have changed: the tall heavy body, the bright red cheeks, the quick smile.

'You got her back safe then. She looks well.'

'Yes, travelling's good for her.'

'I don't know about that. All that cold up North.'

'You've got the wrong idea about Sweden. We've had the warmest summer I ever remember.'

'I expect I have got the wrong idea. I usually have.'

'Go on, you look well on it.'

'That's hard work, that's all.'

She led the way in. There was a huge coal-and-wood fire in the living-room. Beth was leaning over it as if at last she could get warm.

'Your dinner'll be ready in just a few minutes.'

'Can I help, Mam?' Beth asked.

'No, you just stay and get warm.'

'There's no heater in the van,' Peter said. 'Still, it just about goes.'

'Aye,' Gwyn said, 'I was listening to it.'

Myra went through to the kitchen. Beth waited and then followed her. Peter turned to Gwyn.

'You doing all right here, then?'

'Mustn't grumble, Peter.'

'Why ever not? Still, is the garage OK?'

'A bit from that. A bit from the field.'

'You never went on with that elderberry idea.'

'No, that was daft. A real town idea. But I've got apples and blackcurrants and a few hundred Christmas trees. That and the caravans, they're the best crop of the lot.'

'What they call the tourist industry.'

'Aye, where there's money to chuck.'

Gwyn bent and put another log on the fire.

'I had an offer, though, about the garage,' he said.

'What, to buy it?'

'No. You take on this agency, they give you a grant to modernize up. New front, new pumps, all a proper job.'

'Just for taking their brand of petrol?'

'Aye, going over to them. There was a chap come to see me, called Dance, from Pontafren. He's done a lot of it around. Sort of agent for them.'

'Are you going to take it?'

'Well I don't see why not. I shall get the same on the petrol and I get the place done up.'

'No more trade in that.'

'Not up here, no. Whatever I stock, people here got to buy.' Peter laughed.

'Well all right, then. Only all I'd say, don't take the first offer. Work out what you want and then bid them up.'

Gwyn frowned.

'I thought you didn't believe in all that, Peter.'

'I don't. But look at it: five major oil companies, competing flat out. I'd prefer to smash them but meanwhile it's up to us to get all we can out of them. Like the works, remember? Get all you can from the buggers.'

Gwyn narrowed his shoulders.

'I don't know,' he said. 'I'll think about it.'

Myra came in with the dinner. Beth laid the places. They sat to the table, in the warm overcrowded room. Myra was in the middle of serving when the telephone rang, very loud, from outside in the shed.

'Damn,' Gwyn said, 'I didn't switch it through.'

He got up and went to answer it. Almost at once he came back to the window and knocked.

'It's for Peter. Some chap called Price.'

'Christ yes, I gave him this number,' Peter said. He looked angrily around.

'Well go and talk to him, Peter,' Beth said anxiously. 'After all you're three days late, you've got to work sometime.'

'Work you call it.'

'No, go on. And be polite to him.'

'He's all right. I can manage him. Shall I tell him I'll go over tomorrow?'

'It's all right with me. But don't keep him waiting.'

Gwyn came back in. Peter got up reluctantly.

'I'll keep your food warm,' Myra said.

3. Matthew waited at the end of the lane, opposite the Evening Star. The road from the valley was wet but a pale sunlight was filtering through the high clouds above the mountains. He saw a van turn the corner, up the pitch through the steep wet banks. As it came close he lifted his hand and it drew in past him on the lane. Peter got out and came round, slamming the door.

They shook hands. Peter stared with great interest into Matthew's face, and the pressure of his hand was unusually strong. Matthew smiled.

'Did you have a good journey over?'

'From Sweden. Yes, very good.'

'I meant from Trawsfynydd.'

'Yes, all right.'

'They keep improving that road. Though I came over once at night and I forgot the cattle grid. When the headlights caught it I had to slam on the brakes.'

'It's still there,' Peter said.

His voice faded. He turned and looked away. Matthew waited and then spoke.

'Shall we walk up to the cottage?'

'What about the van?'

'It's all right there. Or bring it on up.'

'I'd prefer to walk.'

They moved together up the lane. Opposite Pentre, Peter stopped and looked round.

'So this is the famous Manod?'

'The actual Manod.'

'That's a nice looking farm.'

'Yes, it is.'

'They don't know when they're well off. That's stockbroker level anywhere else.'

'They're having difficulty, actually. Ivor Vaughan, who runs it, had a tractor accident. He still can't get about.'

'Who'd want to, a place like that?'

Matthew turned and looked at him: at the tallow hair, the thin face, the tense body. He was very conscious of how young Peter seemed.

'You believe in all this?' Peter said, looking away.

'In Manod as it is, or as it might be?'

'Well, either. They're connected. But what I really mean is this job we're doing for Lane.'

'I shall do it now I've said I will.'

'Well sure. But keeping clear of the crap.'

'Which, particularly?'

'Well this new city kick. Whatever happens, it won't be that.'

'New towns, new villages?'

'No, nothing of that. Leave the new out of it. It will be a few housing estates looking down at a few factories. That at a maximum.'

'Has the alternative future collapsed that completely?'

'I'd say so, yes. Until power has changed at the centre. The future of this place will be settled between London and Birmingham, either way.'

'No alternative communities?'

'No communities at all. I grew up in the kind of place that is now the best they can imagine: a car works with housing estates all around it. And that's the real pressure. Here, like anywhere else, the factories would take their unquestioned priority. You can't just conjure any other meanings.'

'Not conjure, certainly.'

'Or plan any other meanings. The plans are the deception. The ugliest place ever built looked great, I saw it, on the planning folder. All that clever shading, to soften the brutal cost-effective frontages, and the neatly placed tree, you can almost hear the birdsong, and that slim young mother, an advertising mother, eight foot high, who is strolling through, quite alone, and the flare of her skirt just happens to repeat the perspective of the arcade. Urban arcadia, on paper. In fact a slum of the mind.'

Matthew looked down. He was pushing with his stick at the film of glazed mud on the edge of the lane. It was a beautiful soft pink where it had begun to dry. The small pools in the ruts were a luminous peat brown.

'If we didn't believe that it could somewhere be different,' he began, but then Peter interrupted.

'I know. But it can't start here.'

'Always somewhere else?'

Peter looked across at the Pentre yard, which was deep in mud where the cattle had been standing. He smiled and looked out at the rough fields beside the Dowy, and the tangle of bracken and thorn on the long slopes of the Frith.

'You don't want it here,' he said, turning.

Matthew lifted his stick and moved on.

'I'm not sure,' he said quietly. 'We drove here in September. On the road by Llanerch there's a black and white house, below

74

a long dingle. The bracken begins just behind the house and there's a lane up under the trees, through a white field gate. It runs up to the gorse and the heather, and along the bank of the lane there are old grey marker stones, crusted with yellow lichen. I just stood there looking and I found myself saying: leave it alone, leave at least this place alone.'

'You still feel that, obviously. I can hear that you feel it.'

'Does the feeling matter? I still get my living elsewhere. I made that choice long ago. This place is good to look at but people still have to leave it.'

'That's a different problem.'

'Is it? I don't know. But I must tell you the sequel to that moment in Llanerch. I discovered, quite by chance, that the house I'd admired had been recently modernized by a speculative builder, and that the same man, Dance, is full of plans for this area. If nothing else happens, he'll change it anyway.'

'But in ways you'd approve. That's the moral of that house. Did you say Dance?'

'Yes. He lives in Manod. In fact I rent the cottage from him.'

'He's a builder, is he? Because he's been over in Trawsfynydd with an oil company agency. He made an offer to modernize my uncle's garage.'

'It would fit. He's in everything. He's that kind of man.' They had reached the cottage and Matthew opened the gate. Along the path through the garden there were a few last autumn flowers: late pansies, late Michaelmas daisies, a few ragged marigolds. Most of the stalks and flowers in the border were already dead: falling and twisting into a dark tangled mass. White seeds of the Michaelmas daisies lay thickly at the edge of the path.

They went to the back door and cleaned off their shoes. Then they went through to the living-room, where Susan was sitting by the fire. She got up and welcomed Peter, and asked about Beth.

'It's only a few weeks,' Peter said. 'She's glad to be there with her mother.'

'I didn't realize, till you wrote,' Matthew said, 'you had family so close.'

'It's why I jumped at the job, for Beth. Though I'd have jumped at anything.'

'I thought you said your uncle in Trawsfynydd.'

'It's the usual tangle,' Peter said. 'Beth was actually born in Trawsfynydd. Then her father was killed, on a motorbike, and her mother, Myra, married my father's brother Gwyn. We all

75

lived in adjoining houses in Goldsmith Street. Beth and I were together from before we went to school. About the time we got married Gwyn gave up his job and took on this garage.'

'And are your parents still in Goldsmith Street?'

'Yes. My father's still a convener. My mother runs the City Labour Party, or so she tells me. She's also a magistrate.'

'Kate Owen,' Matthew said. 'Wasn't she on the Children's Commission?'

'That and others. She says she's the Statutory Woman.'

'I think I saw her being interviewed.'

'I expect so. It's a small world, all these liberal causes.'

Susan went and fetched tea. They sat together round the fire, in the small crowded living-room. It was getting dark early, and rain was beginning to beat on the window.

'You're looking forward to this work?' Susan asked.

'Well, Robert Lane's put us here. Now we must see what happens.'

'I've got no ties here,' Susan said, 'but something has to be done. You can't leave a whole country to decay.'

'You can,' Peter said. 'That's how it's always done.'

'If the new city isn't right,' Susan said, 'you can recommend something else. Robert Lane will listen to you.'

'No, he won't. Not to me or to Matthew.'

'Why do you say that?'

'He doesn't listen to anyone. He just plays the system.'

'Then why send you both down here?'

'Some manoeuvre or other. In fact my first business is to find what it is.'

'You mean apart from what he told you? And from what he told Matthew?'

'Yes, apart from that.'

'You know him quite well. Don't you trust him?'

Peter laughed.

'It's a long lane that isn't bent.'

'You don't really think that,' Matthew said, anxiously.

'Not the usual way. Not like this man Dance would be bent. But something, certainly.'

Susan looked across at Matthew. He was lying back in his chair, looking utterly tired.

'Nobody,' Peter said, 'is going to put money into a place like this, just for the good of the people. If they ever put it in it will be to get something out.'

76

'Get what out?' Susan asked.

'Perhaps none of the obvious things, though they must all be checked. Minerals, for example. I was looking up Nantlais. In the early nineteenth century there was lead and silver mining. There was even, believe it or not, a Chartist riot in the town.'

'The mines closed,' Matthew said. 'They were very small scale.'

'Somebody may have done the sums again. But it needn't be that. Water, forestry, upland ranching, a nuclear power station: it could be anything, and whatever it is it won't be in the studies.'

'I've been through them very carefully.'

'Yes,' Peter said, 'as if you were dealing with honest men.'

Susan collected the tea things and went out. Peter sat enjoying the fire. They did not speak for some time. Then when he moved he noticed that Matthew was watching him.

'Have I depressed you, Matthew?'

'No, not particularly. I've run the same analysis and drawn a different conclusion.'

'Which is?'

'That the basic pressure isn't the need here. It's the need in the cities: the need to avoid explosion and breakdown. And it's possible, I think, that this could be a trial run. Not economic investment but social. It would be difficult of course, but there are things they want to try: new communications and transport technologies; a working model of a different kind of city: a dispersed city. If not from Britain then from Europe that kind of experiment, that kind of capital, could come.'

'But that's taking Lane at face value.'

'No, not entirely. As I say, I've thought it through and on those assumptions I believe it's important. If we can't hang on to that then there isn't a future at all.'

It was now dark in the room, except for the light from the fire. Matthew made no move to switch on a lamp but stayed lying deep in his chair.

'Do you like having the light off?' Peter asked.

'Usually, yes.'

'It makes me uneasy.'

'I'm sorry. I'll put it on.'

'No, please. I'm uneasy anyway.'

'I grew up in a house without electric light. That hard glare, overhead, always presses in on me.'

'And you're talking about a future, about a city, about lighting this whole valley.'

'Yes, I know. But we've been living so long in enemy country, we suspect our own shadows.'

He got up and switched on the light. Peter also got up and they were suddenly close to each other, in the small low room. Matthew moved across to the table by the window.

'Shall we go through what we'll do then? What we can each do?' he asked.

'Sure,' Peter said. 'I need to get started.'

Matthew picked up his papers and brought them over to the light.

V

1. As winter closed in it was all Gwen could do to keep going. Ivor could get about now with a stick, but it would be months before he could do heavy work or drive. Gwen got a girl from St Dyfrog, Olwen Mortimer, to help in the house, and did much of the outdoor work herself. But she could not have managed if Trevor Jenkins had not offered to finish the ploughing, and Gethin also helped, bringing the sheep down and taking some to sell in Pontafren market. Trevor still came for a few hours every day, to do the heaviest work. There was a lot of ditching with the heavier rains.

Trevor was nearly twenty years younger than his brother Gethin. William Jenkins, their father, had died in his early fifties and Gethin had taken over the Bedwen while Trevor was still in the junior school. At fifteen, when he left school, Trevor had gone on working on the family farm, as a matter of course. It was only slowly, in his late teens, that he began to question his position. He was paid no regular wage, for he was working in the family and just got odd money when he needed it, as he had while still at school. This was not too bad while his mother was alive, but when she died, when he was just eighteen, he began to realize the difficulties of his position.

William Jenkins had died without making a will, and ownership had passed to his widow. She in turn left the farm to Gethin, who had been actually running it for many years, and tried to keep a balance between her sons by leaving six hundred pounds directly to Trevor, as a start for eventually buying his own farm. She believed that for ten years or more Gethin and Trevor would go on working the farm together and that then, when Trevor came to marry, Gethin would help to set him up in a farm.

It might have worked, but as Trevor got older he became more resentful of Gethin's authority. He could not take the airs of a father, or as often the tone of an employer, from a man who though so much older was only his brother. Finally, after a bad row, he asked Gethin to help him to get his own farm and Gethin refused. He had no money to spare, he insisted; anyway nothing like the money to buy in on a farm, with the price of land rising so fast. Trevor saw the accounts and there was indeed no money to spare. Every year they were in debt until the store sale money, which just got them back level.

Angry but still confident, Trevor struck out on his own. He married Modlen, moved to Nantlais and worked as a platelayer on the railway. The work was no harder and at least, now, he would have a regular wage. This lasted for three years, until the line was given notice to close. The campaign against the closure failed and Trevor lost his job. He was offered another job, at Swindon, on the main line, but Modlen did not want to move so far away from her family. Trevor went back, reluctantly, to talk things over with Gethin.

It was eventually agreed that they would try the old arrangement, working the farm together, but now with Trevor on a regular wage. Trevor drew his six hundred pounds to buy Cae Glas on a mortgage. On its two acres he could add to his wage by breeding ponies for the trekkers, now a lucrative business, and by gardening and keeping bees. But it had not been easy. There were quarrels with Gethin about the amount of time he spent with his ponies, and at the times of year when money was very short—in the late winter and the middle months of summer—Gethin had got into the habit of putting off Trevor's wages, against the promise of a bonus when the lambs or the young cattle or the store ewes were sold. It was difficult, always, to keep these accounts, and hardly a week passed without a quarrel between the brothers, about their complicated obligations and debts.

Gethin had always been tight with money. Like most of his neighbours he spent little on himself and put nearly everything he had into the farm. At first, after Ivor's accident, he had raised no difficulty about Trevor helping at Pentre. Indeed he had urged it on him, and had insisted to Gwen that there was no question of payment: it was the least they could do for a neighbour in trouble. So Trevor worked with Gwen and of course kept on with his ponies. He also still did many jobs on what had been, all his life, the family farm. But his wages, there, were now several months behind, and when he complained Gethin answered only that it was bound to be difficult, now that they were helping a neighbour. They must just all work in together and get along as well as they could. Later on, of course, it would all be put right.

2. Gethin was sitting with Ivor in the cool white kitchen at Pentre. The late afternoon sun threw patches of angled light on the whitewashed plaster walls: a yellow light, at times deepening towards orange, as thin clouds gathered above the spur of the Frith. Where the light fell the plaster showed as uneven. On these kitchen walls there was still very old plaster, pitted and lined, in a surprising tracery, with the marks of the straw that had been used in making it.

Gethin often now sat with Ivor. Before the accident he had taken little notice of him; he was just the youngest at Pentre and of a different, inaccessible generation. But now he came most days, for an hour or so, and sat through the slow conversation, in which Ivor had to make almost every move. Ivor was quite sure that Gethin really came to see Gwen; everyone knew that they had once been going to marry. But Gwen avoided him, and still he kept coming.

Today Gwen had gone out as soon as Gethin arrived. She was still up on Waunfawr, with Cavalier. Olwen had finished her work in the house and gone back down on her bike to St Dyfrog. Gethin and Ivor had the house to themselves.

Gethin was sitting in what had been the father's chair, on the side of the hearth where he could look out to the yard. He had moved closer to the wall when the angled sunlight had touched his face, though his skin was so dark and weatherlined that it was surprising it could feel this pale winter light. On the hollow cheeks there was the usual crop of stiff grey bristles. Ivor could not understand how Gethin seemed always to have about three days' growth of beard, never more or less. But he looked in place, in the big old chair, and when he came to speak, in his few slow bitten phrases, Ivor recognized the accents of the only kind of authority he had ever acknowledged.

Ivor was sitting with his elbow on the corner of the long scrubbed table. His healing leg was propped on a stool towards the fire in the hearth. He had put on weight since the accident. His face was full and flushed under the shiny dark hair. By any ordinary signs he seemed, in these weeks since the accident, more settled, more prosperous and generally more of a man. On the other corner of the table, between him and Gethin, was a bottle of whisky, and Ivor's half-filled glass. Gethin drank no alcohol; indeed he was well-known for his condemnation of it, which was quite common among the farmers of the district. But on these visits to Pentre he would get up and pour for Ivor, to save him the awkwardness of moving. The bottle stood prominently between them, casting its elongated shadow on the patch of yellow sunlight, in the lattice of tiny shadows in the straw marks of the plaster near Gethin's bowed head.

Ivor finished a cigarette and started another. A conversation about buying straw from England had started and faded out. Gethin had been against it: the prices were ridiculous; they'd be better mowing bracken. Then he was silent again.

'You been up Pentwyn lately?' Ivor asked, after a long pause.
'Parry's?'
'Aye.'
'No.'

Ivor eased himself back, settling his leg more comfortably. It was a long slow job, getting words out of Gethin.

'Megan comes down, mind, most days.'
'Aye.'
'Only it's her and Gwen worries me. They don't hardly speak.'
'No, I suppose.'
'D'you reckon it's fair then, Gethin? Fair on me like?'
'What? Gwen?'
'She don't have to like Megan, admitted. Only seeing as we're going to get married.'

Gethin looked across at him.

'When?'
'Oh, no date, mun, now. The old leg put that off.'
'It'll mend.'
'Aye. And then it'll have to be settled.'

Ivor drew on his cigarette, leaning back. He could hear this as the moment when Gethin should shift and speak, in the familiar rhythm of every conversation he was used to. If he waited, now, Gethin would have to show his hand: make the pronouncement, as his father had always described it. But the silence continued and deepened, until Ivor could hear the tick of the clock in the passage. He reached for his glass, trying to think of another approach.

'The Council's quiet these days,' Gethin said suddenly.

Ivor stopped with the glass halfway to his lips. This was so unexpected, so off the line of any real interest, that he had to play it back in his mind, still wondering where Gethin was getting.

'Quieter the better,' he said.
'Aye. On most things.'

Ivor stared across at him. For as long as he remembered Gethin had been their councillor, on both the County and the District.

He had succeeded his father, in both positions, and was always returned unopposed. But he hardly ever spoke about council affairs. There was no real need to. There was an unspoken agreement that once the right men were on—and this was easily managed—there was little more to say. You elected, by and large, to see that the wrong things didn't happen and to keep down the rates. The only important things were the roads and the culverts: the district did well in that; people just mentioned it to Gethin.

'Powys they call us now,' Ivor tried again.

'Aye.'

What had he brought it up for if he wasn't going on? What had it to do with them and with Manod anyway?

'You remember the scheme?' Gethin said.

'No. We buried that.'

'There's talk again. Different things are happening.'

'Aye, that Price up the lane. Somebody's paying him.'

'No, no, that's London.'

'Well it was London it come from. That daft talk about a city.'

'Aye well we shan't see that,' Gethin said.

So leave it alone. Get back to something important.

'Something more practical, perhaps,' Gethin said, shifting.

Ivor drained his glass.

'This is farming land. It'll stay farming land,' he said loudly.

The yellow light ebbed from the walls, as the clouds thickened above the Frith and covered the sun. Gethin moved like a bird, in the change of light, and then again settled himself.

'You see much of John Dance?' he asked, quietly.

'Dance? Aye, I see him most days.'

Gethin was looking down into the side of his chair. Ivor thought for a moment that he was trying to find something, and would have helped if he could. But it was not this, and Gethin looked up again.

'You and Megan have decided?'

'Well aye, as far as we can.'

'You've not put it up to Gwen?'

'Not straight, no. Not since this bloody leg.'

'How much do she have in here?'

'Just still the nineteen hundred.'

'Aye,' Gethin said.

He looked down again into the depth of the chair. While he stayed silent Ivor stared across at him, trying to find some thread of sense in these different starts of talk. It was not easy. All he was

83

really sure of was Gethin's interest in Gwen. It would suit him
very well, and it would of course suit Ivor, if they now made it up
and got married. Then Gwen could move to the Bedwen and
Megan come to Pentre. That was obviously Gethin's idea, but
Ivor didn't expect him to come out and say so. That wouldn't be
his way. But then, even allowing for that, this talk about the
Council and John Dance didn't fit anywhere. There was no way
it could fit.

'Then there's Trevor,' Gethin said.

'Aye?'

Ivor was now quite lost. He had drunk three glasses of whisky
and he could feel the effect, but it was nothing beside Gethin's
shifts of direction. What was the matter with the man? But all he
must hang on to was his own interest, and he needn't let it go
cheap. If Gethin was after Gwen—and everything started from
that—the main thing to watch for was the nineteen hundred
pounds. Leave that in Pentre just a couple more years and it
would all work out. He had to fix his attention on bringing
Gethin to that.

Gethin got up and refilled Ivor's glass. Ivor took his opportunity.

'Mind you,' he said, 'Gwen can be stubborn.'

'Aye.'

'And it's right what she says. For a good few years the farm
couldn't manage, not if she took her money out.'

'Aye.'

Was it going to be this easy? He picked up his glass.

'Old Alun Preece died,' Gethin said.

'Preece? Preece Church Farm?'

'Aye.'

Gwen, Megan, the Council, John Dance, Trevor, Alun Preece.
What the hell was Gethin at?

'That's a tidy little farm,' Gethin said.

'Aye, indeed. There'll be plenty after it.'

'It could all work in,' Gethin said.

Ivor had the glass at his lips but put it quickly down. It was
getting dark in the kitchen. He had heard Gwen ride into the
yard.

'We'd better have some light on,' Ivor said, confused.

'I'll do it,' Gethin said.

He got up and switched on the light. He stood watching Gwen
as she moved across the yard. Ivor looked across at his lean back,

84

with the long old jacket, smeared with red earth and ragged out by thorns on the sleeves.

'You'll be all right now,' Gethin said, turning to him.

'Aye, that's Gwen back.'

'I'll be getting along. Only it might be worth it if you was to have a word with John Dance.'

'With Dance? What for?'

Gethin moved as he heard Gwen opening the door from the yard.

'Think it over,' he said quickly. 'Only I'll tell him we had a word.'

Gwen came into the kitchen. She looked across at Gethin but though Ivor watched carefully he could see nothing between them.

'I'll be getting along,' Gethin said.

'There'll be tea,' Gwen said, 'if you want it.'

'No, not now. I got work.'

Gwen went to the stove.

'We all got work,' she said sharply.

'So long then,' Gethin said, and made his slow way out to the yard.

3. Gwen had stopped at Cae Glas on her way back. She hadn't wanted to get home while Gethin was still there. She walked up with Trevor to look at his ponies, and Modlen walked up to join them. They stood talking, behind the house, as the light faded.

'I'll have to settle up with you, when I get the sale money,' Gwen said to Trevor.

'No no, Gwen, nothing. It's all settled already.'

'How is it settled?'

'Well I heard Gethin tell you. No money involved.'

'He may have said that, Trevor. He's very big-handed. But it's your work, not his. And I'll settle it up, as I said.'

Modlen laughed, moving closer to Gwen.

'You're lucky, Gwen, you've not got a husband like mine. If there's money going, he's off in the other direction.'

'I'll catch him, Modlen, don't worry.'

'Aye, perhaps. But you know Gethin. He's the one needs catching.'

'I know Gethin all right,' Gwen said.

She walked down the side of the house to where Cavalier was waiting. She spoke to the stallion with a quick affection, and then

85

led him through and rode slowly down the lane. There was a light on in the Prices' cottage, and she could see Susan standing in the living-room. She liked the Prices: they were quiet, tidy people. But they didn't have the troubles of really living in Manod.

Back at Cae Glas, Modlen and Trevor were still working outside. They had to carry a new coop to the field, along the narrow path through the garden. When they had put it down beside the others Trevor went to the main pen to separate two of his pheasants and carry them to the coop. He brought them out inside his coat, while Modlen closed the pen behind him.

'I meant what I said, mind,' she called as he went to the coop.

Trevor didn't answer. He put the birds inside, latched the front, and then stood up brushing his hands.

'So you've had fair warning,' Modlen said.

'Fair warning about what?'

'This game with the money. I've had enough of it.'

'Damn the money,' Trevor said, walking across to her. 'There's more to life than money.'

'Then that goes for others as well as for you,' Modlen said and stood her ground.

Trevor put his arm round her shoulders but she pulled herself away. He stared at her, puzzled. His face was curiously blank. He had high cheekbones and a long upper lip. You could see that he and Gethin were brothers: there were the same deepset eyes and sharp nose. But where Gethin looked bitten and weathered, Trevor, by contrast, had an unfinished face: a rough surface laid out but not yet the hard lines of a life. His skin was roughly freckled, under the fine sandy hair. Each summer it peeled a little, adding to the general rawness of the face. He usually smiled easily, and was active and ready, but when he touched what he could not understand the slabs of the face, from the cheekbones, seemed blank.

Modlen stayed close to him, though she had pulled away from his arm. She loved him strongly and easily; it had been a happy marriage from the beginning. But since they had come back to Manod, they had been frustrated everywhere, except in themselves. And what Trevor first felt as a nuisance, that there was no regular money, had become in Modlen a bitter resentment. It took a long time for anger to build in her, and she hated herself for feeling so sharp. But since Ivor's accident it had all become obvious: they were all exploiting Trevor, and he was too easy-going to stand up to anybody and just get his rights. He would talk and even quarrel with Gethin, but he never got what they needed and she was tired of just sympathizing with him. Something harder had got to come through.

'I counted it up, Trevor. We got to have thirty-eight pounds, just to come back up level. That's the different places we owe.'

'They'll hang on a bit yet, girl,' Trevor said, easily. 'Up here it's different from down in the town. They're not in so much of a hurry.'

'That's not what they say to me.'

'Oh, say it, aye, that's expected. But they don't think they'll get it, not this time of year.'

'I want it now,' Modlen said. 'I'm just tired of living on tick. The whole summer I went without buying any clothes. The summer before all I had was that green dress Mary Pearson altered for me, and it was three months before I could pay her for that. I want ten pounds, now, for a coat, and that's on top of the money for the bills. And I mean it, Trevor. I'm tired of this hanging around.'

'I'll get it for you, love,' Trevor said, kindly, and again put his arm round her shoulders.

This time she did not pull away, and they stayed close as they walked to the house. But it had taken a lot for her to come out so strongly, and she was determined, whatever happened, not to let it slip back.

'I'll go to Gethin myself, if you won't,' she said as they went into the kitchen.

'No no, girl, it's my job. You leave it to me.'

4. The next evening, Trevor asked Gethin for the money. They were in the kitchen at Bedwen. Gethin was shaving at the sink, getting ready to go out.

'Where you off tonight then?'

'Oh, look around a bit.'

The razor was harsh on the thick grey stubble. Gethin leaned very close to the old mirror, on which some of the silver had blackened. He was feeling his way over his long upper lip, behind two powerful fingers.

'You don't usually shave going up Pentre.'

'Who said I was going up there?'

'Well you often do.'

'Aye, give them a hand. While Ivor's laid up.'

Trevor shifted.

'Gwen looked in yesterday. She said I'd be paid, when she can, for the extra I've been doing.'

'It's Ivor's farm,' Gethin said, as if to the mirror.

He moved his fingers and pulled his dark skin in the other direction.

'Look it's bugger all to do with you or with Ivor,' Trevor said angrily. 'It's I've done the work and Gwen's willing to pay me.'

'We can't have it like that with a neighbour,' Gethin said, carefully finishing his lip.

'Well then ask the neighbour to pay my bloody bills.'

'You had twelve pound, only the end of last week.'

'Aye, twelve out of eighty-odd you owe me since the summer.'

'I told you all that. I'm waiting for my money, same as you.'

'Morgan must have paid you by now.'

'Well he hasn't, so there it is.'

Gethin turned from the mirror, as if the question was settled. Trevor stepped towards him, angrily, but then held himself back, watching the razor.

'I want forty-eight pound. Tonight, Gethin.'

'You can want away then. I haven't got it.'

'What have you got?'

'I've got the change in my pocket. That's all there is in the house.'

'Then you can draw it out, in Pontafren tomorrow.'

'Forty-eight pound? What do you reckon you want that for?'

'Is that any bloody business of yours. I've worked for it, haven't I?'

'Aye,' Gethin said. 'Up Pentre you have.'

He leaned close again to the mirror as he shaved in the hollows of his neck and throat.

'And here,' Trevor shouted.

'Aye, the bit, agreed.'

'Well then draw the money tomorrow. We got thirty-eight pound bills, they got to be settled. And Modlen needs ten, for herself.'

'Ten? For herself?'

'Aye, why shouldn't she? She's got to buy clothes. She've had no new clothes for a year back.'

'Nor have I had new clothes,' Gethin said. 'You don't see me wasting money like that.'

88

'Only it's different for women.'

'Aye well, then that's their own affair, out of their own money.'

'What own money? She don't have no own money.'

'Get them pheasants of yours laying.'

'Aye, smart bugger. And milk the ponies. Now you listen to me. Tomorrow, you go to the bank, get me forty-eight quid.'

'I'll see what there's there.'

'Forty-eight quid. Tomorrow evening. Or you'll get no more work out of me.'

'I'll see to it, boy,' Gethin said, reasonably.

He had finished shaving and was swilling his face. He dried it roughly on the roller towel by the sink.

'I'll see you right, boy,' he added, looking over the towel. 'Only now I got to get on.'

Trevor hesitated. Gethin's change of attitude had surprised him. He still didn't know whether to believe it.

'Forty-eight quid,' he repeated, stubbornly.

'I told you. I'll see to it.'

Trevor relaxed.

'You walking up?' he asked.

'No, take the truck. I can drop you off at the corner.'

'Then it is Pentre you're going?'

'No, the other way tonight.'

And Gethin would say no more. He drove Trevor up to Manod and stopped where the lane branched off from the road, by the Evening Star. When Trevor had got out he drove on down the road, to the Old Vicarage.

On the next evening, when Gethin had got back from Pontafren, Trevor went in for his money. Gethin seemed cheerful and friendly and at once produced a little blue paper bag, of the kind used at the bank for silver but now with a roll of notes showing through its open top.

'There you are, boy. As promised.'

Trevor took the bag.

'It wasn't easy,' Gethin said. 'But it's only fair. You should have what you worked for.'

Trevor touched the tops of the notes, ready to pull them out and count them.

'No need to count,' Gethin said. 'It's there, what you wanted.'

'Forty-eight quid,' Trevor said.

'Exactly what you asked for,' Gethin said, and smiled.

Trevor pushed the bag in his pocket and hurried back home.

He had to push his bike up the long pitch from the Llancadog road, but he hurried on, out of breath, wanting to get to Modlen. When he was riding again he began to whistle. He pushed the bike into the hedge by his side gate and hurried into the kitchen. As Modlen looked across at him he pulled the bag from his pocket and threw it grandly down on the table.

'He gave it you?'

'Aye.'

'The forty-eight pound?'

'You count it yourself. It's all there.'

Modlen seemed reluctant to pick up the bag. Now that it had actually come it seemed awful to have been nagging about money. But Trevor was so pleased and excited that she picked up the bag and pulled out the notes. She sat at the table, counting them.

'All right then?' Trevor said, as she slowly finished counting.

'I'll just count it again, to be sure.'

'You're getting very careful with it,' Trevor said, teasing her.

But she was bent over the notes again, setting them by her elbow in piles of five. There were seven piles, and she was rubbing the three remaining notes between her fingers. She said nothing.

'What is it?' Trevor asked.

'Thirty-eight,' Modlen answered, in a strange low voice.

'Thirty-eight. It can't be. He said it was right.'

He picked up the piles and went rapidly through them. They were all one-pound notes, and there were just thirty-eight of them.

'What did he actually say?' Modlen asked, still staring down at the table.

Trevor had the notes in his hand, rubbing them between thumb and finger.

'He said it was what I asked for. Exact.'

Modlen stood up slowly and faced away from the table.

'You told him thirty-eight for the bills?'

'Aye, and the ten for you.'

'We've got the thirty-eight,' Modlen said, and swung round to face him.

There were tears in her eyes, though she did not look like crying.

'He's done it deliberate,' she said, in the same strange voice. 'As a way of getting at me.'

'No no, girl, he wouldn't do that.'

'Thirty-eight for the bills. Thirty-eight is there.'

90

'Well that still don't mean you can't have your coat. You can take what it costs and leave that off the bills.'

'That isn't it,' Modlen said.

'Oh now don't be daft, girl. If you give them a bit it'll shut them up. And you need the coat.'

'It isn't the coat,' Modlen said. 'It's me.'

Trevor did not understand her. He stared, helplessly.

'It's me, Trevor. That man can decide what I do.'

Trevor looked into her face. He had never seen her looking quite like this. The open face, with its fresh colour under the thick fair hair, was now set and grave, like the mask of a much older woman. She seemed not to notice him looking at her. She went, stiffly, to the cupboard by the stairs and untied her apron and pulled on her old brown coat. It was unfashionably short, stopping above her knees, over the bare legs. She turned, still silent, and walked to the door.

'You going out? Where you going?'

'Don't try and stop me now, Trevor.'

'But where you going?'

He stood in her way and caught hold of her arm.

'Let me go now,' she said, in the strange cold voice.

'Not till you say where you're going.'

Modlen looked up at him.

'And you then,' she said, smiling without opening her lips.

Trevor stared, not understanding her. She moved quickly and got free of his arm. She opened the door and went out.

5. Modlen walked up the field. One of the ponies came to her, and she stopped and patted him. Then she crossed to the corner of the wire fence, where she could step on a bracing post and get over to the Pentre field. She jumped down, and stood listening.

The village was very quiet. She could feel the empty darkness of the fields. She looked up to Waunfawr, stretching dark and silent for so many miles to the north. Pushing her hands into the pockets of the old brown coat—one of the linings was torn—she began walking across the field towards the Llancadog road. As she passed behind the houses she looked down at them. She could feel herself almost a stranger. There was a light in Mary Pearson's. Mary was the kind of woman who would understand what she was feeling, because of her own life and because she was separate from the village. But Modlen was never easy with her; she was too smart and hard and sure of herself. And she couldn't go in like this, in her old coat, and confess and complain about money. She knew already what Mary would say: take the thirty-eight pound, spend the lot on yourself, leave him to worry about the bills. But it was nothing to do with the money. Mary Pearson would not understand that. Where had her ways got her, her ways of getting her own back? Living there, divorced, by herself, and a cupboard full of clothes. There was nothing in that. And to be complaining about the money and then saying it wasn't the money: what kind of fool would that make her look?

She walked on across the field. It was good being out and alone, and the dark didn't frighten her. There was another light now, from the back of the Prices' cottage. She couldn't go there either. They were very nice people but they wouldn't understand. Their money came from London, not from work or from farming. They might even offer to help her, and that would be worse.

She walked on to the old path. But she missed the stile and had to work back along the hedge, holding her hands in front of her face against the brambles and thorn branches. Something moved in the hedge as she made her way along it: most likely a bird, it seemed too far up for an animal. There was nothing round here that could hurt her, except—and she thought of Gethin. To be so insulting, so mean, so cold and cruel: what could he possibly get from it?; did things like that make him happy? At least Gwen was well off, getting out of marrying him. It would be terrible to be tied to a man like that. But now they were all tied to him: she and Trevor, anyway. Gethin could stand and tell her what clothes she could put on her back.

She began walking faster, as the anger broke through. The path was sloping down, past the field where Ivor had had his accident, and she could see the darker shadow of the dingle ahead. Then she lost the path, as the slope became steeper. But she pushed on down, caring only now that she should get to the Bedwen and face up to Gethin. She got in among gorse and her legs were scratched. She knew she was a fool, coming down at night through the fields, but it was how she had felt, just to push the straightest way down there. She got her feet wet, crossing the brook at the edge of the dingle. But she could now see the road below her as a car passed, its headlights sweeping along the walls and the bare trees. There was some strong bitter scent on this last bank, where the rocks cropped out in the short turf. She hurried down, putting her feet sideways to hold on the slope. She reached the low wall and followed it to the gate. She climbed over to the road, a few hundred yards short of Bedwen.

On the smooth road, with the way clear in front of her, she became aware of herself again in more familiar ways. Her shoes were wet, her legs scratched, and the old coat was hanging and flapping wet against her legs. She pushed her hand back over her hair and as she touched her hair thought of Trevor. He would come out looking for her but he would look down the lane; and he wouldn't go asking, not yet. That would give her time to get straight with Gethin. Nothing mattered until that had been done. She turned into the Bedwen yard and made her way round to the kitchen door, by the high old water-butt. She knocked loudly.

Gethin was late back that evening. He had stayed with John Dance till gone ten: there had been important business to settle. The night was clearing as he ran the truck back down, and the moon was getting up. He turned into the yard and parked the truck by the barn. He walked across to the back door, whistling. As he was opening the door there was a noise behind him. He swung round and saw someone standing in the shadow of the water-butt.

'You've taken your time, Gethin.'

'Who's that then?'

'I've been here hours. I've been waiting for you.'

'It's Modlen, is it?'

'You can give me a name now, can you?'

'What's wrong, girl? Say. Is it something with Trevor?'

Modlen didn't answer. She stood looking up at him, keeping her distance.

'Come in then, girl,' Gethin said. 'You don't want to be standing out here.'

He pushed the door and put on the kitchen light. He waited for Modlen to follow, but she was slow in coming. Then as he turned again she was there in the doorway. As the light fell on her he stepped back, alarmed.

'You surprised then?' Modlen said, pushing the door shut behind her.

'Surprised?'

As Gethin spoke he backed away, until he stood facing her from the hearth. In his lean dark face, with the surface of the skin still glazed after shaving, the deepset eyes were alive and glittering, as intent and concentrated as if watching an animal. Modlen moved slowly forward, to the corner of the big scrubbed table.

'You give him thirty-eight pound,' she said, in a voice so low that he could hardly hear the words.

'Trevor?'

'He explained it all to you. Thirty-eight for the bills and ten for my clothes.'

'I settle all that with him,' Gethin said.

After the first surprise he could feel his mastery returning.

'He was a kid in this kitchen,' Modlen said, her voice rising. 'A kid in this kitchen, you still treat him like that. You just give him pocket money, never mind he's a man and got his own wife and home.'

'That's for him to see to. That's what he took on.'

'No, Gethin. If he was a hired man, you'd have to pay him his wages. Just because he's your brother you can do what you like to him.'

'He don't have to stay. If he don't want.'

'But he has stayed, hasn't he? He's done your work and now you won't pay it.'

'He had the money. We made an arrangement.'

'You broke the arrangement. Trevor said forty-eight.'

'Thirty-eight and ten, what he actually said.'

'That makes forty-eight.'

'Not from me it don't. I don't owe you nothing.'

Modlen stared across at him. Her mouth opened, and the colour left her face. She lifted her hands, slowly. She looked down at her hands as they clasped the rough seams of her coat.

Gethin moved and relaxed.

'What it is,' he said confidently, 'you was never born to this life, you don't understand it. In the towns, aye, it's all money, money. Just hold out your hand at the end of the week. Up here it's different. We've not got it spare. We live by the farm and we live as a family. We don't shout what we're owed, not between ourselves. What we get we put to the farm, or we'd none of us carry on.'

Modlen was still looking down.

'So I don't need clothes?' she said, very quietly.

'When there's spare, yes. That's for Trevor to see to. Only I can't see to it, not out of the farm.'

Modlen looked up at him. It was a look of appeal.

'I've had nothing new, Gethin. Nothing new for two years.'

'No more have I, girl. I can't keep affording it.'

'We was better off,' Modlen said, looking round, 'when we got

94

the wage from the railway. At the end of the week I always got my money. I could plan it all out.'

'Aye well that's the difference. That's what I've been saying.'

'Do you think it's right though, your brother's wife, going about in old clothes?'

'We don't dress up much here.'

'But going in to town, going to see my Mam. She said last week she was ashamed to see me so shabby.'

Gethin looked across at her. He seemed, for the first time, to be looking at her clothes: at the rough brown coat, the worn shoes, the pale washed-out jersey at her neck.

'We're not judged by what we put on our backs,' he concluded.

'If it was the car you'd spend it.'

'I need the car for the market. That's running the farm.'

'Aye, running with you in it. That's too bloody easy.'

'There's no call to swearing.'

'It's all I can do,' Modlen said and then shouted: 'I can't talk to you reasonable, you're too mean to listen. All you say is I don't matter. Your brother married me but that's none of your business. Like your dog sneaking off but you're not responsible. Only I won't take it. I'm warning you, Gethin.'

Gethin turned away.

'You're just talking wild, girl.'

She let go of her coat and brought her fists hard down on the table.

'Aye and I'll do something wild. You'll be sorry, Gethin, I can promise you that.'

He turned and stepped towards her.

'Go home to your husband,' he said, sternly.

'To your brother, shouldn't you say?'

'No, you go home to your husband.'

She stood with her fists still clenched, staring up into his face. She felt utterly helpless, not knowing what next she could say or do. He was dark and ugly, facing her, but she could not get past him. She looked quickly round the neglected kitchen: the un-washed floor, the untidy hearth, the unpolished furniture, the old smoke-stained walls. It was true that he lived as he said, not caring for appearance. But it was still mean and dirty, all the life crushed out.

She pulled her coat tight around her and turned to go. As she was moving to the door Gethin spoke again, in a changed voice.

'I can't tell you yet, but by spring for certain.'

'What?' she asked looking round.

'It'll all be cleared up.'

'The money you owe Trevor?'

'Not just the money. The whole arrangement. We shall all be living different.'

'Some hope of that,' Modlen said, bitterly.

'Now I've told you,' Gethin said. 'I don't say things for nothing.'

'How could it all be different?'

'You must wait and see but you can both depend on it. I shall see Trevor right.'

'I've heard that before. It's just the same old talk.'

'No,' Gethin said. 'I don't run word.'

Modlen looked into his face. He was smiling suddenly: not a pleasant smile but full of cunning satisfaction and assurance.

'You mean it, Gethin? Can I tell Trevor?'

Gethin squared his shoulders.

'No, I shall be telling him. When the time comes.'

She hesitated. She looked again into the dark, ugly, strong face.

'All right then,' she said.

She opened the door and went out into the yard. She hurried across it, now bright in the moonlight. Gethin followed her, unnoticed, and watched her along the road.

VI

1. PETER and Beth had settled in a flat in Pontafren: three rooms and a kitchen over a newsagent's shop near the bridge. From their wide, draughty windows they could look out over the Afren and to the mountains beyond.

'Being urban in fact,' Peter said to Matthew, 'and come here to plan a new town, I'm not following you out to your country cottage. Though perhaps other futures have been planned in exile.'

'I just wanted somewhere congenial to live,' Matthew said, smiling.

They had been driving all day through the valley, to each of the centres that had been designated for the city. In the early evening they drove back to Pontafren. Matthew parked by the bridge. After the rain of the day it was still surprisingly light. They stood looking down at the rush of water under the bridge.

'It's light, that sky,' Peter said. 'I suppose there's a moon behind it.'

'Yes, it's coming to full.'

'And the water is getting the light. I've noticed that. I never just walk across this bridge. I always stop and look down.'

'You feel it here, do you?' Matthew asked.

'Feel what?'

'Something different. Something other. Some altered physical sense.'

'You grew up in this sort of country, Matthew. You're remembering that.'

'Yes, I know when I remember it. And I try to understand it as memory. But sometimes I think it's a different experience. Something that actually alters me.'

'No,' Peter said, 'I don't get that.'

'It only comes occasionally. Some particular shape: the line of a hedge, the turn of a path round a wood, or in movement sometimes, the shadow of a cloud that bends in a watercourse, or then again a sound, the wind in wires, wind tearing at a chimney.'

'Moments of heightened attention.'

97

'Yes, but attention to what? What I really seem to feel is these things as my body. As my own physical existence, a material continuity in which there are no breaks. As if I was feeling through them, not feeling about them.'

Peter stared down at the river.

'I can hear that you feel it. But . . .'

'Yes. But. There's usually nothing to be said.'

They moved from the bridge. The street was empty. They stopped by the door of the shop.

'Come and have a cup of tea. Beth will be glad to see you.'

'She'll be tired, won't she?'

'Yes, maybe. But better tired than alone. She gets miserable sitting alone. This is a lonely place.'

He opened the side door. Matthew followed him up the steep stairs.

'Peter?' Beth called from the kitchen.

'Yes. And I've brought Matthew.'

Beth came into the living-room.

'I saw you park the car. Then you were leaning over the bridge, like the oldest inhabitants.'

'It's the moon,' Peter said.

'Shall I get you some tea?'

'No, I'll make it. You talk to Matthew. Try and talk him out of this business.'

He went to the kitchen. Matthew took off his coat.

'Do you want talking out of it?' Beth said.

'Out of being contradictory? Out of feeling it several ways at once? Yes, I could do with that.'

'Well I wouldn't try. That's how it is, isn't it?'

Matthew was staring at the table in the centre of the room.

'Yes, I feel the pull of the past so strongly, but I think there's something else that belongs to this country: a pure idea, a pure passion, for a different world.'

'In the people around here?'

Matthew looked across at her.

'In what has moved through them. In their religion, in their politics. It's not ever been cynical, not ever resigned. It's been a dream, if you like, but a dream of a country. And if we give up that . . .'

'I agree with you, Matthew.'

He looked intently into her face.

'If we give up that future . . . It needn't be this city, but I keep thinking it has to be. That we have to make the leap, get on to new ground. And yet the old ground holds me. It holds us and holds us back.'

Beth held his look.

'You mean giving up the city would be like giving up faith?'

'Yes, I feel that. Past all the arguments, that's exactly what I feel.'

He looked away. He looked in detail around the room.

'It looks temporary, doesn't it?' Beth said, smiling.

'I'm sorry. Was I staring?'

'It doesn't matter. It *is* temporary. I've had all I can do getting ready for the baby.'

'What is it now, a week?'

'If he's punctual, yes.'

'Are you still feeling well?'

'God yes. It's extraordinary. It's like a whole separate well-being. I have to hang on to myself. That's a daft thing to say.'

'No. It happens.'

Beth pushed back her dark-red hair.

'This,' she said, riffling her fingers, 'this hair of mine seems to take off. Like a power station or something.'

Peter had come in with the tea.

'That's right,' he said. 'Give us a few years and we'll change this whole place. Electrification, repopulation.'

'You're daft, Peter,' Beth said, still smiling.

'Well is it any dafter than the Whitehall farce?'

'I keep telling you, that's your job.'

Peter poured the tea and passed round.

'She's fierce, this lady,' he said, to Matthew. 'She demands an entire economy to support her child.'

'That's fair enough,' Matthew said.

'Like if you and I said yes, let Manod be built, we could stay for ever, until the child has a child.'

'That's usually worked,' Matthew said. 'As a society, I mean.'

'Well anyway I want it,' Beth said firmly. 'I want some settlement for a change.'

2. Next morning, when Matthew went out, he took Mrs Lewis, from next door, to Nantlais. She had broken her glasses, getting up from her chair with them still in her lap and then stepping on them. She had an old pair but she could only just get about with

99

them. Matthew took her to the optician's. He offered to stay and run her back, but she would not hear of it. She would be all right, she said, on the twelve bus back to the corner. Matthew saw her inside and then drove to Pontafren to collect Peter.

Mrs Lewis caught the bus back. She walked up the Llancadog road and the pitch to Manod. It was raining heavily, and when she got in she was soaked. She warmed a tin of soup, and went straight up to bed.

It got dark by four, under the heavy sky. The incessant rain was beating at the windows. Susan missed, then, the familiar light from the next-door kitchen, on to the shed and the apple trees. She pulled on a coat and went round and knocked. There was no answer, and she opened the door and called. The house was cold and silent, and she called again. She put on the light in the kitchen. The empty soup tin stood on the white scrubbed table: its sharp green and red label garish against the washed wood. Resting her fingers beside the tin, Susan felt the fibres of the wood, at first rough like worn skin but then yielding and pulpy, like hands kept too long in water. She turned uneasily as her hand moved, and went across to the stairs. Calling again, and getting no answer, she went up to the front bedroom. The door was open, from the tiny landing.

'Mrs Lewis?'

There was an answering sound from the bed: more breathed than voiced. She put on the light. Mrs Lewis was lying in bed, her hair loose around her face, the edge of the sheet pulled up against her throat. Susan hurried across.

'Are you all right? Can I help you.'

The answering voice was very hoarse and slow, but the weak eyes stared up, as if trying to make their own meaning.

'I heard you come, dear, the first time. Only I couldn't call down. It's this pain, it's bad in my throat.'

She wrenched her hand from the sheet, and grasped at her neck. The skin of the hand was mottled, among the prominent veins. Susan bent closer to her.

'I'll get the doctor, shall I?'

'No, he won't come out. Not out here in the country. Not on a night like this.'

'Oh I'm sure he will.'

'No, he'll say to rest till tomorrow, he'll be out then.'

'You need him to see you. I'll get him to come.'

Mrs Lewis looked away. The room was cold, under the poor

light. The rain was still beating heavily, and they could hear the wind, in gusts, seeming to tear at the chimney.

'I'll go and ring up. But I'll just make you comfortable. Have you got a bottle?'

'I brought one up. Only it's cold now.'

'You must let me have it. I'll fill it again.'

'I can reach it myself, dear. It's here on my chest.'

She made an embarrassed effort to pull the rubber hot-water bottle from under the sheet. But her breathing sharpened again, and her hands were trembling. Susan took her right hand and they drew out the bottle, in its knitted green cover.

'I'll only be a minute. You'll listen for me, will you?'

'I can hear it all, dear. It isn't the hearing.'

Susan rearranged the bedclothes, and hurried downstairs. She boiled a kettle and refilled the hot-water bottle. When she took it upstairs, Mrs Lewis was lying with closed eyes, but she moved as the bottle was put in beside her. Susan went to her own house and rang the Nantlais doctor, Bowen, who came out to Manod once a week. He was only just in from a visit, but he agreed to call, about eight, when he had had his supper.

She went back next door. Mrs Lewis was sleeping, and she sat beside her, settling to wait. There was a cane chair, with a black frame inset with bright coloured glass, green and yellow and blue. The counterpane and curtains were green; the walls green and white. It would be a pretty room, with the morning sun in it, but now it was bitterly cold.

Mrs Lewis stirred, but her eyes were still closed.

'It's got to come, all the changes,' she said.

'There, the doctor's coming. You rest.'

Mrs Lewis opened her eyes. She stared, desperately, into Susan's face.

'Only I've been all my life here in Manod. I don't want to see it cut up.'

Susan could say nothing. She stared down at the worn counterpane, thinking of Harry and Jack. She had felt old herself, her effective life finished, as her boys grew up to young men. Now she saw this again, past Mrs Lewis lying there: a generation further on: a single frail life, on beyond her family.

Mrs Lewis was speaking again. She had again closed her eyes.

'It's for the young ones, the changes. But still they all go away. It'll be all cut up, all the fields around here. I don't want to see it.'

'There's time, Mrs Lewis. Try to rest.'

The room dropped back into its cold silence. The breathing from the bed was harsher. Susan rested her hand on the warm forehead, among the thin loose hair.

When Dr Bowen came she waited downstairs. After ten minutes he came down to talk to her. Would she be sitting with Mrs Lewis? The tablets were on the chair, they might help a little. He would come again in the morning; she was too weak to be moved. And it might not be long. Were there any relatives near?

'I don't know,' Susan said, and returned to the bedroom. It was too sudden a change, from the old lady, the neighbour—Mrs Lewis, she didn't even know her first name—to this failing, isolated life. She had settled now into a deeper sleep. Susan went down to the kitchen, wondering if the habits of her childhood still held. On the dresser, where she expected it, there was an envelope with an address. She went out and along to Pentre, to confirm it with Gwen Vaughan. It was a married daughter, May, in Coventry. Susan waited while Gwen sent a telegram.

She went back to sit with Mrs Lewis. To vary the waiting, she sat on a chair by the window, pulling the curtain a bit aside. The heavy rain had stopped, though there was still a high wind. The clouds had lifted and the evening sky seemed lighter. There was even a moon, occasionally, through the flying clouds.

At last she heard Matthew come back. She went down quickly. He was just getting out of the car.

'I can't come in. I've got to sit with Mrs Lewis.'

'Is she ill?'

'Yes.'

He walked to the back door and into the kitchen. Susan followed him.

'What is it, love?' she asked.

He was staring at the sink, but his eyes had lost focus.

'I should have brought her back. I suppose she got soaked.'

'Yes. And of course she wouldn't ask for help.'

'We shouldn't wait to be asked.'

'Well it's easy to say that after.'

'I know. But what was I doing, that couldn't wait for that? Driving around and speculating.'

'No, Matthew, you couldn't have known.'

He took off his coat.

'Are you going back in?'

'Yes.'

'Overnight?'

'Yes, I'd better.'

'All right, but have you eaten?'

'I don't need anything. But I'll get yours.'

'It's all right. You go back.'

She moved quickly and kissed him, then went back round. The sky was now very much clearer. A full moon had come through, above the low tower of the church. She went through and into the cold house, and up to the bedroom.

In the late afternoon of the following day, Mrs Lewis died. Mrs Willis, May, the daughter from Coventry, came in time to see her mother before she died, but she was then very weak and did not seem to know her, though she held tightly to her hand. May stayed for the funeral and then to clear her mother's things and arrange for most of them to be sold. In ten days the cottage was empty and May went back to Coventry. She explained to Susan that she had offered her mother to go there to live with them; her husband had a good job, on the transporters, and there was a nice modern house, with a room ready for her in it. As a girl Mrs Lewis had been as far as Northampton, in service, but now she had wanted to stay in Manod, in her own home.

'Yes, well with her home she was used to,' Susan said.

'Stay in Manod, die in Manod,' May said.

3. The wind was blowing heavy rain against the glass of the bedroom window as Peter and Beth lay awake in the darkness, their hands linked, lightly, as they tried to sleep. They had gone early to bed, because Beth was tired after a visit to Myra and Gwyn, and her body was heavy, so that she needed to lie down. In the movement of the day, talking to others, it had been easy for them both to be cheerful. Now, lying alone, they were quieter, turned to each other, and there was an apprehension, which neither needed to speak of, as they felt the slow wait before the baby could come.

Every touch was important, in this long still wait of their bodies. Shut out from everyone else, and with the rain beating loud on the glass, they felt, in the darkness, a new kind of tenderness, in which to move and touch fingers, or to rest a cheek on the smooth warm skin of a shoulder, was an intensity of pleasure, a gathering of the senses until they seemed, lying still in the darkness of the bed, to be more than each other, to be a new and strange presence, breathing and waiting.

The rain continued through the rest of the night. Often it was flung against the glass in the gusting wind. When they began to sleep, they slowly lost contact, and the first moments of each waking were a sudden anxiety. But then they recovered each other, in touch and in simply breathed words, turning again to sleep, though always the disturbance came back, in the next anxious waking, and these breaks came more often, as they lay towards morning.

It was a little before five when Beth woke and sat up, crying out in anxiety. Peter touched her arm but she was already moving and sitting away. He sat up, following her, and the long slow rhythm of the night was immediately broken.

'Yes, get up, Peter, quickly.'

'What is it, love?'

'I'm wet. I can feel it. I can feel it beginning.'

Peter hurried out of bed, and switched on the light. Beth had moved and was sitting on the far side of the bed, turning the coverings back and looking in at the sheets, which were damp. She pushed back her hair, in an almost frantic movement. Peter saw her white fingers against the brightness of the hair. She was rocking where she sat, and was breathing heavily.

'I'll get dressed and the van,' he said, hurrying round.

'Yes, hold my hand, love, hold it.'

She squeezed his fingers until they hurt to the bone. He leaned and touched her forehead, but she rocked away from him.

'Yes, you must get the car.'

'And I'll ring and say that we're coming.'

He released his fingers, and pulled on his trousers and coat.

'Shall I help you dress?'

'No, ring them. I'll manage.'

He hurried through to the other room, and rang the nursing-home where they had reserved a bed. They were a long time answering and he called back through to the bedroom. There was no answer from Beth, and he put down the receiver and ran across to the door. She had got her nightdress off and was leaning forward, her arms stretched out holding the end of the bed.

'You'll get cold, love.'

'Yes.'

As he came beside her, she caught hold of him tightly. Her swollen body was pressed closely against him, and her shoulders

104

were trembling. He supported her against him until he could free one arm, and reached out for her clothes. He pulled her slip over her hair and shoulders, and she drew back a little to let it cover her.

'Have you told them we're coming?'

'They haven't answered. It's still ringing.'

'You must go,' she said sharply, and with an effort turned away.

'I don't want to leave you.'

'I can manage the rest of my clothes.'

Peter watched as she sat on the edge of the bed, and then ran back through to the phone. The ringing had stopped, but the line was now open. He spoke several times, and at last was answered. He confirmed the arrangements, and then hurried back.

Beth had pulled on her dress, and was buttoning it at the neck. As he rushed in she smiled, and seemed suddenly recovered and composed. It was a bright yellow dress, the colour he had always preferred. Several years back, in Goldsmith Street, he had persuaded her to buy a coat in this same yellow, and he remembered her doubts about it, as she went in to show it to Myra.

'Look, don't bother with the buttons. Let's get your coat on.'

'You want me decent, don't you?' Beth said, smiling.

Peter stared across at her. He could hardly believe that she had recovered so quickly, and he was now in danger of relaxing too soon. Even as she stood in front of him, as if showing off the yellow dress, the pain crossed her face again and she reached out, quickly, for the end of the bed.

'You'd better hang on to me, look. And just say where your coat is.'

'It's in the other room.'

'Then I'll take you through. Come on, love, hurry.'

She took his arm, rather formally, and again smiled.

'Are you afraid it'll all happen here?' she said, teasing him.

'Well why not, for Christ's sake, if I knew what to do?'

'Dr Owen to the rescue. Anyway, it happens itself.'

'Come on, girl, for God's sake.'

'All right, I'm coming.'

They moved, slowly, round the end of the bed.

'Hey, we've not brought my suitcase,' Beth cried, and turned on his arm.

'Come on to the other room,' Peter said irritably. 'Then you can put on your coat, sit down, and I'll fetch the case.'

'That's right, shout the odds.'

'Well I have to look after you.'

'I know. Like a baby.'

He eased her into the chair by the window, in which Matthew had sat when he had visited. That seemed, now, very far back. He fetched her coat from the pegs by the door and put it over her shoulders. She looked very pale, in this different light, and her eyelids were wet.

'I'll take the case and bring the van to the door. Then I'll come back up for you. Don't you move till I'm back.'

'All right,' Beth said, in a voice so low that he could hardly hear it.

He fetched the suitcase from the bedroom, and paused to draw back the curtains and look out at the weather. It was blowing and raining hard, and it was still very dark.

'I wish I could get the car up closer,' he said as he went to the door.

'It'll be all right, love.'

'Yes but it's pitch dark and raining like Wales.'

'Like what?' Beth said, looking up and smiling.

'I know. All right. It's your own beloved country.'

'Put your mac on, Peter.'

'No, I haven't got time.'

'Put it on.'

He grabbed his raincoat and hurried out down the stairs. The van was parked in the yard of the pub by the bridge. He had to switch on the headlights and wait for a minute, in the darkness and driving rain. Then he turned in the street, going up on to the pavement to be nearer the door. He left the engine running and hurried back up.

'All right then, come on.'

'I'll walk behind you, Peter.'

At the top of the stairs she leaned forward quickly and kissed him. He barely responded, but spread his arms to each side of the stairs. She came down very slowly, and he waited on the pavement to help her into the van.

'Why did you turn it this way?' she asked when she was inside.

'To save you walking round. I can soon turn it back.'

'You're fussing too much. I'm all right, love, really.'

'Yes, I know about that,' he said, and ran round.

They drove through the dark empty streets of Pontafren, out to the northern edge where a gabled Edwardian villa had been converted to a nursing-home. There was a light in the porch at the end of the gravelled drive. Beth stayed in the van while Peter ran round and rang the bell. The door was quickly opened, by the matron, who had an umbrella ready to shelter Beth in. Peter followed, carrying the suitcase, as they crossed the entrance hall and made their way up the broad stairs, with Beth running her hand along the curving mahogany rail.

'Shall I come on up?' Peter called.

'No, if you'd like to wait there, Mr Owen. We can bring the suitcase up later.'

Beth turned as the matron spoke, and looked back down at Peter. He waved and she smiled before going on up. He watched her out of sight, and then stood at the foot of the stairs, as if guarding the suitcase. There was a long wait, and then the doctor arrived, stopping in the hall to wipe the rain from his spectacles. He spoke briefly, abstractedly, to Peter, and then went on up-stairs. Almost at once an elderly woman came down for the suit-case. As she bent to pick it up, Peter offered to carry it. She was thin and stooping, and her face, under the meagre grey hair, seemed torn with fatigue.

'No, sir, I can manage it.'

'But let me take it at least to the landing.'

'No, sir, I can do it.'

Peter watched her take the first steps.

'Should I go back home now and wait?'

Mrs Evans turned, on the third step, holding the large grey case across her thighs, with both wrinkled hands on the handle.

'I should think so, sir.'

'Not wait here?'

He was alarmed as he saw her perched on the step, with the heavy suitcase in front of her.

'That's right, sir. You don't have to wait. The matron will ring you when the baby has come.'

'All right. Thank you.'

She nodded and turned to climb on up the stairs. The case bumped on the riser of the fifth step, and she jerked it up, sharply, as she continued to climb. Peter closed his eyes as she reached the top.

After a while he looked round and listened, but the place was silent. He went back to the van, and drove slowly home. It seemed lighter now, and he could see the windows, along the dim grey streets. He looked up as he crossed the bridge and felt suddenly tired.

In the flat, the lights were still on, but the rooms were cold. He switched on the living-room fire and looked around for something to read. He had exhausted the papers on the previous day, but he looked again at the local paper, the *Pontafren Chronicle*. There was a report of a speech at a Chamber of Trade dinner; headlined *Old Ways and New Needs: a Local Problem*. Nothing, it seemed, had been said, in the inches of grey text. He rubbed his eyes, feeling sleep coming, and then shook out the paper to see the adverts. Cars, television, furniture, cut-price groceries. A funeral service and two licensed horse slaughterers. Houses, farms, implements, cattle. A public notice of intention to compile a register of all persons legally entitled to graze stock on The Frith. National Childbirth Trust: Pontafren and District Group: classes every Wednesday in the Scouts Hut, Mortimer Park. Births, Marriages, Deaths, in a large Gothic title. Yet they were all, incredibly, deaths. Three announcements of deaths, ten in memoriam, three acknowledgments of sympathy and floral tributes. No births, no marriages that week in Pontafren.

It was ten past eight. He got up and made coffee, and then went through and stripped the bed. It was light, now, along the Afren, and the water was touched with silver in the long reach above the bridge. He stood for some time, looking along the river, and then carried the mattress through to dry in front of the fire in the living-room. Half past eight. He felt like ringing up Matthew. Or the other calls, but they would want only definite news. It was still very difficult to think of Beth. He could think of her here, but not in the nursing-home, where he could see the old woman, holding the heavy suitcase across her body. He took off his shoes, and sat by the fire with his feet over the curved mattress. He closed his eyes.

The telephone woke him. It was a quarter to nine.

'Your wife's well, Mr Owen, and you have a fine baby daughter.'

'Can I come up and see them?'

'Well yes, certainly. In about an hour.'

'Thank you, Mrs Probert.'

The matron's name had quite suddenly come back. He put down the phone and leaped across the room. He started singing to himself and then hurried to open the front curtains. There were a few people in the street, going in to the shop downstairs. He hurried back to the mattress and felt it with his cheek; it was dry but not bone dry, and he pulled it back over the chair. He rang the garage at Trawsfynydd. Gwyn answered.

'Kestrel Service Station.'

The distant voice was strange.

'You're a grandfather, mister. What did I tell you?'

'That's Peter, is it?'

'That's right, a baby girl.'

'And Beth?'

'She's all right. I'm going up now to see her.'

But there was also the other call, to the house in Goldsmith Street. He checked the time. His father would have left. It took some time to make the connection. Then among the voices of the operators, another voice.

'Owen.'

'Mam?'

'Who's that?'

'Mam, this is Peter.'

'Oh, *Peter*,' Kate said. 'But your voice sounds strange.'

'You all right then, Mam?'

'Yes, I'm all right.'

'Look, I rang to say about Beth.'

'Go on.'

'She's had the baby. This morning.'

'Well that's lovely, Peter. And is Beth all right?'

'I'm just going to see her.'

'And is it a boy or a girl?'

'A girl, Mam. Didn't I say?'

'No you didn't. You're all worked up.'

'Well that's a good thing, isn't it?'

Kate didn't answer.

'Mam?'

'I'm still here, Peter.'

'Are you keeping all right? And Dad?'

'Harold's just gone off. You've only just missed him.'

'And you're all right?'

'You treat me as fragile, don't you?'

'I don't think so. Do I?'

'For a grandmother, you should see me,' Kate said, laughing.

Peter stared at the phone. He could see very clearly the prominent dark eyes, the pale heavy cheeks, the black hair to her shoulders.

'Well you must come and see us, Mam. When we've got Beth and the baby back home.'

'Yes, of course, whenever Harold can arrange it.'

'Only I must get off now, go up and see Beth.'

'Yes, of course, you go on. And remember me to her.'

'Sure, Mam, sure. And so long then for now. See you.'

'Thanks for ringing, Peter.'

The receiver was put down. Peter listened for some moments, until the dialling tone came back. Then he put the phone down and pulled on his shoes. He drove back through the town. It was still not half-past nine, though the day seemed half over.

Mrs Evans answered his ring, and led him up the stairs. He was shown into a bedroom at the end of the corridor. The curtains were drawn, and the air inside was a warm dusk, with a separate sharp layer of disinfectant. Beth had heard him come in, and had stretched out her arms. He went across and laid his head on her shoulder, kissing her neck. She eased him back and smiled, happily, into his face.

'You all right, Beth?'

'Yes.'

'Sure?'

'Yes, of course. And you needn't be nervous.'

'Nervous?'

'Of the baby.'

He pulled himself up. The baby was lying in a cradle on the far side of the bed. He stared across, his eyes getting used to the light.

'Can I go round and see her?'

'Yes, we've been waiting for you.'

'I bet she has.'

He walked, slowly, round the end of the bed. He leaned over the cradle. Beth took his hand and guided it down. He touched the small head, with its thin dark hair. It was slightly damp. The face was drawn, reddened, the lips tightly pursed. At the touch the eyes opened: unexpectedly large, and bright and alive in a sudden deep blue.

'Can I say her name?'

Beth smiled and tightened her hold on his fingers.

'Menna,' Peter said, looking down intently into the shining unknowing eyes. 'Menna. Menna.'

VII

1. JULIET Dance had been Juliet Davies, only daughter of the headmaster of the Pontafren County School. She had trained as a teacher in Cardiff, but had taught for less than a year, in the little all-age school at Llanerch, before she agreed to marry John Dance, already a successful and sociable man, and at forty just nineteen years older.

People said of Juliet, having seen her grow up, that from the age of fourteen she had been fascinated by herself. Indeed it was more than fascination, it was something like wonder. Even those who had not seen her staring fixedly at her face in the mirror, usually imagined her doing so, as if this was the only attention which could quite be expected from her. For she was, and had been from fourteen, quite remarkably—but there the description hesitated. You could not really say good-looking; it was not easy to imagine any separable content, let alone such a content as goodness, in that remarkable face. And while pretty was too weak, attractive again was uncertain, for it was a cold face, ice-cold; that was part of its quality. Strangers said that she was lovely; or beautiful; but no one who knew her well ever used these words without prompting, and then only reluctantly. Nothing implying desire or assent, or even admiration, could be easily said, by those who knew her as Juliet. There seemed to be no descriptions that extended beyond her. For the quality of her face was a complete-ness, an immobility; indeed an incapacity (itself a kind of achievement) to extend to or be touched by the imperfect and varying community of life beyond her.

To some people, staring at her, as almost everyone stared, she seemed a rare prototype, which human features only occasionally achieve, of the beauty of the figurine or the doll: a random human achievement, in flesh and blood, of the perfection so often achieved by the conscious hand, in porcelain or in paint. But there was no way of knowing whether such figures were imita-tions, records, of the rare Juliets who had appeared, unexpectedly, in the crowded generations, or whether the occasional Juliet, as in this case—the Juliet who stared at her mirror as if making and completing herself—was not a human repetition, an imitation in its turn, of the dolls and the figurines. Her finely dressed blonde hair had the intricate fixity of sculpture. Her deep blue eyes, under the high forehead, had a brilliance of colour, as in the pinks and whites of her skin, that is seen more often in paint than on a living face. The moulding of the mouth, the slight flare of the nostrils under the fine nose, had the theatrical quality of a portrait: the fixed and captured gesture which was no passing expression but seemed always to be there: a face living beyond faces, yet in its isolated movement unchanging and impressively still.

Juliet lived with John Dance in the high stately rooms of the eighteenth-century parsonage: going out with her husband to dinners and dances, being regularly photographed, but at most other times very much on her own—there had been no children in the seven years of the marriage. Now the house seemed built around her, a finely kept frame for her, and the girl who came in from St Dyfrog was an attendant on house and mistress, picture and frame, as if the two were inseparable and required the same kind of service.

There was money in the house; that went without saying. The jobbing builder, repairing the farms and cottages, putting up, one summer, the occasional house, had become, from grandfather and father to son, from John Dance to John Dance to John Dance again, a small firm, a business, an enterprise, and now at last an agency. The idea of an estate agent had been changing, imperceptibly. There were no longer estates of the old kind. The area had no large and cultivated gentleman landowners who needed, beyond the area of their politeness, a more limited and coarser man of affairs. But there were houses to trade in, though not very many. There were cottages to modernize and sell. There were occasional opportunities in land, and a few offices and shops for an insurance company or a building society or a chain store. Over the last few years there had been two more substantial developments. First, private forestry, which had become suddenly attractive with the threat of a wealth tax. London syndicates, looking for protected deposits of capital, developed, within a month, a profound interest in conifers: 'planting for the future of the nation', as their public relations agency put it. All over rural Wales there was a sudden demand for cheap marginal land, in which the future of the nation could be set out in long rows: lines of spruce among the ploughed bracken and heather and the coarse tussocks of grass. The price of such land rose remarkably quickly;
112

within six months it was beyond the reach of the local farmers, and indeed beyond any possible return for ordinary farming. In the Afren valley and the surrounding hills John Dance was handling nearly all of this business: getting the farms, at a death, often before they could arrive on the open market. It was a profitable business. But the second development was equally profitable: the conversion of garages from wayside petrol stations (many of them once blacksmiths' shops) into a new identity: agencies, now, of more distant estates, with names running back to California and Texas and the Gulf. John Dance had got most of this business, for it was necessary to know when a man had died and when his son could be persuaded to accept a capital grant. This would transform the old pumps into a gleaming series of robot dispensers. It would change the galvanized shed into a plate-glass shopfront with maps and canned drinks and cleaning fluids. It would put in toilets, washed green and pink, with finely lettered and conventional signs, and above all the star or the shell or the helmeted head: the final mark of the agency. Through several convenient deals, over a wide area, from the Bronydd Service Station to the Llancadog Motor Company, and from Auto-Pontafren to the Central Garage, Nantlais, Dance had built up with one of these groups a close and expanding connection. He could now look down from the Old Vicarage to one of his latest achievements: the St Dyfrog Motorama, as the sign put it, over the reconstructed garage that had formerly announced itself as Petrol: J. Watkins, Prop. Dance was particularly proud that he had brought what he called this facility to the area. It served the holiday traffic with its snack-bar, and it had toilets so fine that the children from the school on the opposite corner, where there was only an earth-closet, would slip across to try to use them, though they were quickly spotted and chased away.

All Dance's ordinary business was done from Pontafren, where he had an office in the High Street. But important clients he would bring to the house. It was necessary to impress them that he was a man of substance. Juliet was waiting now, for just such a visit: an especially important one. Any time now the big cars would turn off at St Dyfrog: carrying the men carrying the papers that made everything possible; moving almost unnoticed up the narrow road from the valley, through the close earth banks. They would turn, smoothly, into the gravelled drive of the Old Vicarage and stop at the tall white door with its fanlight and its shining brass horseshoe knocker. And part of the pleasure for Dance was in this:

that Juliet would come out and stand on the whitened steps and that she would be more remarkable than anyone, any wife or travelling secretary, who could conceivably arrive, under any sign or protection. When it had happened first, and he had seen its effect, he had made a note to remember it. But it was now habitual, and Juliet had her instructions: to wait and watch for his profitable guests.

2. Susan opened the post and found a note from Juliet: a thick card with rounded corners, the surface a luminous grey like a cloud. The invitation was informal, in the neatly formal handwriting. Would Mrs Price come to tea on the following Thursday, at about four?

Susan looked down the bare back garden to the fowl-run. In the darkening green grass, the last broken windfalls were lying raked towards the path. It was increasingly lonely in Manod since Mrs Lewis had died. She saw Modlen most days, and Gwen quite often, but Matthew was out, for long hours, since Peter had come, and the whole place seemed deserted. And it was bleak now with the ending of autumn. The very air was dark, with the black hills and the rain.

'Not that I intend to fill my life with tea at the Vicarage.'

Matthew had come home wet, and was changing in front of the fire.

'As you like. I don't mind.'

'You're not listening, are you? But I might as well go. Unless it makes any difficulties for you?'

'Why should it, love? Could it?'

'I just wonder about Dance.'

'What, his business you mean?'

'Certainly his business. And don't underestimate him. The country's been going his way, steadily, for the last twenty years.'

'But is going to tea with his wife any part of his business?'

Susan moved and stood close to him.

'No,' she said, 'I won't explain it again. I thought we had learned it in London.'

Matthew rubbed his hair with the towel. The hair was getting much thinner, and he could feel the bare scalp as he rubbed.

'You mean complicity?'

'It isn't just finding a word.'

114

'Well, the thing itself? Getting in with people like that?'

'If it were real complicity it would be very much simpler. But what actually happens, as we make our social round? We go out and break bread with all the people we're against.'

'Yes,' Matthew said. 'This is the old, covert negotiation of England. Living in enemy country.'

'Taking tea with the enemy. Starting to make allowances, avoiding saying certain things.'

'I know. Yes.'

'Starting to look like the enemy, to be the enemy, for all I know.'

'Actually I should like to know just what Dance is up to.'

Matthew put away the towel, and picked up his wet clothes.

'Well then go and ask him. Don't try sending me.'

'Do you think he'd tell me?'

'No, of course he wouldn't.'

'All right then. Leave it.'

'Leave that, yes,' Susan said. 'But nevertheless I could do with the company.'

3. On the Thursday she walked down the lane, and turned past the Evening Star. It was a rough afternoon, with rain in the wind. The damp air was mild, but as she turned to the road the wind was violent. At the gate of the Old Vicarage she met Mary Pearson, from Long View.

'You're called to the Vicarage too, then?'

'Yes,' Susan said, 'I was asked to tea.'

'She's all right, Juliet. I make a lot of her clothes. But don't expect much tea. It's short commons in there.'

As they walked up the gravelled drive, Juliet came out and stood on the steps. She shook hands with them, formally, and led them in to the drawing room.

Very little was said, after the first formal words, and Mary Pearson found it easier to continue her conversation with Susan, as if there, at least, was some point in talking.

'This whole place,' she said, 'gets me ragged, it feels like a ship in a gale.'

'Yes, it's very exposed.'

Mary looked across at Juliet, who was sitting impressively between them. Then she turned back to Susan.

'I should have left here years ago. The year I came I got a very good offer. There was this new company—I knew the chap through Brian—starting a motel near Stratford, I could have been manageress.'

'That sounds interesting.'

'Only I was in court with Brian, getting the divorce. It just shot up my nerves. Get me in black and a bottle, I'd have drunk up the proceeds. And you know the men you get, dropping by, if you're on a main road.'

'Do you?'

'Yes, the usual dirty pigs. All that sort of men are.'

Susan looked away.

'I expect it could be difficult, a job like that.'

'Oh yes. But mind, I could supervise girls. Just give me what you like, up to twenty. I used to say to Brian, it's no use at all putting a man in charge of them, they just know what to do to tie him right up. But if I got a job like that, and my own little flat, I'd make them work, you watch me. I should earn my keep. There's nothing much I don't know about girls.'

'Do you know about motels?' Susan asked.

'They're open, that's the trouble. Like I said straight out, all those pigs of men coming in, with their fancy pieces. I should spit in their eye.'

Susan hesitated. She looked at Juliet before answering.

'Are motels like that? You surprise me. The only ones I've seen were very respectable. Just middle-aged people, carrying their hot water bottles from the car.'

'Those travelling men are like that,' Mary said, 'and those girls, if you let them. That's what I said, they need supervision.'

Susan moved and looked again at Juliet, who was sitting quite still, arranged in her chair.

'What do you think, Mrs Dance?'

Juliet turned her head.

'Mary's always been unlucky,' she said.

She got up and stood very straight. It was a fine pose. She handed round tea and a plate with four small sandwiches. She took no food herself. Mary waited some moments, and then turned to Susan again.

'Is your husband's work going well, Mrs Price?'

'Yes, quite well, I think, thank you.'

'What's this city idea?'

Susan looked across at her.

'It's a study, that's all. To see if it's needed.'

Mary appealed to Juliet, to share her contempt.

'Get a main road through here, all those travelling people. Anyhow what's the point building it up? There's not enough here to live as it is.'

'That's one of the problems. Bringing work so that people could stay.'

'They're rough enough here already, I was telling Juliet. But not really nasty, like this new lot you'd get.'

'Well I wasn't born here, I can't say.'

'Nor was I born here. Don't think I was born here. I was born in Solihull. When Dad first had the shop it was a respectable area, then they started this development, well that's what they called it, meaning council estates, all that sort of people.'

Susan looked away. As she moved she noticed Juliet inspecting her clothes, with a cool detachment.

'And your husband's work, Mrs Dance? Is that going well?'

'Yes,' Juliet said.

There was a considerable silence. The maid knocked, and came in and cleared away the tea things. Juliet watched her, without speaking, but as the door closed she leaned across to Mary. She was smiling, now, with a surprising animation.

'Trying to get it before it's cold,' she said.

'She'll be lucky.'

'She is. She'll do anything.'

Susan moved uneasily, but Juliet, unexpectedly, was coming alive.

'You'd never believe, Mrs Price, how greedy, disgustingly greedy, that girl can be. Last night it was cheese. She took a slice of cheese.'

'What, for supper or something?'

'She's not entitled to supper. John went to her mother and told her, it was all made quite clear. She has her breakfast and supper at home, it's the only way.'

Mary intervened.

'You mean she just pinched a piece of cheese?'

Juliet leaned forward, excitedly.

'The day before it was coffee. She'd had a cup and she washed it up, thinking I wouldn't see. But I knew the mark on the jar. And that morning a tomato, there were three, I counted them, with the two slices of ham for our supper—John likes an extra tomato. She made out I'd told her to throw it away, because it was bad at the top; you know by the stalk, soft, nasty.'

117

'And you hadn't?'

'John likes the extra tomato. I shall have to get rid of her, though it's hard to get anybody. That girl I had before, Olwen Mortimer, she's working now at Pentre, since Ivor had the accident. And she not only stole my food, she accused me of starving my husband. She had the cheek to say that. She just stood and shouted at me. It's not enough you starve yourself, you must starve the rest of us.'

Susan moved again, but Juliet could not be stopped now.

'If the baker calls when I'm out, though I've told him often enough, they take the stuff in, they're all the same. A Swiss roll last Thursday, and a packet of pikelets. I put them away to give back but he wouldn't take them, he said they were stale. I said that was his business, leaving stale food that nobody wanted in the first place.'

Susan wished she could go. She looked across at Mary, but she was leaning forward, sharing what Juliet was saying.

'I mean it's greedy and disgusting,' Juliet said, 'to eat more than you need. And to take other people's food off them. I've known the time I've been out of eggs on a Sunday, we have just the thirteen for the week, and I know where they've gone, though it's hard to catch them at it, they say they get broken and the shells look the same whichever it is. And sugar or flour, or tea if it's left in the packet, it's very hard to measure, they just take a spoonful at a time. If the ham isn't sliced, there's no controlling it. That's why I've given up joints.'

Susan moved more decisively.

'I must really go, Mrs Dance. My husband will be home.'

'Does he get his dinners when he's out?'

'Yes, he often does.'

'And you give him another meal now?'

'Yes, I cook about six.'

It was all that was necessary. Juliet's eager voice stopped, after its surprising release. The stillness and withdrawal came back, and the remarkable face was again composed and distant.

'Anyway thank you for the tea, Mrs Dance.'

Mary looked across and got up.

'And I'd better be going. I've got a coat to alter, for Modlen.'

Juliet looked at them, impassively. Susan felt chilled, watching her. What had begun as a minor embarrassment was now cold and frightening. The rigid moment, in which Juliet neither moved nor spoke, seemed unbreakable and endless. It was in fact only broken by a noise from outside: wheels on the gravel, outside the high window.

Juliet looked around, and spoke in a general way.

'My husband has business visitors calling.'

'Yes well we must be going. And thank you for asking us.'

Susan opened the door. Juliet followed them out, to the steps. Two men were coming to the house from the car. They were John Dance and a stranger. They were talking excitedly but stopped suddenly, as they saw the women. Susan and Mary went on down the drive.

'Of course she's mad when it comes on to food,' Mary said. Her voice was hoarse as she looked back to the house. 'She just keeps him on eggs and ham, and not much of either. Of course he gets his real food, and the rest, being out in the day.'

Susan didn't know what to say. She didn't trust her own voice.

'What about her own meals?'

'Practically nothing. Not since she got married. Though it started as a girl, just ordinary dieting. Then it built up and up, she just hates the very idea.'

'I'm very sorry.'

'Yes, it's creepy, really. The whole world, you listen to her, trying to pinch her food.'

They had to step aside, quickly, as a truck, driven fast, turned in at the gate. Susan caught sight of Ivor and Megan, laughing in the front seat; Megan was driving. Mary turned and swore.

'Silly young devils.'

'Yes, they're driving badly.'

'Of course they still can't get married. Not with that sister of his.'

'Yes, it's very difficult. Gwen was telling me about it.'

Mary laughed and ruffled the neck of her blouse.

'Perhaps they'll have to, one of these days. That's the easiest way.'

Susan didn't answer.

'All they got to do,' Mary said, 'is have a kid. And I bet they know how to do that. It'd be a lovely wedding, all confetti and roses, from the day the doctor confirmed it.'

Susan lifted her coat collar, against the pull of the wind. The truck passed them again, from behind. Megan was alone in it now, driving slowly and carefully. Mary stood against the bank, and then pushed herself back to the centre of the road.

'I know I would, quick enough, with a farm at the end of it. Catch me hanging about.'

Susan leaned into the wind, as they reached the Evening Star. As they were turning into the lane, another truck passed them, with Gethin driving.

'See what his sister made of it then,' Mary said. 'She'd be off sharp enough, with a kid in the house.'

'Wasn't that Gethin?'

'Yes, that pig. Did I tell you what he said to Modlen? That he didn't care whether she dressed or not.'

'What did he mean by that?'

'They're all the same. All in with each other, and the women get the worst of it.'

Susan looked into Pentre as they passed. Gwen was out with Cavalier, in the far corner of the yard.

'Well I hope they get it settled,' she said, drawing away. Mary laughed and reached for her arm.

'Don't worry, Mrs Price. Don't worry about them. They'll settle it, don't worry, they know how to look for their own.'

4. 'Busy then this morning?'

Matthew looked up, shaking the hair from his eyes. John Dance, with his Alsatian, was standing watching him from the lane. Years ago someone had planted a snowberry inside the gate of the cottage, and it had spread, with suckers, until it was now an impenetrable tangle, narrowing the path and beginning to break down the fence. Matthew had cut most of it down and was gathering the brush to burn.

'That's a difficult thing if it's let go.'

'Yes.'

'Though you're probably glad of the exercise. In a job like yours.'

'It releases a lot of energy. With no very obvious result.'

'Go on, you're clearing it lovely.'

'Till the Spring. The roots are persistent.'

He turned and lifted the knife, but Dance didn't move on.

'I was hoping I might see you, Mr Price. I thought I ought to put it to you. About next door.'

'Mrs Lewis's?'

'Yes, yes. That was very sad, wasn't it? She was a dear old soul.'

'It was sad, yes.'

'She used to keep a bit of a shop, in her front room. Till it got uneconomic, with the vans calling.'

'Yes, I remember her saying.'

'When I bought these two cottages, from old Tom Vaughan, I said for as long as you want it, Mrs Lewis, it's yours, don't worry whatever you do. And we won't fall out about the rent.'

'I see.'

'Only now, of course, well, I only bought them to convert.'

'Convert both, you mean?'

Dance nodded.

'Just come across the lane, Mr Price. Stand and really look at it.'

Matthew put down his knife. He followed Dance across the lane.

'You got to half close your eyes,' Dance said. 'Cut out that fence and that bit of old hedge, follow the line of the roof.'

Matthew looked. He realized that he had not looked at it before as a single building. To see the south end had been, inevitably, to see Mrs Lewis's house. But now he could make out the long, low, whitewashed building, with the eight small windows and the chimney at each end.

'It could be fine, couldn't it?' Dance said. 'The two front doors out, make a central door. Make a slated porch the same pitch as the roof. Clear the whole front to grass, just open to the lane. And under that roughcast, you'd hardly believe it, there's really good stone. Local stone. Clean and point it, it would be a different house altogether. A different class of house.'

'Yes,' Matthew said. 'Yes, I see.'

Dance threw his stick for his Alsatian. They moved back across the lane.

'Only I thought I'd mention it,' Dance said, 'because I would like you to have the first chance.'

'What chance do you mean?'

'Well you've got your let for the year. No fuss about that. But now the other cottage is vacant I shall be getting out the plans. And I'd be glad to show them to you, in the hope you might be interested.'

'Well but . . .'

'It would be a proper job, mind. None of these hardboard and paint affairs. And it would cost, there's no use saying otherwise. But still, for someone like yourself . . .'

'Oh no,' Matthew said. 'My job's in London, I shall be going back at the end of the year.'

'Well as you say, but there's always ways and means. It would be worth it just as a straight investment. I mean when the scheme comes, as I was saying before, it'll be modern houses, six or eight to the acre, one or two standard designs. And the professional families won't want that. Whereas a converted cottage, brought up to date but still keeping its character, that, believe me, is gilt-edged.'

'Well yes but not for me.'

'I don't know, Mr Price. But this sort of property, it's getting so scarce, even right up here, the value's going up before you convert. It's five thousand, now, for some broken old barn, if the stone and the site are good enough.'

'Yes, I've heard. But that's just the point. I don't have that kind of money to invest. Even supposing I wanted to.'

'Well, it depends. For a conversion for a client there's finance available. I've done several, already, on a ninety per cent mortgage.'

'Putting the money up yourself?'

'Well there's different ways. I'll put down the figures, you'd be very surprised. I reckon for two months letting, the top of the season, you'd bring the cost back down to like a lowish rent. And you'd have a modernized house, here in lovely country, all the rest of the year.'

'It's being done, I know.'

'Of course it's being done. People are all getting on to it. It's the way the country's going.'

Matthew moved to the gate and looked down at the area he had cleared. Dance followed his look.

'Get a bulldozer in, that's what we usually do. Clear the old muck right out, all the old roots and drains. Then we relay top soil and bring turf from the mountain, it makes a lovely lawn.'

'Yes, I can see cutting it over seems a bit pathetic.'

'Not at all, not at all. Only I just thought I'd mention it now. And I'm sorry to have interrupted your work.'

Matthew laughed as he looked at the tangle of stems.

'No, you needn't be sorry for that.'

    .   .   .   .

'I can't touch it, of course,' he said, later, to Susan.

'Why can't you touch it?'

'Because I'm here as a consultant. Because this would be a private interest.'

'No, that's rubbish, Matthew. You could simply tell Robert Lane. Nothing would be changed in the general decision because of this one house.'

'It could change what I said. What I think and feel.'

'Well at least it solves one thing. You know what Dance is up to.'

'Part of what he's up to.'

'I wouldn't trust him, but you've got to admit that what he's doing is good. It's terrible to let these old houses decay.'

'Yes I agree with that. And his conversions are good.'

'Well then?'

'It's how it fits in, with everything else that is happening. I just have the suspicion it's something very much bigger.'

5. Juliet stood on the whitened steps, watching the last to arrive: Gethin Jenkins. She shook hands, closed the door, and led him through to the study. The other men got up as she entered: her husband, his solicitor, and young Ivor Vaughan. Ivor was getting attractive, she noticed; a surprisingly nice-looking boy. Gethin shook hands with her husband and Postan-Jones; to Ivor he just nodded. They settled and sat down, with the papers in front of them.

It had taken months of negotiation to arrive at this point: from the first suggestions and soundings, through the careful and secret bargaining, to the drafts of the final agreements. But what was now at last on the table was the first meeting of a new private company: Afren Agricultural Holdings, Ltd; registered office, The Old Vicarage, Manod.

Behind this simple foundation lay a complicated network of agreements. Afren Agricultural Holdings was acquiring the freehold of the farms known as Pentre Court and Bedwen, in the parish of Manod, and of Church Farm, St Dyfrog, formerly the property of Alun Preece, Esquire. The directors of Afren Agricultural Holdings were to be John Dance, Juliet Dance, Gethin Jenkins, and Ivor William Vaughan. The shares of the two latter directors in the capital of the new company had been calculated to be equivalent to the market value, plus fifteen per cent, of the freehold farms which they had sold to Afren Agricultural Holdings (an external mortgage on Pentre Court was being separately redeemed by the company). In the case of Ivor William Vaughan, the shareholding on his account had been reduced by a sum equivalent to a cash payment of two thousand pounds. This cash sum, together with the purchase money for Church Farm, St Dyfrog (now vacant on the death of its owner, who had been a widower and childless) formed the basis of the shareholdings of John and Juliet Dance; together, a majority holding in the company, though the shares were individually held. John Dance was elected chairman of the company, and John Postan-Jones, solicitor, secretary. Under separate agreements, the management of the farm known as Pentre Court was assigned to Ivor William Vaughan, Esquire, and of the farms known as Bedwen, in the parish of Manod, and Church Farm, in the parish of St Dyfrog, to Gethin Jenkins, Esquire. Consequential agreements on stock and machinery, at valuation, were appended. The articles of association of Afren Agricultural Holdings defined the purposes of the company as to engage in agricultural production and related enterprises.

It was not a difficult meeting, though the large number of formal resolutions took a considerable time. Mr Postan-Jones, a contemporary of John Dance at the Pontafren County School for Boys (he had been one of Juliet's father's best pupils, and might have gone on to a metropolitan career if the family solicitor's business in Pontafren had not been waiting for him), took them quietly and skilfully through the business. He was a man well trusted by the farmers and tradesmen around Pontafren, for he had acquired great insight into their ways of thinking and negotiating. His only job, he would explain, with a quick smile, just before the signing of papers, was to put their great wisdom into the formalities required by the law. He was their agent and draftsman; he could not pretend to be their adviser. Yet it was widely believed, in Pontafren and district, that when it came to dealings in Welsh land, over a period of years and through the many changes of national policy, there was nobody around quite to touch Postan-Jones. Certainly he and John Dance had worked closely together, in recent years, and looked forward to long association in the future.

The formal meeting broke up. John Dance served whisky. John Postan-Jones took his glass to the window, so that he could talk to Juliet, whom he had always greatly admired. Juliet let herself be talked to, but hardly bothered to reply. Once she moved away, abstractedly, to refill her glass.

Her husband was standing by the big wood fire, talking to Gethin and Ivor. The three of them, they understood, were the heart of the business. Gethin had declined whisky, but Ivor had boisterously accepted and was in very good humour, his face reddening in the glow from the fire. John Dance moved away, to talk to John Postan-Jones, and Gethin was left looking at Ivor, under the high marble and walnut chimney-piece. They had changed their clothes for the meeting, but Gethin was feeling out of place, in the formal and highly polished room.

'Have you told Gwen yet?' he asked.

Ivor gulped at his glass.

'Catch me before it's all signed.'

'Well you'll have to now.'

'Aye of course. Now.'

'There's her nineteen hundred you'll have to pay over.'

'Aye, that.'

Gethin narrowed his eyes, looking across at Ivor. He had spent so many evenings, bringing Ivor to the point where Dance's scheme became clear to him, that he thought he understood him, but he was still not quite sure. It had taken a surprisingly long time to make Ivor's advantage clear: that with the mortgage redeemed, and the two thousand pounds paid over in cash, he could pay Gwen off and become his own master and marry. Ivor had been very slow to grasp this: mainly because he had gone on believing that the point of Gethin's interest was to marry Gwen. Gethin simply ignored this. His only interest, he explained, was to get hold of Church Farm and put Trevor in there. Yet Ivor still stared at him, in a happy confidential way, as if easy and willing to share the pretence. For if he wanted Church Farm for Trevor (and that was understandable) why didn't he just get an agreement, inside the new company, that Trevor should be made manager of Church Farm, in the same way that he and Gethin were made managers of Pentre and Bedwen? Gethin explained, carefully, that this was impossible, on the advice of John Dance and John Postan-Jones. Trevor had no money to put into the company, and the arrangement could only work if the managers of the farm were also directors. The complicated accounts, of the combined farms, had of course to be related to shareholdings. So Gethin would be the official manager, but between him and Trevor—Ivor could be certain of that—all the proper arrangements would be taken care of. He would see his brother all right, as he always had done. And Trevor, Gethin said, was more than

125

willing to accept the arrangement. He had wanted for so long to get his own place, and Church Farm was a good one, with its long meadows by the river. The paper arrangements with the company—and that was all the company was, just pieces of paper—Trevor accepted, Gethin said, as he would have accepted a mortgage. The main thing was that he and Modlen—and she deserved it, she had been a good wife to him—would get settled. Yet after all these explanations, and for all his pleasure in the cleverness of the interlocking arrangements (especially his own neat stroke in the case of Pentre) Ivor still believed (though he didn't say it any more) that Gethin's main object was to marry Gwen.

'What do you reckon *you're* getting out of it then?' he had asked Gethin.

'I get Church Farm for Trevor.'

'Aye for Trevor. But what's for you?'

'Well, getting it all cleared up. And the bit of capital to draw on.'

'Gwen's nineteen hundred.'

'No, we pay that out, the nineteen hundred goes to Gwen.' Ivor smiled.

'No, what you really ought to ask,' Gethin said, 'is what Dance gets out of it.'

'Dance and Juliet.'

'Aye, the two together.'

'Well for him it's an investment. That's obvious.'

'Aye, an investment. You could say that.'

John Dance came back to them, and refilled Ivor's glass. Gethin looked at him, distrusting him, but reminded himself of all the other considerations, which Ivor could not yet know about and which were Gethin's own real security. The advantage of the company to Dance, and especially the advantage of buying Church Farm, was the scheme for building and development. That was still uncertain, but if ever it happened Gethin knew, as a councillor, that the fields beside the Llancadog road—partly on his land and partly on Ivor's—would be one of the sites. When Alun Preece had died and Church Farm came on the market, Dance really came in, for if the full scheme went through it was there, in St Dyfrog, on that land between the river and the railway which was two-thirds of Preece's holding, that the industrial estate would be built; and in that, after all, there would be the real money. To get to buy Church Farm needed a lot of extra capital: more, Gethin had thought, than Dance himself could

126

raise. All Dance's money, Gethin reckoned, would go on redeeming the Pentre mortgage and the cash payment to Ivor for buying out Gwen. But within a few days Dance had come and told him the extra money could be raised: through his wife, he said, who had money through her father. Gethin hadn't believed this: Davies the headmaster had got some houses in Pontafren, down by the bridge, and he knew one block had been sold for an insurance company office. But not to this value, not to the price of Church Farm. It was really some other arrangement, probably through Postan-Jones. Gethin would have liked to know about it. Still, the money would be there, and Church Farm would be bought and the company formed. And Dance needn't think, whatever he fixed, that he could get past Gethin, in the final run. There was a long way through the council before any development of a size like that. And opinion in the council, among the majority who were farmers, would have to be taken care of, as was only right. On the other hand, if it all came to nothing, there were still the three farms. And Gethin knew more about the farming than any of the others in the company. He had already reckoned the taxation advantages, setting profits and losses between the three holdings, that Postan-Jones had gone over with him and Ivor. Again, if the development came—and Gethin, there, as a councillor, was in the strong position; Dance understood that very well —then it was only right, and he'd see to this, that the farmers whose fathers had worked this land for centuries should be properly protected, if their fields were taken off them for what these planners called development. The protection wouldn't only be in money, though that would count. For if the fields by the Llancadog road had to go, and of course Church Farm, there would still, for the company, be enough land left, taking the rest of Pentre and Bedwen together, to make one good working farm. And Gethin, if that came, had the largest shareholding, among the directors of the company with the experience to manage it. Ivor would get in time to understand all this, according to how things turned out; it might all come to nothing, and they could just carry on with the farms. But he could hardly be told all the ramifications yet, while the whole affair—as was repeatedly stressed at the council—was very strictly confidential. And that side of it, Gethin knew—he nodded to himself—was his only real protection against Dance.

'Can't I get you something else, mun?' Dance said to Gethin. 'Ginger ale, bitter lemon? Or a glass of Malvern water?'

Gethin looked at Dance, cautiously.

'What is it, that Malvern water?'

'I'll let you into a secret, mun. It's just pure water. Nothing more, nothing less.'

'Then what do I want to drink it for, when I get water like that from the tap?'

Dance laughed.

'Aye, your little supply up the Frith. Well, I expect so, yes, Gethin. Only Malvern, they say, see, is the purest water there is. Unadulterated.'

'And they got to have water from a bottle? Like babies?'

Ivor rocked forward, holding his refilled glass.

'What we ought to do, Gethin, is bottle our water, call it Manod water.'

Gethin looked at him disapprovingly. He didn't like the effects of drink.

'Aye well mine could spare it, Ivor, but I've known yours run out, when your Dad was alive. It was putting them others on, Cae Glas and Fronheulog. And of course now the bungalow.'

Ivor turned to Dance.

'That was your Grandad did that, wasn't it?'

'Aye, well it was paid, mun. The agreement's still there.'

'Not now it isn't. Not now with the company.'

John Dance turned away.

'Oh, the details'll sort themselves out. Remind me, Ivor, to mention it to Postan-Jones.'

Ivor returned to his glass.

'I'll bring it up,' he said.

Dance hesitated, and turned back to him.

'What you were saying about the water, Ivor. It's not a bad idea. Only not call it Manod water. Nobody knows about Manod. Call it Mountain Spring, or something like that. We could start in a small way, in the bar down the service area. If we got it to spare, that is.'

Gethin moved impatiently.

'What them bloody cities is leaving us,' he said. 'Coming and piping it away, then they turn round and tell us it don't cost nothing, it just comes down from the sky.'

Ivor staggered and looked up.

'Well it do, don't it, Gethin?'

'So do grass come up from the ground. Only it's our land it does it on, and our land the rain comes on. They'll steal the sweat off

128

your face, that lot in the towns. All their food and drink, it just comes up for nothing, away in the country. Then they elect their bloody governments to see they pay us low.'

'You're right, there, mun.'

John Dance laughed.

'Aye, right as rain,' he said.

He put his arm to steady Ivor.

'Only now, I expect, we must all get on.'

Gethin moved to help.

'I'll run you back home, boy.'

Ivor stood and smiled in his face.

'Aye come on in the house, Come on in and see Gwen.'

As he watched Gethin's face, so drawn and uneasy, Ivor began to laugh. His shiny black hair was damp with sweat, and his plump reddish face was like fire. John Dance took his arm, and Gethin stood, cautiously, on his other side. He seemed to be measuring the distance between the hearth and the door.

'You got a lot to talk over, our Gwen and you, now it's on the dotted line. It'll make all the difference, you mark my words.'

'We'll get on along, now,' Gethin said.

John Dance intervened, genially.

'Aye that's it, Ivor. Get back and celebrate.'

Ivor laughed.

'A lot to talk over, our Gwen and you.'

He resisted Dance's pressure to move him to the door.

There was an awkward silence. Neither of the men seemed to know what to do. From their place by the window, Postan-Jones and Juliet turned and watched them, curiously. Then Juliet put down her glass and walked slowly across. She stopped in front of Ivor and stood very close to him. She looked directly into his face. Ivor glanced away, confused, and then turned to face her, his mouth hanging open. Juliet gazed into his face, her body quite still. Then, quickly, she smiled.

'Come out with me, Ivor.'

'What?'

'Come outside with me.'

Ivor managed to look away. Dance released his arm, and he had to move his feet, suddenly, to stand where he was. As Juliet stood close to him, so close that if he staggered again he would take her with him to the floor, he was confused and embarrassed. She had come so close and open that he didn't dare move.

'Come on then, Ivor,' she said. 'Come on out now with me.'

She reached down quickly and caught tight hold of his hand. He looked round at Gethin, and then at her husband. They were staring away, but Juliet seemed not to notice them. It was as if, for her, there was nobody else in the room. She tightened her fingers again, and pulled at his hand. Ivor squared his shoulders and made an effort to move. Then he went with her to the door.

They turned through the hall, towards the high front door and its fanlight. Juliet kept her tight grip on his hand, and squeezed past him to open the door. She led him out to the steps and then stood, still touching him. There were lights down the drive but beyond them the darkness of the valley. Far below them, beyond the bare trees, were the scattered yellow lights of St Dyfrog.

'Don't you feel it cold now, Ivor?'

He didn't answer. In the wind on the steps he could feel his sweating face, and his whole body was aching. She still kept the pressure, very tight, on his fingers.

Gethin came from behind them, and then John Dance. They went across to the truck, and Gethin started the engine. The headlights cut suddenly across the gravel. Gethin drove to the foot of the steps.

Then very slowly, as if in a timed rehearsal, Juliet walked down the steps, leading Ivor beside her. John Dance opened the door and Ivor, still half-conscious, was eased inside. In the same instant, Juliet released his hand and stood back. John Dance slammed the door. Ivor looked round at Juliet, confused, as if he did not know where she had gone.

The truck moved suddenly forward, its wheels skidding on the loose sharp gravel. Juliet lifted her hand and waved, into the darkness.

VIII

1. MATTHEW heard the post van stop in the lane. He went out, for he was expecting a parcel, but it was only a letter. He stood talking to the postman, Ivor Morris, a small farmer from Llanerch. There had been a burglary, overnight, in a cottage at Parc y Meirch, where an old lady lived alone. Someone had taken her saved pension money, more than sixty pounds.

'Only we have to expect it a bit in the summer, with the visitors around. But now, this time of year, I don't understand it.'

'She didn't hear anything?'

'No, she doesn't even hardly hear *me*, and I bring her milk and bread.'

They talked for a while longer and then Matthew took in his letter. He opened it indifferently, but it was several typed pages. He looked at the signature: Ivor Rees: his first research student, now a senior lecturer at Cardiff. The letter had been sent to London and forwarded.

Matthew was slow to take it all in. There was to be a new Institute and Library of Industrial Wales: bringing all the records together and organizing research. A planning committee had been meeting and had just been discussing a Director. It had been agreed, informally, to offer Matthew the job. The letter was to persuade him to accept a formal offer.

He stared down the garden. The trees and hedge had now moved into what seemed a different bareness: a change of colour, a loss of colour, in the smaller branches and twigs. But on the forked earth under them there was a strengthening of colour: a deep rich brown where the leaves were beginning to rot.

'It is not only the distinction of your own work,' Ivor Morris wrote; 'it is the sense so many of us have that you founded us, you gave us direction, you taught, without having to teach, what such work can be. And moreover it is wrong, we feel that it is wrong, that after so much struggle you should still be out of your country, and especially out of it now, when so much is happening here, so much new energy, so strong a sense of our possible future. And so on every count we were unanimous, enthusiastic and unanimous, and to be both things in Wales, at the same time, that is a rare

131

event; rare enough, in all conscience, to overcome even your diffidence.'

Matthew stared again down the garden, but now he wasn't looking at it. What was sticking in his mind, from the long letter, was the handwritten postscript: 'We were sorry to hear that you had been so ill. We hear now that you are well again. And Wales will complete the cure!'

He made a pot of tea and carried it up to Susan, who had a heavy cold. He put the letter beside the cup, as he handed it to her.

'What is it?'

'You'd better read it.'

She looked through it before drinking her tea. Matthew had gone to the window and was staring out at the lane.

'Do you want it?' Susan asked.

'I don't know. I can't link it up.'

'Well you're pleased, aren't you? I mean the way Ivor puts it, and then the job itself, it's so exactly your own work.'

'Yes. It isn't that. I was thinking about the postscript.'

Susan turned the pages to look at it again.

'What about it? They must have heard.'

'Don't you feel the pity in it?'

'No, not pity. It's just ordinary sympathy.'

'It's the fantasy, too, I suppose. Really that London made me ill.'

'You always used to say that yourself.'

'Before I learned how the worlds connect. How the border got crossed.'

'It hasn't been your own world, all the same.'

'Who lives in his own world? Isn't that the struggle?'

'There are still differences, gradations. I've heard you say that so often.'

He walked back to the bed, took the letter and folded it.

'I expect Lane sent me here for the same reason. Not an inquiry, just a rest cure. Because it will make no difference, whatever I report.'

'The Industrial Institute wouldn't be as little as that.'

'No. It wouldn't. It would be a life's work.'

'Well then accept it. I'd be very willing.' He smiled. He reached down for her hand.

'How's the cold?'

'A bit easier. I'd better get up.'

132

'No, stay. I'm just working downstairs. There's something very odd about that forestry study. I think they're using different job projections in the analysis and in the tables.'

'Isn't that always likely for forestry? The job intensity varies over time.'

'Yes. Of course. That's why it was their job to be especially careful.'

The phone rang downstairs. He smiled and went down to answer it.

2. It had been Peter on the phone. He was coming over, urgently. He was bringing someone with him. Matthew could drop everything: this was the break they'd been waiting for.

He was still a long time coming. Matthew worked, half watching the lane. The forestry labour statistics were indeed inconsistent; he made a provisional correction of the general table. But it was at best marginal. The issue didn't turn on it.

Peter arrived at last, in a strange car. A tall red-haired man in his thirties was with him. Matthew met them at the door.

'This is Tom Meurig,' Peter said. 'He lives in Llanidloes or in Europe, I can't remember which.'

Tom Meurig laughed.

'I knew this unruly assistant of yours, Dr Price, when we were both in Oxford, setting up a red base. Mind you, he's good on strategy, a bit short on logistics.'

'Peter isn't my assistant,' Matthew said, awkwardly.

'Oh you disown him too? Well, that's a relief. But while he's been bumming round the world, taking money from foundations, I've come back to do some work: a bit of actual political organizing.'

'He can't make up his mind,' Peter said, 'whether to proclaim an immediate Federation of the Celtic Peoples, with honorary membership for the Basques, or whether simply to take over Europe, with this new communal socialism they've been dreaming up in the hills.'

'Either of those,' Meurig said, 'or the third possibility: getting one of our people on to the District Council.'

They went in and sat down. Matthew shifted his papers.

'Yes,' Peter said, 'put that lot away. What we've got is the actual scheme.'

'Well,' Meurig said, 'only a bit of it really. I didn't even know

133

Peter was down here, till I heard through his mother. And we've only just got this, we were wondering how to use it.'

'Got what?' Matthew asked.

They started to speak together, but then Peter gave way.

'Only the first bit is definite,' Meurig said, carefully. 'But there's been a whole interlocking set of land deals, most of them, on the surface, appearing quite normal, the usual buying and selling of farms, but there's a new company: Afren Agricultural Holdings . . .'

'Run by one of your neighbours,' Peter said.

'Yes, Dance is up to his neck in it. And in fact the farm down the lane is involved. But that's only the outlying bits. Afren Agricultural Holdings is just a subsidiary. We already know of three others, at Llanerch, at Bronydd, at the Cwm: altogether, already, more than eighteen farms. And we've not been able to check this, or rather, till I met Peter . . .'

He stopped. His face flushed. The blood seemed to move up, visibly, through the pale skin, under the springing red hair.

'I showed him our maps,' Peter said. 'Our classified maps. Robert Lane's classified maps.'

'I see,' Matthew said, 'And . . . ?'

Tom Meurig breathed out, loudly. Peter turned to him and nodded, confirming a point.

'Well you must look for yourself, Dr Price, but to us it's very clear. All the buying is exactly in the designated areas; I mean after allowing for overlap on particular farms. It looks very much like a coordinated job, getting company ownership of all the designated land.'

'Not all,' Matthew said. 'From the names you mentioned.'

'Which are all we're yet sure of. There may well be more.'

'And subsidiaries, you say? Running back to what?'

'To the Mid-Wales Rural Community Development Agency.'

'What?'

'No, it isn't the official one. It just sounds very like it. It was chosen to sound like it.'

'And do you know who they are?'

'Well that's the devil of it. All we get, each time, are the two recurrent names: Dance and this solicitor, Postan-Jones. But of course it isn't possible that they're the principals. The operation's much too big for that.'

'I'm going to London this evening,' Peter said. 'I'll get the real names at Companies House.'

Matthew lay back in his chair.

'Yes,' he said, 'Yes, obviously. And then the problems start.'

'You mean,' Peter said, 'the fight starts.'

'Well yes, of course, but with some problems of just who to fight. We must take it to Lane, obviously, once we've got the principal names. But meanwhile I must see Bryn Walters. In case the leak is local.'

'Why a leak?' Peter said. 'Knowing Robert Lane and his government this could be what they're meaning to happen: a good solid capitalist renewal.'

'With us as its advisers?'

'With us as its ritual offering. It's what progressive intellectuals are for.'

'Why risk it, if so? Since as soon as we hear of it we start prising it open?'

'You're too trusting, Matthew.'

'No, I just distribute trust and distrust. I mean I try to distribute them.'

Tom Meurig smiled, looking across at Peter as if resuming a discussion.

'Yes,' he said, noticing Matthew's interception of the look, 'we've been arguing about you.'

'Why not?' Matthew said.

'But don't get it the wrong way round. Peter was defending you. It was I who was asking what you meant by coming here.'

'With what possibilities?'

Meurig laughed.

'Well, Matthew Price,' he said, smiling, 'you're an exile. Perhaps, I don't know, a voluntary exile. So that none of us yet knows your commitment to Wales.'

Matthew leaned forward.

'Enough of a commitment to know the divisions,' he said, sharply.

'No, don't resent it,' Meurig said. 'But a scheme like the city, it's an English device, you must agree on that. They will say they're renewing mid-Wales but they'll be renewing it with Englishmen, English people from English cities. In fact a colony, you could say. Just the old penetration.'

'It could be more complex than that. Since the earlier history sucked hundreds of thousands of us away.'

'You mean Manod as a National Home for the Welsh of the diaspora?'

'No. Because we've not stayed exclusive. Any more than the making of industrial South Wales was a return. It was always a mixed immigration, yet it led, didn't it, to one of the strongest autonomous cultures in Europe? A culture people made, not inherited.'

'With very strong native elements. As you showed yourself.'

'Of course. But still transmuting. In a new historical phase.'

'An old one now,' Meurig said. 'A culture with its base breaking up.'

'Yes, and then where do we go? Back to traditional rural Wales?'

'Which you think I'm attached to? Which you think is all we're offering? Fortress Gwynedd!'

'That's the risk, isn't it? Just because it's a real short-term option. And because it isn't a fortress, it's a matter of the heart.'

'Yes indeed, yes it is. But then you're not part of it. You're from the border, you live in both worlds, or in neither. And the strongest desire you may have is that it should stay that way, in an unspoiled mid-Wales, carrying the recreational traffic from England.'

'In the city?'

'No, *against* the city. If you come down on that side.'

Matthew got up and went to the window. He stared down at the leaves of the coleus on the sill. In the larger leaves the green was spreading and dulling the crimson.

'It's as well I mentioned divisions,' he said, turning. 'Since you've now got an ideological explanation for either conclusion I might come to.'

'Right,' Meurig said.

'It's where you are,' Peter said. 'It's where Lane has put you.'

'Not you, however?'

'Hell no. I can walk away from it. Tom has no claim on me, even after he's proved I've got three Welsh grandmothers . . .'

'Three would be an historic event,' Meurig said.

'That shows how little you know about family life. Your family's like your Wales: an idealist norm. All it does is waste time. The actual history is back there in the bloody centre: the Birmingham–Düsseldorf axis, with offices in London, Brussels, Paris, Rome. You two post-Celts are just severed talking heads.'

Matthew moved back to the fireplace.

'The quite alternative strategy,' he said to Meurig, 'is to

sustain mid-Wales, by organic development, more assistance to the farms, bringing some light industry, naming certain growth towns, and above all improving transport, especially a new South–North road. Then we could put the major investment into the south, to regenerate the valleys.'

'Yes,' Meurig said, 'that would be a Welsh policy. And no English government will do it. It will go on using Wales to solve English problems, or it will neglect us altogether.'

'And if that's right,' Matthew said, 'what's the tactical decision on Manod?'

Meurig laughed.

'Divisions again, as you said. But what I'd say myself is not just thumbs down. Rather use the inquiry to develop an alternative strategy.'

'He can't,' Peter said, impatiently. 'Lane's brief doesn't run to it.'

'I can do what I choose,' Matthew said, coldly.

'Yes, that's your voluntarism. But on this you can't. You can say Yes Manod, No Manod, three bags full Manod, and nothing else. That's the extent of your consultancy.'

'But not the extent of what I can say.'

'Well of course privately you can recommend a revolution. You can suggest that Lane shoots himself. But nobody will take a blind bit of notice.'

'We'd take notice,' Meurig said.

'Yes, you the severers, the talking heads.'

The door from the kitchen opened. Susan came in and said that she had made lunch: nothing much, just soup, bread and cheese.

'You shouldn't have, Mrs Price,' Tom Meurig said, and introduced himself.

Matthew turned to Peter.

'You're going to London tonight, you said?'

'Yes. I'll get Beth and the baby to Trawsfynydd and go on from there.'

'Will you come back when you've got the names?'

'I don't know, straightaway. There may be more to track down. But I'll ring you, shall I, when I've been to Companies House?'

'I'd be glad if you would. It would be an obvious advantage if we could go to Lane together.'

'Suppose he's one of the names?'

137

'You're not serious. But then all the more so.'

'Okay, boss,' Peter said.

Matthew saw Meurig look up and frown, as he heard Peter. They followed Susan to the kitchen.

3. 'You shouldn't have got up and made lunch,' Matthew said. 'I could have managed that.'

It was mid-afternoon. Tom Meurig and Peter had gone. Matthew had tried to phone Bryn Walters but he was away at a conference until the weekend. Susan had not gone back to bed; she was sitting under a quilt by the big fire in the front room.

'It's habit,' Susan said.

'The habit of looking after people. You ought now, occasionally, to look after yourself.'

'Anyway I was glad. I liked Tom Meurig.'

'Welsh charm?'

'Is it? I hope not. Just some unregenerate condition: like noticing when another person comes into the room.'

'Someone not part of the meeting? Some unaccommodated man.'

'Man or woman.'

'Yes.'

'Whereas Peter . . .'

'I know.'

'That's London, if you insist on the geography. One of your immaterial materialists with so much energy locked in the struggle that he's neither physically present nor physically responsive, in any way the rest of us know. Within alienation analysing alienation. What are the other concepts?'

'Instrumentality. Dehumanization.'

'He'll do well. When he settles.'

'No, not necessarily. It's harder than that. As a company man, or a government man, yes of course. But in the opposition there's only the opposition. That's why I can't be against him.'

'I wouldn't want to be Beth,' Susan said.

Matthew stared into the fire. It was getting dark outside but he didn't put on the light. After a while he went to the kitchen and made tea. He carried it back in front of the fire.

'You didn't mention the job,' Susan said, after a while.

'No.'

'Did you worry that Tom would persuade you? Making the Welsh connection.'

'I don't need persuading. I'm sure I would like it.'

'Then why not write and accept?'

'I don't know. I really don't know. Perhaps just social inertia. I just don't think of changing jobs.'

'Like your father.'

'Is it? I wouldn't think so. He hadn't that much choice.'

'He could have gone in with Morgan Rosser. You remember Morgan told us about it.'

'No, that was a class change.'

'He wouldn't have said so.'

'Maybe, but he could feel what he might well not say. In any case it's different from a move to the same kind of job.'

'Which he also didn't make. Though he was offered it often.'

'Well he always had more than his job. He had the gardens and the bees.'

'And you don't?'

'Have more than the job? Well anything I have I can take.'

'That's the shift, Matthew. That you can put it like that.'

He got up impatiently.

'Yes,' he said. 'Yes, I heard.'

Someone opened their gate from the lane. He crossed to the window.

'It's Gwen, I think. Gwen Vaughan.'

'I'll go,' Susan said, getting up.

'No you stay and sit in the warm.'

'She'll expect it,' Susan said, and went through to the back door.

Matthew put on a light and drew the curtains. He could hear voices in the kitchen. He made up the fire. After some minutes Susan opened the door.

'Matthew. It's Gwen. She'd like to talk to you.'

'Well yes. Come in, Gwen.'

Gwen came through shyly. She had changed from her usual clothing of jersey and breeches and put on a suit. She looked very different: older, tidier, more composed.

'I must make up my bed,' Susan said, and went quickly upstairs, before the others could speak.

'I'm sorry to disturb you, Mr Price,' Gwen said, formally.

'No. That's all right. I've finished all I was doing.'

She hesitated. She was looking down into the fire.

'Sit down look, Gwen.'

'Thank you.'

'How's Ivor? I've not seen him about.'

Gwen looked up sharply.

'Oh he's as good as better. Thank you.'

She stared again at the fire. Matthew waited before prompting her. He felt especially unsure.

'You've been managing, have you, with Trevor helping?'

'Oh we've managed,' Gwen said, sharply. 'I've had to learn to manage.'

'And a bit quieter now through the winter,' Matthew said.

'Oh it's not to do with that,' Gwen said, looking up at him. 'But I wanted to ask—don't say if you don't want to—is this development coming, this building they keep bringing up?'

'Nobody knows, Gwen, yet. I was asked to come down here to give an opinion, but how it will all be decided I've no real idea.'

'Then why is the land being bought?'

'Which land?'

'Well ours for a start. Gethin and Dance talked Ivor into it. He's gone and sold our farm to this company.'

'Afren Agricultural Holdings?'

Gwen jerked forward.

'So you do know about it.'

'I was told this morning. Though it's been kept very secret.'

'It wasn't kept any secret from me. Only till after it was done. Only Ivor's still a kid, they can twist him which way they like. He thinks he's been clever, getting money to buy me out and then he's free to get married. But then it isn't our farm any more. It isn't his, though he thinks so. He's just a manager now, put in by this company. And when the building comes, they can just turn him out.'

'He's not in the company?'

'Oh yes, he's got shares. But the others have got more, they can vote him out. And he's been led like a fool, just to spite me.'

'Because he wants to get married?'

'Yes, to Megan Parry. And he had to buy me out first.'

'Did he?'

Gwen leaned towards the fire. The angry blotches came up again in her face. Her lips started moving, as if she were talking to herself, or rehearsing what she would say.

'I don't have to trouble you with it,' she said, eventually. 'But what always breaks us up is this money from outside. This isn't

Dance's money, or Gethin's. It's from somewhere else and I've been going all through it: it must be part of your scheme.'

'Not my scheme, Gwen. And the one thing kept secret was the possible sites, just so that they wouldn't get bought.'

'Only now they have been. This one, any road.'

'Yes,' Matthew said, 'this one.'

Gwen looked across at him.

'What rights do any of you have, Mr Price, to come in here, breaking us up?'

'None,' Matthew said. 'None I'd want to claim. Except that you've also got to admit that it's being done from inside.'

'Yes it is, by young fools like Ivor. He's only a boy. You can all fool him quick enough.'

'And Gethin?'

'Gethin would sell anybody. And he's part of it, isn't he, from the Council?'

'No, the Council's against the development.'

'Well who's for it, then? Except you?'

'I'm not for or against it. I was just sent to find out and then give an opinion.'

'You expect me to believe that?'

'Yes, Gwen, I expect you to believe it. Because it's the truth.'

'And they pay you for that?'

'Yes, they pay me. The Government pays me.'

'The Government that thought of the scheme in the first place.'

'That thought of it, that changed its mind, that's going over it now again.'

'You're like Ivor,' Gwen said. 'You believe what people tell you. And you'll only find out when they've got you where they want you.'

'No, Gwen. We just heard about this buying. And within a few days we shall know who's really behind it.'

'With it already bought? What good will that do you? That you can write it all down, but only after it's happened?'

'We'll see,' Matthew said. 'There may be things we can do.'

'There'll be nothing you can do. The farms have been sold. The money's done all the talking.'

She stood, abruptly, from her chair. Matthew also stood, facing her.

'I'm sorry, Gwen. This was none of my doing.'

'No, you just watch and let it happen.'

'If we'd known before . . .'

'Yes and if I'd known before. But you've been dealing with Dance. You rent this place from him. It used to be ours. And with Annie Lewis dead now he'll convert it for you, I expect.'

'Yes, he offered. I haven't accepted.'

'You see. You'll be all right, whatever happens to us. Because *your* money comes from the other end of the line.'

'Yes. It does. Because I'm supposed to be trained to give a fair assessment.'

'Fair to who? To them that pay you?'

'For the general good is what I'm really asked.'

'And for your own good in any case, whether you find the general out or not.'

Matthew stood very still. He was turned looking at Gwen, but he did not seem to see her. His eyes had lost focus and his lips were loosely open, showing the big irregular teeth. Gwen didn't move. She was looking steadily into his face.

'I'm taking it out on you, Mr Price. And it's right, what I said. But I've got nobody to go to. Trevor and Modlen are glad it's all happened; they're getting Church Farm. The Parrys are glad, it's a place for Megan. And my brothers are against Ivor but they say they can't stop it. Only I can stop it, if I can find the strength.'

'You said it was all done,' Matthew answered, coming slowly back.

'All the selling is done. Ivor came in, last night, with this cheque in his hand. "There's your money," he said, and he put it down on the table. I could hardly believe it, I had to force it all out of him. But I wouldn't take the cheque. He can't force me to take it.'

'It's your share in Pentre?'

'Yes, it has to be paid to me if the farm is sold.'

'And it has been sold?'

'I told you.'

'Then refusing the cheque doesn't stop it. It only hurts you.'

'It's putting him on his conscience. That I won't go along with it.'

'And what does he say?'

'That it can lie there till I want it. It makes no difference to him.'

'Well he's right, Gwen.'

'You call that right?'

'I mean refusing the cheque can't stop him.'

142

'And I must just turn out, I suppose. With nineteen hundred pounds that'll buy nothing.'

'You can't stay? If he gets married?'

'No, not after this.'

'Though you don't mind him getting married?'

Gwen pushed back at her hair.

'No, it's nothing to me. He's a boy, that's all. He thinks I'll marry Gethin. That's all he knows about it.'

Matthew looked away. He could hear Susan moving, in the bedroom above them. He wished that she had stayed, through this difficult meeting. In the sudden convergence of so many issues he was very exposed and uncertain.

'Look, Gwen,' he said shyly, 'I'm as you say, an outsider. There's probably nothing I can do. But you came, and I'm glad, because I have to know the truth. You've been hurt, obviously, and you include me, my job, in what's come to hurt you. In a way that may be true, but not intentionally; you know that, or you wouldn't have come to me. And all I can say, now, if you want to tell me all the details of this deal, write them down if you like, we're already going into it, we may find something out.'

'It's what I want,' Gwen said, eagerly. 'It was why I came, only then I lost my temper. Only with Dance and Gethin behind it there'll be some shady business for certain. And if you could make that out then perhaps . . .'

She stopped. She looked away. Then she reached in her pocket and took out a sheaf of papers.

'It's all here,' she said. 'All the papers Ivor got.'

Matthew looked at her curiously.

'Yes,' she said, 'I took them. I saw where he put them, like a boy hiding his secret.'

'But then I can't take them.'

Gwen breathed out angrily. Her eyes, suddenly, were unusually bright.

'Why, Mr Price? You afraid to dirty your hands?'

'No, these are private legal papers. They're not yours or mine to look at.'

'So we can let people cheat us but we mustn't know how?'

Matthew hesitated. In the sudden silence of the room he could hear Susan coming downstairs. She opened the door and looked in on them. They were standing facing each other. Then as Susan came in Gwen moved and put the papers on the table.

'I'm sorry,' Susan said, 'I'm interrupting.'

'No, you're not, Mrs Price,' Gwen said, quickly. 'I just brought some papers for your husband to see.'

Susan looked at Matthew. His face was still set hard, but now he smiled suddenly.

'Yes,' he said. He picked up the papers and put them away in a drawer.

IX

1. MATTHEW stopped the car in St Dyfrog, just beyond Church Farm. He again checked the maps before getting out. It was then a shock to be wrenched from the formality of the maps to the drenched road and fields, in the heavy February rain. The Afren, down the road, was bank high, its colour a milky light brown with all the soil it was carrying. Every ditch was running with water and pools were spreading across the road where the banks had been broken by the heavy wheels of lorries that had pulled in to pass. Water was lying in sheets in the fields, with tussocks of roots and coarse grass standing up like small islands.

He stared at the fields, not really knowing why he had come. His first look at the maps had made everything clear: Church Farm, where Trevor and Modlen would be moving, was exactly the site of the city's factory area. Under the driving rain, now, either use seemed as improbable as the other.

He got back in the car and drove as far as the bridge. He got out and looked down at the fast foaming swell of the river. Its rushing noise was overpowering where it washed and divided at the old stone piers of the bridge. He could still feel its power as he turned and drove back up to Manod. On the steeper land there were new brooks everywhere, rushing down the slopes towards the Dowy. Spouts of tumbling water were breaking through the hedges, overfilling the deep ditch and spreading out across the road, where they found a new course. On the bend of the pitch, between the high ivied banks, the road itself seemed to have become a stream, flowing in wide ripples across the path of the tyres.

He stopped at the cottage and ran inside. By the gate the holes where he had tried to dig out the snowberry, and which he had carefully refilled, had opened again, the rain carrying the loose soil down.

It was already three days since Peter had gone to London, and he had not rung back. Taking off his wet clothes, Matthew asked again, but there had been no call. When he had made up the fire he sat staring into it. He was oppressed by a sense of forces moving beyond him, forces he seemed to recognize but could still not be

145

sure of. And his mind kept returning to Peter. When it came to it, he thought, he did not really know him at all. Once he was not there in front of you he seemed quite incalculable: a quite separate kind of life.

He could not leave it much longer. He left the fire, reluctantly, and put a call through to Lane. There were the usual delays, through the network of extensions, but in the end he got a secretary, who said that Lane was at a meeting. He thought he recognized the voice.

'Is that Joan?' he said, relaxing.

'No, it isn't,' the girl said, pleasantly. 'She's moved to another desk. Shall I try to put you through to her?'

'No, thank you. Not now.'

He had just put down the phone when it rang. The unexpectedness startled him. He was slow to pick it up.

'Dr Price? This is Gwyn. Gwyn Owen, Trawsfynydd.'

'Yes, Gwyn, how are you?'

'Well I'm sorry to disturb you but . . . Hold on, I'll just shut the door.'

He heard the steps away from the phone. There was a long pause.

'Sorry, somebody came,' Gwyn's voice came back. 'Only as I say, I don't want to disturb you but we're starting to get worried. Have you heard at all from Peter?'

'No, I've been waiting for him to call.'

'Well, that's it, you see. He brought Beth and the baby over, that's nearly four days now, and he set off for London, the one night he said it would be, or the most two.'

'And you've not heard from him?'

'Nothing. And it isn't him, he's all right for certain. Only Beth, with the baby, you know what it's like. She's not saying much but Myra and I are getting really worried about her. It's not just the usual nerves. It's as if, almost, she knows something has happened. Only she won't talk to us.'

'Where was he to stay in London?'

'Well that's it. And Beth see, today, was so bad, Myra got me to ring it. I got hold of the chap and Peter had been there, the night he travelled up. But he hasn't been back, and his van's still there, in the street.'

'Nothing more than that?'

'No, nothing. So I thought I'd ring you, I didn't know what else.'

146

'Well yes. And I wish I could help. But I'll do what I can and if I hear I'll let you know.'

'Thank you. We'd be glad. Only it's not really us, see, it's Beth we're thinking about.'

2. Gwen came in again that evening. She seemed more her usual self, even pleased about something. She talked mostly about the weather and the trouble with the ditches: Trevor had been out all day, trying to keep them clear. Then, as she was going, she said, casually:

'I'll take those papers while I'm here.'

'Yes, of course, Gwen. I'll get them.'

As Matthew went to the drawer, Gwen said to Susan:

'It's fixed at last. Ivor and Megan are getting married. On the fifth, that's a Saturday.'

'Oh that's very good news,' Susan said.

Matthew handed Gwen the papers. She stuffed them, without looking, into her raincoat pocket. But she held Matthew's look for a moment, before turning again to Susan.

'There's been such a lot to arrange,' she said. 'Only it's all right now.'

'They'll live in Pentre, will they?'

'Well yes, of course. It's Ivor's farm. Only it's general post, we shall all be moving. Trevor and Modlen go down to St Dyfrog, and I'm taking over their place. I've got plans, I can tell you.'

'Well that's good, Gwen. It's good for you all.'

Matthew was looking down, not wanting to speak.

'Yes, I'm going in properly for the pony trekking. Just a string of a dozen at first. I've been up there now with John Dance. The old barn at the back, he's going to do it up for the visitors to sleep, and I'm putting in the adverts, I'll be going by the summer.'

'Well then it's all worked out very well.'

'Oh we manage,' Gwen said. 'We're not so stuck in Manod.'

As she spoke she looked, deliberately, at Matthew. He straightened and looked back at her.

'You're not worried then, now, that the farm has been sold?'

'I'd have preferred it not,' Gwen said.

Her face was very pale, under the black cropped hair. But the eyes were lively, as he had often seen her on a gallop down from the mountain.

'Only these changes have to come,' she said, still looking at him.

'The local changes?'

'Yes, local. We don't want the other.'

'Is it still in your hands to decide?' he asked.

'In whose then? In yours?' she said, challenging him.

'Gwen, you know I didn't mean that. I mean now that it's out of your family. Now that this company owns it.'

'They won't own Cae Glas. I'm buying that private. And whatever happens, they'll still want to come, for the trekking.'

'Yes, I suppose they will.'

'So John Dance says, anyhow.'

'Says *now*.'

Gwen smiled, broadly.

'I've had to learn to manage,' she said. 'I've had to manage since Dad died.'

She patted her raincoat pocket, where she had stuffed the papers.

'Only I must be going,' she said. 'See if Trevor's managed not to drown himself. Only I thought I'd let you know. And I'll be telling Mrs Parry to invite you both to the wedding.'

3. Beth was sitting by the window of the living-room at Trawsfynydd, looking out at the garage yard and the black shed. She had just finished feeding the baby, who was now asleep across her arm. She could feel the arm going numb but she was too tired to move, after a bad night when the baby had been awake and crying, and she had only slept, at last, when Myra had come in and taken her.

The post van had drawn into the yard. Gwyn was standing in the doorway of the shed, talking to the driver: a relief man whom she didn't know. She had watched if there were letters but had seen nothing. What did it matter anyway? If Peter wrote it would be the worst news of all. And through her drained tiredness she felt, at times, that none of it mattered anyway. Life had narrowed down to this single necessity and there would be nothing beyond it. Peter, wherever he was, would go his own way.

It was warm in the room. Gwyn had made up a big wood fire on the stone hearth. Myra was out the back, doing the washing; in these days of heavy rain it was so hard to keep level with it. What could she ever do, now, without Myra supporting her?

148

Myra and Gwyn. To be alone in the flat in Pontafren, with or without Peter, would be hopeless. She hadn't got the strength to manage the baby and the work.

Would it go on like this, then, for months, for years? Perhaps she had just come back home with Peter's baby, to let Myra and Gwyn support her? For the first few days she had still had some energy. When the phone had rung loudly, outside in the garage, she had rushed out to answer it, but it had never been for her. And she had made no calls herself. She had let Gwyn ring Dick Edmunds, to see if Peter was still there. She was not really surprised when she heard that he wasn't, though indeed she had not expected anything quite so cruel and abrupt. For he had seemed so glad when Menna had been born, and he had been enjoying the work with Matthew Price, though he always said it meant nothing. She went back now, again and again, to his look when Tom Meurig had called, with the news of the land deals. 'That's it then,' Peter had said, 'that's the end of that little game.' It had made sense, in its direct reference, but there had been something else. He had looked around the flat, and out through the window at the bridge over the Afren, as if including them in the phase that was ending. And then his immediate idea of going to London, once he had seen Matthew, had also made sense; she had not quarrelled with it though it was the last thing she wanted. He had indeed to go and track down the land deals, but again, as he spoke of it, and as he made the arrangement to take her and the baby to Trawsfynydd, there was something else: some other impulse; some familiar first steps into his old kind of run.

That possibility, probability even, had always been there: that when something happened to disturb him he would move back, as if inevitably, into cancellation and flight. It must be this now, but there was nobody she could talk to about it. Gwyn and Myra knew of it, but as belonging to a period before, as they thought of it, he had settled; before he had married, they really meant. And she had wanted to think of it that way herself; at times, for weeks or months, she could manage to see it their way. But her sense of the real danger always came back. This was nothing, really, that time or relationship could change. It was his condition, his setting in the world: a permanent kind of damage—for damage it had to be reckoned—which could be cured, if at all, only by some much more general change. Not that this was her own understanding of it; she had always argued against him when he had put it like that; seen it, angrily or certainly, as no more than an excuse.

149

But while it was still how he put it to himself, it did not even have to be true; his feelings were locked in it and he would make it be true, in all he did and felt.

Myra came in, already talking: vigorous and confident as always. What ever was the difference between them, that Myra, with her much harder life, was so much stronger and more resilient? Here in Trawsfynydd Myra had lost her first husband and been left alone with her baby. And she had flared back at life, flared and lived her whole experience. 'It wasn't only the once,' she had said to Beth, remembering that time, 'and we wasn't thinking of that.' That had been when Beth had told her that she had slept with Peter, before they were married. 'I don't know about wrong,' Myra had said, twisting the old wedding ring that she could not now take off. 'We wasn't thinking of that.' And then she had cried, terribly, remembering the young man who had been killed on his motor-bike, just down the road on the corner by Bridge Farm: Jack Evans, Beth's father; a lifetime ago.

Myra stopped in mid-sentence as she came into the room and saw the baby asleep. She moved over quickly, though as she bent to take the baby she put her hand to her back and hissed with pain.

'That bloody machine,' she whispered, but she was already taking the baby. 'And you get up and move about, slopping over like that.'

'You'll wake her, Mam.'

'And if I do I'll get her to sleep again. We can't leave her like this.'

'I'm sorry. I'm good for nothing.'

'No,' Myra said, 'you don't want to think that.'

Beth pushed herself up from the chair. The post van was still there; Gwyn and the postman were still talking. What could it ever be about, this prolonged talking, that happened everywhere in this country whenever people met? Not talking to each other, it often seemed. Just talking to anybody, keeping the world going. Keeping life in existence.

A car drew up in the yard. Gwyn thought it was for petrol and walked across to the pump. The postman, reluctantly, moved a step towards his van, but then stopped to see who it was. Matthew Price got out of the car. Beth felt her heart jump, but of course it would mean nothing. She watched from the window as the three men, now, stood and talked. Myra, behind her, was changing the baby in the armchair by the fire.

'It's Matthew Price,' Beth said.

'Well ask him in when I've put her down.'

'He's seen a baby before.'

'Aye and I've seen men before.'

Matthew was looking towards the window. Beth pushed back the curtain and waved. He said something to Gwyn and then turned to come into the house. Beth hurried and met him in the doorway.

'I called on my way through to London. How are you?' he said quickly.

'Oh we're fine.'

'It's obviously very complicated, this business Peter's gone on. So I thought I'd go up and help.'

'He's let you know about it, has he?'

'Well no, not yet. But I can imagine it taking some time. It's all very devious and a lot of it, I should think, well disguised.'

Myra came to the porch door behind them, carrying the baby against her shoulder.

'Ask Dr Price in, Beth, why don't you?'

'Well I mustn't stay. My wife's gone shopping in Gwenton. I must get back to pick her up and then on to London.'

'You'll have a cup of tea, though.'

'No,' Matthew said. 'But I'll say hello to Miss Menna.'

'Don't you wake her, the little devil,' Myra said, but she was already half turning the baby, so that Matthew could see her face.

Matthew stared at the pink drawn face inside the shawl.

'She keeps you awake then?' he said to Beth.

'Yes. I couldn't really manage if it wasn't for Mam.'

'Aye well, there are other things keep us awake, without that much promise.'

'You needn't say,' Beth said.

He looked at the two women. They were so clearly mother and daughter: the same tall, strong body, the high colouring, the heavy brightness of dark-red hair. And their expressions were much alike, in this moment, with the baby between them.

'She's got a good line to follow, that's one thing,' he said.

Beth looked at him, puzzled. He was so different, here, from when she had met him in Manod and Pontafren. His stance and his voice had changed, both relaxed and roughened.

'You came up through Glynmawr?' Myra said.

'Aye, what's left of it.'

'That's a lovely fast road down there now.'

'Aye. The lorries was butting me as I was looking to see where I was.'

'Catch you not knowing,' Myra said.

'Aye, I knew.'

He stood for a moment, looking across at the baby, and then went back to speak to Gwyn. They stood for some time, talking closely, before Matthew drove off, down the valley.

4. Matthew met Susan in a pub in Oxford Street. He had spent the morning tracing the records that Peter had come up to trace. Now he thought he had what he wanted.

'But what next?' he asked, as they found a table to put down their beer and bread and cheese.

'On which do you mean?'

'Yes. On the business this is enough. I should go straight to Lane. But I'm now also pretty sure what Peter is following.'

He got out his notebook and they went through the details. All the farm-buying companies were, as Peter and Tom Meurig had said, subsidiaries of a company registered as the Mid-Wales Rural Community Development Agency. There were three more than they had previously known about; at Fforest, Parc-y-Meirch and Nantlais. All the directors of these small companies were local, with Dance and Postan-Jones on each list. In the large company there were again Dance and Postan-Jones but then five other names which had to be separately traced. This had been relatively difficult, for while two were easily identified, as directors of a London merchant bank, the other three included two foreign nationals, one Dutch and one Belgian, and it was finally only through the third, Edward Harley, with an address in London, that the significant grouping could be seen. For these three were among fifteen directors of a company registered in London and Antwerp under the trading name ABCD. But then there was not much to learn about the precise nature of this company, which declared its purposes in the broad terms of developing and applying 'environmental technology systems'.

That was as far, in the time, as Matthew had been able to get. But he was willing to break off because, in the short term at least, he cared more about Peter than about this tangle of money and interests.

'He's gone to Belgium, obviously. To check on this company in Antwerp. To get leads on these other names.'

152

'He could have rung and said so.'

'Yes. Yes he could. But it's no use now. We must wait till he gets back.'

'And meanwhile you'll go to Lane?'

'Sure. Because I must. And because even for this tracking of companies he has far more resources.'

'Does he have as much will to find out?' Susan asked.

'Yes, I wonder about that. I wonder, obviously, why Peter didn't go straight to him.'

'It's how different people work. Peter's not the most official kind of man.'

'Well yes. I hope it's only that.'

They got up and walked out of the pub. In the crowded street, with its jam of traffic and people passing indifferently on the pavements, Matthew stopped and held Susan's arm.

'What is it, love?' she asked.

'It's what they call banal,' he said, leaning close to her. 'These facts and these relations are so obvious, so solidly and habitually obvious, that it takes all your strength just to admit they're still there.'

'The companies?'

'The companies. And then the distance, the everyday obviousness of the distance, between that lane in Manod, all the immediate problems of Gwen and Ivor and Trevor and Gethin and the others: the distance from them to this register of companies, but at the same time the relations are so solid, so registered. The transactions reach right down to them. Not just as a force from outside but as a force they've engaged with, are now part of. Yet still a force that cares nothing about them, that's just driving its own way.'

'It ought to be known,' Susan said.

'Well, yes. But we all *start* by knowing it. It's there all the time, so solid, so obvious, it's even embarrassing to mention it.'

'In general it's known. It's only actual details convince us.'

'But convince us of what? That this is the system; that it's become so central, so decisive, that to follow what seem our own interests, as those farmers were doing in Manod, isn't against it but is part of it; is its local reproduction.'

'When it's all fully known, the choices can be different.'

'Can they? I mean, is there time?'

He looked along the street: at the separate people passing, on so many different journeys; at the more distant crowd and traffic, the slow aggregation within which they stood, leaning close to each other and talking, close as always but close now in their separateness: a conscious separateness, within a crowd of strangers.

'I'll call Gwyn,' Matthew said. 'I promised him that. And then I'll make an appointment with Lane.'

But Dr Lane was out of the country. He was at a conference in Germany; it would be at least a week until he was back in his office and even then, Matthew was told, with an unemphatic finality, he would be very busy; he had left instructions to make no appointments. Frustrated and angry, but not knowing how to fight back against something so dispersed and so indifferent, he suggested to Susan that they should return to Manod. 'At least there,' he said, 'we can try to gather some strength.' For he was now again very tired; he hardly knew how to get through more days in London. And Susan was worried about him and wanted him to get back and rest.

'There's just one more thing,' he said suddenly. 'The only other person I know in that office, Joan Reynolds.'

'But she won't be able to help.'

'No, I don't expect so. But it'll be something to get a message to someone I know exists.'

He called Joan Reynolds. At first it was exactly like the previous call. But as he persisted she seemed to remember him, as if in a different dimension, though she was still, she was sure, not able to help. It was then by chance, really, that he asked if Peter, Peter Owen, had been trying to see Lane. She didn't know but she offered to ask. She was some time away but when she came back on the phone her voice was friendly and relieved: a direct voice. Peter Owen had left a London number; Dr Lane was to call him there. And Dr Price, as well, if he got in touch.

It was strange but it was something. Matthew checked that it wasn't Dick Edmunds' number, which he had already rung several times. Then he tried the new number. A woman's voice answered.

'Owen!'

'Is Peter Owen there?'

'Peter? Who's that?'

'Who am I, do you mean? My name's Matthew Price. I work with Peter Owen.'

'Matthew Price! Well, hello. This is Kate Owen.'

'Kate?'

'Yes, I'm Peter's mother. He has one, or hasn't he told you?'

'Yes, of course. I'm sorry. But is Peter there?'

'He should be. He said he would be. Look, why don't you come round? He'll be here by then.'

'Well, I have my wife with me.'

'It's all right. We're broadminded. Bring her too if she wants.'

5. Kate opened the door to them. She looked up, smiling.

'So that's what you look like, Matthew Price!'

'This is Susan,' Matthew said.

'Hi Susan.'

She didn't at once let them in. She was so tiny that it seemed, at first, like a child answering the door. She wore a black jersey and black trousers, without ornament. Her black hair was down to her shoulders. The small face was lined and pale.

'Is Peter back then?' Matthew asked.

'Yes, he's in the bathroom.'

She turned and let them in. They took off their coats.

'Hi, Peter,' she shouted. 'Come on, hurry up.'

Matthew and Susan stayed close to each other.

'What's your drink then?' Kate asked Matthew.

'No thanks, not now.'

'You?' Kate asked Susan.

'No, really, thank you. Not now.'

A door slammed and Peter came into the room. He was still rubbing his cropped fair hair with a towel.

'You got my message then?' he said, smiling across at Matthew.

'Well yes, eventually.'

'I rang you yesterday at Manod. There was no reply.'

'No. We came up. Because we hadn't heard.'

'Sure,' Peter said. 'It's a long story.'

He threw the towel down in a chair. Kate moved, quickly, and folded it away on the table.

'Sit down,' Kate said. 'We can't stand here contemplating each other.'

They sat down.

'I've been in Belgium,' Peter said.

'Yes, I assumed that. Once I saw that company registration.'

'Christ, you've been going over that same stuff?'

'Well, since I didn't know that you had.'

'You see,' Kate said, 'you've offended him, Peter. I told you you'd offend him. The one decent man you ever worked with.'

155

'Matthew's not offended,' Peter said, confidently. 'But yes, I ought to have rung you. Only several things happened at once, and only one of them really concerned you.'

Matthew sat forward.

'Before we go on, if we go on,' he said, heavily, 'I shouldn't have to tell you that Beth is very worried. I've been talking to Gwyn. He's naturally worried about her.'

'But not Myra,' Kate said. 'Myra just puts on the dinner.'

'Myra's keeping her going,' Matthew said.

'Yeah well, that's it then,' Peter said. 'The part that doesn't concern you.'

Matthew got up.

'Shall we arrange to meet somewhere tomorrow?' he said, quickly. 'We could probably borrow an office.'

'Oh for Christ's sake! Because I won't discuss my personal affairs?'

'We can all refuse anything. What I'm refusing is that kind of division. Especially a division so abrupt and unexplained.'

'Sure, you refuse to divide what the world has in practice divided. It's a quick way to sympathy and to absolute irrelevance. You think you'll know about this scheme if you live in Manod, get involved with a few people. While all the time the real action is a rip-off between London and Brussels.'

'Brussels? Not Antwerp?'

'You see,' Kate said. 'I told you. Nobody lives past thirty without knowing how to deal with a tantrum.'

'Bloody hell,' Peter said. 'A chorus!'

He turned away. He noticed the towel and picked it up and went out of the room. Kate sat with her feet drawn up under her, in the big leather chair by the fire.

'Is this your flat, Mrs Owen?' Susan asked.

'No. It's Tom Elliott's. But he's often abroad. I can usually use it when I have to be in London.'

'You do a lot of committee work, don't you?'

'Hasn't Peter told you? I'm the statutory co-optable woman.'

'I wouldn't have thought so,' Susan said.

'Because I say a few things? It's an adaptive strategy. And by the way they don't even listen. It's just a limited natural break. Like the tea being brought in.'

Peter came back. He had put on a jacket and tie. He sat down opposite Matthew. His briefcase was by his chair.

'Do you want it or not?' he asked, looking across.

'Yes. Tell me.'

'You see,' Kate said to Susan. 'Here too.'

Susan smiled.

'The local companies,' Peter said, 'all run back to this Rural Community Development Agency. And it runs back to ABCD, which provides all the capital.'

'ABCD being what?'

'Anglo-Belgian Community Developments.'

'They've acquired all the nice-sounding words.'

'Yes, they're very sharp. And their capital, in turn, is as to sixty-forty a split between an oil company subsidiary and a London merchant bank.'

'An *oil* subsidiary.'

'Yeah. It's been happening for some time. Their first interest in Manod, way back, was traditional: they wanted the heating oil contracts, they were prepared to help finance the scheme that the oil would be used in. But now, of course, there are new market problems. They know, more precisely than anyone, the risks and the limits of any oil economy. So because they're real planners—not Lane's sort, I mean, but people actually running the world—they intend to be first in the alternatives, the support systems, the new planning techniques. What was once just their ploy to supply the demand, to get the city built to consume their oil, is now more than that, though it still of course includes it. It's now a radically different energy design, and for that, they believe, they must start somewhere clear, build it in from the beginning. In the whole of Western Europe there were eight of these plans that they put on their short list. But what they need, fairly quickly, is at least one working model: a new city built to a different energy pattern.'

'So Manod . . . ?'

'Yes. Though they're keeping two others active. Some government, even some people, might get awkward. But Manod attracted them because of the original design, which was actually very close to their own. What they call the cluster city: with minimal internal transport; district power and heating obviously; and then of course the communications technology, which is actually the major energy saving.'

'But then the capital involved . . .'

'Exactly. All they've committed, so far, is the money for the land. And that's quite safe, whichever way it goes. They could

157

sell the farms again, or keep them as an investment, or of course, given the city, start as clear proprietors.'

'But with the city to be built by public money?'

'Well yes. What else? And it was this that took me to Brussels. Because the scheme was blocked, as Lane told us, in a straight British context. It was just a forgotten idea. But then there was a move in the Community, as part of the energy policy, to have two or three pilot schemes, using the new planning and technology. That's where it is now: still on its way through and being argued about, but in fact fairly probable.'

'With community funds?'

'Well, guarantors more likely. That's why the banks are there.'

'But then Lane must have known this. Why couldn't he have told us.'

'Because it's all still under wraps. To prevent speculation on the land.'

Kate laughed. The others smiled.

'So that the real argument,' Matthew said, 'is happening there? We, as consultants, are just at the local end?'

'Yeah. As I told you.'

'Will they even wait for our reports?'

'Not necessarily. But perhaps.'

'How did you find all this?'

'I have a friend works there. Well two friends actually. Rose and Michael Swinburne.'

Kate moved abruptly, bringing her hands, palms down, on the arms of the chair, and swinging out her legs.

'You didn't tell me that,' she said, angrily, to Peter.

'Didn't I?'

'Who did you see then? Rose?'

'Yes. Michael was away.'

'You bastard, Peter.'

'That?' he said, staring at her.

'Pig then.'

'No, Mam. No.'

Matthew and Susan were staring at them.

'I'm sorry,' Kate said. 'This is an old private quarrel.'

'Which as you see,' Peter added, 'we have in public.'

Matthew and Susan stayed silent. There was a long tension, while Kate and Peter stared at each other.

'I'll find out,' Kate finally said.

'Yes, you do that. Only I'm a man still at the end of it.'

158

Kate jerked up out of her chair. Her pale lined face went suddenly dark with anger. She glared at Peter and then, with a quick word to Matthew and Susan, she hurried from the room.

'Would you like us to go?' Matthew asked, after a pause.

'No. It's all right.'

'It isn't, you know, Peter,' Susan said, firmly.

He smiled. He got up and moved across to sit in the chair where his mother had been sitting.

'She's a remarkable woman,' he said, easily. 'But she has this effect on you, when you're not used to her.'

'I wasn't thinking of your mother,' Susan said, watching him.

'No? Well anyway I was merely quoting my father. On one rather special occasion.'

'We know nothing about that,' Susan said. 'All we've known is you and Beth.'

'Don't worry. All that will come right.'

'Will it?' Susan asked. 'You have this entire social pessimism but when it comes down to people all you say is it's all right.'

He glanced across at her, interestedly. He nodded.

'Have you let Beth know that you're back?' Susan asked, directly.

'No, I haven't yet, actually.'

'She's got your baby down there. Don't you care about that?'

'Yes, I care.'

'Then why go on hurting her?'

'You don't understand,' Peter said, leaning back. 'It was that frightened me. I found I wasn't strong enough, complete enough.'

'None of us inherits completeness. It comes by staying and working.'

'If you're lucky,' Peter said.

'No, not if you're lucky. If you're prepared to work.'

'Until you tire,' Peter said, looking across at Matthew.

'Yes, that too,' Matthew said.

Peter sat forward.

'Okay,' he said.

He looked from Matthew to Susan and back again. Matthew got up.

'Lane is in Germany,' Matthew said, without emphasis. 'But as soon as he's back we must both go to see him. Quite apart from the politics, which are serious enough, this whole land deal's probably criminal: at least in the sense that it's a speculation based on access to what's supposed to be secret, and that it's been

159

happening just now, with the scheme revived in Europe. So that one way or the other we must bring it all out.'

'To Robert Lane?' Peter said, getting up.

'In the first instance, yes.'

'But, Matthew, he's bound to be in on it,' Peter said earnestly. 'He's on the Community committee which has been reviewing the schemes.'

'That still isn't the land deals.'

'Oh, come on. They didn't think of it out of the air. It was ABCD and probably others like them saw this chance of public money for their own schemes. And when people like that start operating they don't sit waiting for the legions, they move in and push.'

'That's the case he has to answer,' Matthew said, evenly.

'Yes, okay. But when he puts up his smokescreen will you really come in and fight him?'

Matthew went for his coat. He pulled it on, roughly.

'We'll be in Manod,' he said. 'Ring me. I shall keep ringing Lane.'

X

1. The line of trucks and cars stretched out of sight from the lane in Manod past Cae Glas towards Waunfawr and Pentwyn. For ten minutes it had moved quickly and steadily from the chapel in Bronydd along the valley road and up the pitch to Manod. Ivor and Megan had gone in the first car: the green Jaguar with an excited John Dance driving. The others had made an informal file, pulling out from muddy verges, reversing in gateways, the last in the line those who had come earliest and parked in the loose stone paved yard between the chapel and the river. Matthew and Susan, well back in the line, were halted now just outside their own cottage.

'We may all get up to Pentwyn,' Matthew said, 'but how many of us will get back?'

For after the winter's rains the narrow track was already cut up. There was an especially bad place where a winter brook crossed it, overflowing the concreted drain. All the trucks would get through, for they had the clearance, but the cars had been made for a different country. If one of them early in the line got stuck, most of them might not get to the wedding breakfast at all.

Gwen was somewhere ahead, driving Mrs Parry in the Pentre truck. Her brother Lewis, in a truck, was just behind Matthew and Susan. He came up now and talked to them.

'When we get going let us pull in front. Then we can pull you through if you need it.'

'It might be quicker to walk,' Matthew said.

'No, no, mun, you try it. Pentwyn's the end of the world.'

It was indeed far up, on the open mountain. Most farms that far up had in the last eighty years been abandoned. There were a score of ruins, within a morning's walk: the nettles growing thickly inside the crumbling walls, in which doorways and window spaces could still be made out, or the heavy chimney stacks, more resistant to the storms of the long derelict years. No fields had been given up. Where the old stone boundaries had crumbled there were good wire fences and the fields were ploughed or grazed. But the people had gone, from the outlying settlements. It had been so long a history. From forty years back the abandoned chimneys and doorways were usually visible from a distance; from eighty years or more the only distant sign was a stand of pines, sheltering what had once been the house from the prevailing north-west winds. There the walls and paved floors had been overgrown by bramble or bracken, or dead trees had fallen across them.

The occupancy of Pentwyn had been, then, unusually stubborn, yet how long, now, would it last? Megan was the Parrys' only child. When Will Parry died it was most likely that she and Ivor would take in the land and farm it from Pentre. It was the way it had gone for generations: the farms expanding and contracting by the chance of sons or daughters, of the distance of neighbouring marriages, of the adoption of roads to the more marginal land. One house would be kept in repair though empty, because a son had been born in a related farm and would eventually grow up to occupy it and take back its fields. Another would be let go, or converted to a barn, the fields being taken in and farmed from further back. It was the movement of the country: the movement of difficult land through the network of marriages and children.

The line began moving again, though slowly. Matthew held back to let Lewis's truck get in front of him. He looked across at the church, where the final redundancy notice had just been posted. It was ironic that it had lasted so long, the decisive factor its connection with a larger network stretching back, ultimately, into England. Most of the people in Manod were chapel, not church, yet since the war the chapels had been closing in greater numbers, dependent as they were on local support. That was why they had today all gone down to Bronydd for the wedding. The Manod chapel was now unrecognizable; it had become a barn at Trefedw, in whose yard it had originally been built. Bronydd now served the whole declining district: the most accessible by car, on any normal occasion.

The line was still moving. At Cae Glas Trevor and Modlen had stopped and gone into the house. Modlen came out now, carrying two baskets covered with cloths. She waved to Matthew and Susan as they drove slowly past. They were now out on the track to Waunfawr. The weather had lifted and the sky was very blue in the west. The sun came out suddenly and colour seemed to flow into the land ahead of them. The sunlight caught the water in its hundreds of courses down the steep transverse slopes. The dead bracken, stripped of its fronds by the winds, gleamed in its pale gold stems. There were early gorse flowers, rich sharp yellow on the black mounds. The close grass was bright green, the wet earth a rich pink. Early violets were flowering on the banks, under the wide dark sheepwall.

On the way ahead of them, past the curve of the sheepwall and up to the ridge at Pentwyn, the trucks and cars were stretched out, but now in two lines; there was a long gap ahead of a small red car, which was going very slowly along the slippery track. Susan wound down the window. A sweet sharp air flowed in over hands and faces.

'This can take as long as it likes,' Matthew said.

'Yes. I just thought. There seems all the time in the world.'

They could look out now over the Dowy valley and up at the great slope of the Frith beyond. Far into the distance, west and south, it was the same country, as if there could be no other. Towards Nantlais, from a wood on a hillside, there was a tall column of blue woodsmoke: or blue against the land, suddenly white against the sky. They watched the shapes of the slopes changing, as the line of trucks and cars moved slowly towards the ridge.

It was like parking at a show, outside the low grey house. Gwilym, Ivor's other brother, whom they had met that morning, was directing the vehicles as they came in. He found Matthew a space by the wall under the firs. They got out and walked to the house. There was a crowd by the doorway.

'We'll never hardly all get in,' Lewis said.

'Crush up,' Susan said.

She was walking with Lewis's wife, Eira.

'It's more like our place,' Eira said. 'Down Pentre's like living in town.'

They shuffled towards the door. Mr and Mrs Parry were standing, shaking hands, inside the long low kitchen. Beyond them, in line, stood Megan and Ivor, and then Gwen. They all shook hands, formally, though Ivor was laughing, telling all the men where the beer was. There was music from somewhere beyond the kitchen. The air was warm and heavy with woodsmoke. On the far kitchen wall, by the window, there was an impenetrable crowd around the table of food. Susan saw Juliet Dance standing away on her own, in the opposite corner. Her fine dark blue dress stood out among the pale greens and yellows of most of the women's dresses. Mary Pearson, carrying a plate of food, emerged from the crowd round the table and found herself facing Juliet. She looked away, quickly, and moved in the opposite direction, towards the music.

There was a noise at the doorway behind them. Trevor and Modlen had arrived and Modlen was arguing about something; it turned out to be her baskets, which were full of freshly boiled hams.

'Only if you want them to go old cold, say so,' she was calling across.

Trevor was laughing. Stuck in the doorway, in the line for handshaking, he suddenly took the baskets from Modlen, lifted them high above his head and pushed through. As the others saw him coming there was a loud cheer.

'Aye and pinched it now, to show it off,' Modlen's voice followed him. 'Making out, I bet, he did it all himself.'

'So I did,' Trevor called. 'Well I killed them anyhow.'

There was another cheer. Modlen appeared to forget the baskets. As she came to Megan she stopped and kissed her: not leaning across, as the other women were doing, but going close and embracing her, holding her tight and long.

'My turn, Modlen,' Ivor joked, beside them.

'No, you watch out,' Modlen said, pulling back from Megan, 'or your leg'll give at the joint.'

She pushed past him, just brushing his hand, and embraced Gwen. Gwen turned aside, slightly, but Modlen pulled her back close. The others saw Gwen smile, happily, over Modlen's shoulder.

It was still crowded around the table. Matthew and Susan moved through to the other room, where music was playing from a big cassette recorder. Several people were standing around, balancing plates of food and glasses, finding difficulty in using either. Only two couples were dancing: Len Birch from the garage, with a girl from St Dyfrog; and John Dance and Mary Waters, Gwen and Ivor's married sister who had travelled up from Tiverton. Most of the energy was coming from Dance, in the small cleared space between the tables and chairs. There were beads of sweat on his blond moustache and on his sunburned bald crown. Mary, coolly smiling at him, did not look like the others of her family; it was something in the way she held herself, a combination of poise and reserve.

The tape ended. Mary at once moved away from John Dance and went round greeting old friends.

'More,' Dance shouted, standing alone in the small cleared

space. He clapped his hands loudly. But then as nobody took any notice he moved across to the recorder himself. As he was passing Matthew and Susan he stopped.

'You got the papers I left, Dr Price?'

'No,' Matthew said, startled.

'I dropped them in. I expect you haven't been back.'

'What papers?'

Dance smiled.

'Never do business at a wedding, Dr Price,' he said, roguishly. 'Never, that is, till the last inch of the last bottle.'

'Or then,' Matthew said.

'Aye, you're probably right. There'll be time. Mrs Price, now come on. Won't you join us for a dance?'

'Us?' Susan said.

'Well of course you're right. I didn't mean us, I meant me.'

'No,' Susan said.

'Oh come on, it's a wedding, we've got a lot to celebrate.'

'No,' Susan said.

Dance frowned.

'Hey Mary!' he said, quickly. 'Mary, where are you? Partner! Partner!'

He again clapped his hands.

Susan and Matthew turned and went back to the other room. Modlen, seeing them, at once took them over and served them with food. She was just filling glasses for them when Gwilym called for silence. There was a slow quieting.

'It is my duty and pleasure,' Gwilym said, speaking up with a sudden formality, 'to propose the health of Megan and Ivor. They are entering upon their married life with the respect and good wishes of us all.'

He paused. The mood of easy and joking informality was still dominant in the room. It could be expected at any moment to come back, to reassert itself, to determine the tone of the speeches. But Gwilym stood gravely, compelling another attention. Gethin, very dark in his stiff dark suit, stood immediately behind him, also grave and formal. Megan and Ivor, who had been laughing, stood nervously still.

'Megan and Ivor,' Gwilym said formally.

'Megan. And Ivor,' the other voices responded, very slowly and distinctly.

There was a long break of silence.

2. Matthew picked up the large heavy envelope that was lying on the mat by the door. He moved it from one hand to the other, as if weighing it.

'Yes,' he said to Susan, 'Dance understands timing.'

'The reverse, I'd have said. He's a dreadful man.'

Matthew made up the fire and sat heavily in his chair. Then he slowly opened the envelope. There were sheets of finely folded drawing paper and a clip of typed schedules. Matthew unfolded the large drawn plans.

Proposed Improvements to Nos. 1 and 2, Pentre Cottages, Manod, including conversion to a single dwelling-house.

For Dr and Mrs M. H. Price. Scale 1 in. to 8 ft 0 in.

Susan watched him anxiously as he stared down at the neat coloured ground plan and elevations. His face was dark and sad, the eyes fixed.

'Just put the lot on the fire,' she said.

He didn't answer. He seemed hardly to have heard. Seeing his gravity she remembered, briefly, Gwilym and Gethin standing in the centre of the kitchen at Pentwyn.

'I'll put them on the fire.'

'No, I'll look at them,' he said.

He reached up and held her hand. His own hand was very cold.

'Yes well I'm curious too,' Susan said, trying to rally him, 'but then let's just look them over and forget them. Now that we know it's out of the question.'

He folded the plans again.

'I only just remembered,' he said quietly.

'Remembered what?'

'How much I would have wanted it. How much I have always wanted it.'

'Well yes, love, I know, but not here, not now. And there are other places.'

'Yes, always other places.'

'And when within a week you'll be blowing Dance sky-high. Exposing his whole racket.'

'Shall I?' he asked.

She pulled away her hand.

'Matthew, you'll not go back on that?'

'On publishing it, no. But I very much doubt if we'll blow him anywhere. In ten years, you see, he'll be making all the arrangements.'

166

'Not at all necessarily. We can drive his kind out.'

'Out of Manod? Shall we? When he knows how to plan from real interests?'

'Whose interests? The Anglo-Belgian?'

'Of course, but tying up all the local settlements. This, meanwhile, is my own little piece of the action.'

'So you burn it. So that refuses him.'

'Yes, lose some, win some. He wins rather many.' He pushed the plans away and looked rapidly through the schedules.

'Aye,' he said, sitting up now actively engaged. 'Five thousand eight hundred. A very nice calculation.'

'The cost of the conversion?'

'Of the conversion and the freehold. That's very sweetly figured. About six thousand less than real cost, I'd guess, but at the same time not ridiculous, not so low as to be give away. A very precise calculation of where market, conscience and auditing converge. The one cost not shown is the cost of the bribe.'

Susan took the schedules and looked through them. Then she kneeled by the fire and spread out the plans. Matthew bent over her as they traced and identified all the details of the conversion, imagining and discussing the fine new house that could in this way be built around them.

'You're right,' she said at last. 'It would be a good place to live in.'

'Yes, plans like all the others. Like the Manod development. We sit poring over such plans.'

'To have somewhere worth living in.'

'I know. I still want that.'

He got up and fetched his coat.

'When you're finished,' he said, 'I'll take them back to Dance.'

'You don't have to do that. You can post them.'

'No I want to put them in his hands. And to say a few things.'

Susan jumped up.

'If you must,' she said. 'But whether or not, you must write him a letter, giving not only your refusal but all the dates and conversations, and you must keep a copy.'

'Sure.'

Susan repacked the envelope. He took his cap and stick and walked out into the lane. It was colder now but the air was still bright. As he passed Pentre the yard was still crowded with cars and trucks, and there were lights in the big front windows. The

Vaughan brothers and sisters were together for the first time since their father's funeral. He turned at the Evening Star and walked along to the Old Vicarage. He rang the bell.

Juliet answered the door. She had changed from the dress she had worn at the wedding; she was now in a finely cut green tweed suit. She smiled.

'Dr Price. This is pleasant.'

'And unexpected?'

'I don't think so. We've just finished tea.'

She smiled again. Neither made any move. But then Dance came hurrying downstairs.

'What is it? Have they brought back the glasses?'

Juliet turned, gracefully, so that he could see Matthew.

'Dr Price! This is pleasant. And I thought it was one of the Parrys. The stuff we've ferried up there.'

'Yes.'

'Well, come in, come in. There's a fire in the drawing room.'

He ushered Matthew in, leaving Juliet to close the door. She did not follow them. Dance went to the big mahogany sideboard and took out a bottle.

'A drop of whisky, of course,' he said, taking two glasses but not turning.

'No,' Matthew said. 'I've not come sealing a bargain.'

Dance swung round. He looked keenly at Matthew.

'Ah, you know that little habit of ours. But of course you would, you're a local man. Local by origin.'

'I brought back these papers,' Matthew said, holding out the envelope.

'Something you didn't get? Didn't like? A lot of it's formal, I don't have to tell you. We clear it up best by talking it through.'

'No. It isn't that. But I had to tell you immediately that we are not interested.'

Dance stared across at him.

'Look, sit down, Dr Price. Let's enjoy this lovely fire.'

'No, I'd rather stand.'

Dance hesitated, then moved nearer.

'What is it, particularly? Almost any of the details, you know, can be altered.'

'Not the details, the whole thing.'

'Or the final figure perhaps? That's often a problem. Though even there, you know, there's no harm in talking it through.'

168

Matthew put the envelope on the table in the centre of the room.

'Yes,' he said, 'the final figure is part of the problem.'

'Ah well,' Dance said, smiling. 'But there are always . . .'

'No, let me finish. It is part of the problem because I know, and you know, that it's well below cost.'

'*Below* cost? Impossible. What you're thinking, Dr Price, is by the London market. Down here, you understand . . .'

'I mean by prices down here. Don't think I don't know them, it's my job to know them.'

'As well as I do, perhaps, with my living dependent on knowing?'

'It depends what you're selling. Or buying.'

Dance touched his moustache. He walked over to the fire.

'Let me get this straight, Dr Price,' he said, warming his back. 'You're saying you're not interested because that figure is too *low*.'

'That's one reason, yes.'

'But if you're right, you're lucky. It's I'd be standing the loss.'

'No, I don't think you would. And that's my basic reason. Whatever I might think about those actual plans I have to tell you, clearly, that I can do no business with you, of any kind. Indeed as well as returning the plans I've come to let you know that we're leaving the cottage, as soon as we can, though I shall pay the full rent to the end of the year as agreed.'

Dance looked carefully across at him. He put his elbow, half-turning, on the high marble mantelpiece.

'Your work's finished here then, is it?'

'No. Not quite.'

'But as good as finished. And then you're returning to London.'

'Not that either. I have other work to go to.'

Dance smiled.

'Mysteries,' he said. 'Of course a mystery from the beginning, your coming to Manod.'

'No, I told you then. I'm a government consultant.'

'Yes, yes. Of course. And the next mystery, I suppose, is what you'd call your report.'

'No mystery about that. I'll report what I've found.'

'And back to London and hey presto, leaving the rest of us here still stuck with the problems.'

'Not quite, as you know. It's not exactly, any longer, just a local matter.'

'In what way?' Dance said, interestedly.

He lifted his elbow from the mantelpiece. He was smiling and attentive.

'I can't discuss it,' Matthew said. 'I just came to clear up our immediate relationship.'

'Clear up, clear off, you've lost me, I'm afraid.'

'I hope so, Mr Dance.'

Dance moved quickly. He was trying to rest his heel on the fender behind him, but he stumbled and almost fell, before he again grabbed the mantelpiece. In the stumble the colour had come up into his face. He looked resentfully at Matthew.

'It's not our way, you know that,' he said, hoarsely.

'Not whose way?'

'Not our way, you know what I mean. Not how we live down here and get on with each other, because this is our place, this is all we have.'

'I could comment on that but I won't.'

'You see. No comment. You've learned up all that. So that you can't talk to us, not as if you were one of us. You've come back as an official, one of the government's people. One of this caste that controls us, but that lives off our living.'

'I must go.'

'Yes indeed, Dr Price, you must go. Walk away, like the rest of them. Back to England, back to your caste.'

'Goodnight,' Matthew said.

Dance turned to face the fire. Matthew crossed to the door and let himself out but as he walked along the hall Juliet reappeared and moved beside him to the front door.

'I'm so glad you called, Dr Price. You'll give my love to your wife.'

Matthew turned and looked at her. She immediately smiled.

'Yes, thank you,' he said, as she opened the front door and stood on the whitened steps, seeing him safely down the drive.

3. Matthew looked for Susan along the main street in Nantlais. He had been longer with Bryn Walters than he had expected; she was not in the car or any of the near shops. There were more people in the street than on any of his previous visits; indeed more visitors, to judge from their voices as they passed, than inhabitants. It was especially in and around Nantlais that a new kind of settlement was happening: town houses, cottages, shops, the old

mill and the old fire-station, even a few outlying farms, were being bought by a new kind of settler who saw in mid-Wales one of the last accessible places of calm: a place to work in new ways, to practise crafts, to experiment in life styles. Along the main street there were already nine of these new enterprises: a bookshop, a print and map shop, three shops selling antiques, a pottery, two woollen craft shops and a health foods store. The family grocer's by the clock tower had changed ownership, discreetly; there was now a small sign of a supermarket chain on the proprietor's board above the entrance, although the former owner's name—E. E. Price—was still set in large gilded letters on its pavement step.

Matthew stood and looked in one of the antique shops. Its name was *Stripped Pine*: a new name for the rubbed and sanded deal furniture which now filled its interior: not antiques, unless the majority of those who inspected it were prepared to use the same word of themselves: inter-war and post-war tables, chests of drawers, kitchen chairs, with the white dust of the rubbing and grinding still lodged in the coarse grain. Vases, glasses and china of the same period were arranged in neat rows at the display windows. A man and women, each about thirty, each dressed in faded blue jean suits, sat with pottery mugs of coffee—the jar was between them—at a half-waxed round table. As Matthew stared they looked up at him. He moved on, crossing the quiet street.

He glanced up again, half-consciously, at the windows of Bryn Walters' office. He thought he saw a movement there, but as he focused it was blank. It had been very difficult, taking his leave of Bryn. After their edgy first meeting they had found an easy, informal way of getting along, and it had seemed that they trusted each other. That was perhaps why it had been so difficult today, when a few months' habit had been put under pressure. Matthew had known that part of it would be difficult: not the detailed exposition of the interlocking land deals, which Bryn had sat through, sharply attentive and without comment; but the few minutes following that, when the necessary question had hung in the air and neither had been willing to voice it: the inevitable question of the source of the information on which the deals had been based.

'Go on, boy, ask,' Bryn had said, finally. The deepset eyes, under the heavy eyebrows, seemed to have lost all their light.

'Well it could be from anywhere,' Matthew said, quietly.

'Aye it could but you've brought it to me.'

'Among others. You're not blaming me?'

'No no, mun. Don't swerve. Don't run back to social method.'

'All right. Well then three of the people involved in these deals are on the Council.'

'You've checked, see. And you're right.'

'Yes, but what I couldn't check was the circulation of the plans, among Councillors.'

'It was very strict. Planning Committee only. Well, they had to, obviously.'

'And then?'

'One. Your neighbour. Gethin Jenkins.'

'I see.'

'And I'll tell you something else, if you don't know it already. Gethin's a mean devil, he'd clean his boots on samples or let them stay dirty. But he's as straight as a die on anything official. I have reason to know.'

'All right, if you say so. Not Gethin.'

'And if not Gethin, not anybody local.'

'That doesn't follow exactly. Somebody else could have talked. It could have been indirect.'

'Indirect is right. Here's this master plan, this plan of our masters . . .'

He shook his head irritably. He closed his thin lips.

'All right, I see it your way,' Matthew said, quickly.

'No, Will, you can't. Though I give you full credit for trying. But this plan has been circulating these last nine years, under the Lord knows how many inauspicious auspices, from the English Government to your Anglo-Belgian conglomerate, and somewhere, somehow, in that insane and habitual process, it must have been available to be known by every speculator from here to Threadneedle Street, and nobody, *nobody*, could expect otherwise.'

'It's only now the land has been bought.'

'Then beware of the buyers, why don't you?'

'It's an integrated process. They're not just distant financiers. They have their local agents.'

'Every party to this business has its local agents.'

'Including me, you mean?'

'Including you, Will. Including me. Including Dance and Postan-Jones. A mad dance of agents around a dying country.'

'Not bothering with formal distinctions? Between official and unofficial, public and private?'

'Lord, Will, do I have to explain that to *you*? Tell me how do you write them, those barons, the Lords of the Marches? Was that public or private power?'

'Your Council is elected.'

'It is and I'm glad. It has power over its ditches. It has a word in edgeways on many other local features. But look across this desk, it's just a place where the circulars stop. Where we become the agency of all that power out there that still calls itself public.'

'Right,' Matthew said. 'Only now we'll be testing it.'

Bryn stood up. He took Matthew's hand.

'I'll watch it through, Will.'

'Right.'

'And come back here, mind, when it's blown itself out. We'll still be here, don't worry. We've been here long enough.'

There was now no movement at the windows. Matthew walked down the quiet street, past the clock tower, to where they had parked the car. Susan was just arriving from the other direction. She was carrying a heavy bag of shopping. He took it from her and they got into the car.

'Are we still going on to Trawsfynydd?' Susan asked.

'Unless you don't want to.'

'No, we must if we can.'

They drove out over the stone bridge of the Afren and began climbing the long pitch to the ridge from the Daren. Matthew went over what Walters had said.

'He trusts Gethin further than I would,' Susan observed.

'Well yes, he must have used his knowledge for his own part of the deal. But that's different from giving Dance the whole scheme.'

'He would give it if it suited him.'

'Well, Bryn thought not.'

'Bryn changes his standards, for his own people.'

'Yes, he knows where to be loyal.'

'And the rest of us don't?'

'We know what. We're less sure of where.'

They drove over the Daren ridge. The long valley lay below them, the river silver under the sun. From the height it seemed quiet and empty. It was difficult to imagine the lodged papers that now effectively determined it. It was too great a disparity for any single perspective.

They turned at St Dyfrog, where the water had seeped back from the flood meadows and the young grass was already bright

173

green. They crossed the river and climbed to the road through the mountains. In the slanting light from the west, every watercourse on the steep slopes was edged with dark shadow, and the moulding of the land was like flesh and bone. Still climbing they felt the air pressure change, in their ears; it sounded like the coming of another dimension of hearing. They crossed the cattle grid and now the hedges fell away and the road was unfenced across the open mountain. There were ponies everywhere, almost all of the local breed, sorrel and white and ashgrey, with the fine full manes. And now there were thousands of sheep on the lower slopes: four or five times the stock that Matthew remembered. On a scarp above the road there was a group of men on the skyline and as they watched one of them launched into the air, on a big red hang-glider. They watched him turning and sailing on a rising current of air.

The road became narrower, as they still climbed. Every few hundred yards there were passing places, bays of red earth scooped out in the bitten grass and bracken. The dark hummocks of gorse began to give way to spreading expanses of whinberry and heather. Then the pass was ahead of them, its road gleaming with running water where it cut across one of the shallower streams. They eased through the pass, with its rough broken walls of loose earth and littered stone. Immediately now below them was the source of the Honddu: the bare, deeply incised watercourses that came together like the fingers of a hand. Its sheltered valley was more wooded than the valleys to the north. In the distance, now, they could see, past the edge of Brynllwyd, the unmistakeable shape of the Holy Mountain, standing above Glynmawr.

The road dropped steeply. Twice they had to stop and open mountain gates. There was a new forestry plantation, on one of the far slopes: the earth scored between the rows of five and six year old spruce. The birches and thorns gave way, along the road, to close hazel and holly and hawthorn and wild cherry. The road became banked, close and twisting. They had to stop now, often, passing cars and lorries and tractors. They passed the boundary chapel and the ruins of the abbey, the road descending all the time and with the Honddu now running close and loudly below it. Then the valley began to broaden and they could see the rocks of the Daren ahead of them. *Petrol, Eight Hundred Yards*, said the sign.

They pulled in at the garage. The yard was crowded with cars and vans. There was scaffolding up on the old metal shed, and new signs and pumps were stacked beyond the vans against the wall of the house.

'We'll park farther down and walk back,' Matthew said.

As they walked through to the house he spoke to the men on the scaffolding; they were strangers. He rang the bell at the porch door. There was some delay and then the glass door was opened.

'You again?' said Kate Owen, looking happily up at them. 'You seem to turn up everywhere.'

4. 'We've come at the wrong time,' Susan said, when they were all settled in the living-room. They had shaken hands all round, with Gwyn and Myra and Beth, and with Harold, Kate's husband and Gwyn's brother. Harold sat quiet and withdrawn by the fire: his face thin and very tired, his stocky body inert.

'Family occasions,' Kate said, laughing. 'They can do with the odd variation.'

'That's rude,' Myra said, glancing anxiously at Susan.

'Not at all,' Kate said, speaking only to Matthew. 'Did Peter ever tell you we used all to live together in Goldsmith Street? Well, two houses. Like Harold used to say, semi-attached.'

Matthew looked across at Harold. He seemed to be taking no notice of anyone. Beth, sitting beyond him, got up, looked at Kate and went quietly out of the room. As the door closed behind her Myra said to Kate, in a hoarse whisper:

'You don't think, do you? You just say Peter straight out. You don't think what she's feeling.'

'What she's feeling about Peter?' Kate said, easily. 'So where's the problem? She knows what his name is.'

Harold moved in his chair.

'Leave it,' he said, in a very hard, cold voice. Kate did not look at him or appear to hear him, but she said no more.

'You mustn't mind us,' Gwyn said, smiling, to Susan and Matthew. 'We're used to each other, we have this bit of a spat.'

'He's still not written?' Matthew asked.

'No. Not a word.'

'Well, I'm meeting him tomorrow. We've got our big meeting with Lane.'

'We knew Dr Lane,' Myra said. 'When he was teaching Peter.'

There was a general silence. Kate seemed to be holding herself in, against great waves of pressure. The effort of her control seemed tangible in the room.

'One thing,' Harold said, looking up. 'He must stick to that job.'

'I don't know that he will,' Matthew said. 'It's all very complicated. We may both have to resign.'

'Well, that's your own affair,' Harold said, 'but he can't afford to. He's got a wife and child to look after.'

'Beth and the little girl are being looked after,' Myra said, fiercely.

'I never said they weren't. But it's his responsibility. He can't go on living off the backs of the rest of us.'

'It's not that, mun,' Gwyn said. 'You know we're glad to have them.'

'I never said you weren't,' Harold answered, looking up at his brother. 'But we've had it all through. He come down the works, he was really going to change things. Then he'd gone and we're still there, in the same bloody mess.'

'He wrote his book,' Gwyn said.

'Aye, if it was for books and programmes about us, we'd be leading Europe. And that Lane's the same. Starting up this development that nobody wants but where there's actual industry there's never the investment.'

'You and I moved, didn't we?' Gwyn said, 'where the money had moved? It'll happen again.'

'Aye, we track after them. Up and down Black Rock, that's our family history, get settled to one thing and they start up another, leaving our homes and their rubbish behind them. Only it can't go on. They're all running out of time.'

'See your time through, Harold, you can forget the lot of them.'

'Aye, no doubt. Only I shan't forget them. We made a party that forgot us. Now we've got sons forget us. They're up there, joining in, shuffling their bloody bits of paper that are other people's lives.'

'Well, I won't take that,' Kate said angrily to her husband. 'Peter's fighting the system, his whole work's been fighting it. And I'm out fighting, trying to keep a real party. There's more going on than just you on the lines.'

'If there's to be a British car industry,' Harold answered, angrily, but then stopped, suddenly. 'What's the use?' he said, dropping his voice and looking back at the fire.

176

'Peter will come through,' Kate said, looking at Matthew.

'Yes. I'd expect so.'

'And if he wants the fight in the open, if either of you want it, don't forget I can help. I know my way around the Party.'

'It depends,' Matthew said. 'Whether we're fighting for or against.'

'For or against a city at Manod? Well you have to be against it.'

'I'm against the speculation, that's all I'm really sure of.'

'The whole area needs work,' Gwyn said, firmly.

There was again a general silence. It was Susan who broke it.

'We ought to be going, Matthew.'

'Yes, of course.'

'No, you'll stay for tea,' Myra said.

'No, we ought to get back before dark.'

There was a brief, facing hesitation before they all moved. Then Harold got up and shook hands with Susan and Matthew. Kate and Myra went through to the kitchen. Gwyn walked out with the visitors to the yard.

'You're having the place done up then?' Matthew said, looking up at the scaffolding.

'Aye. They give me the refit. It's more than I could afford.'

'The petrol company.'

'Aye. It was a chap up your way, John Dance, he arranged it.'

'Yes.'

'Only it'll be a lot more convenient,' Gwyn said.

Matthew shook hands, warmly, before they walked back to the car.

XI

1. PETER led the way briskly across the bridge to the tower of offices.

'The thing is,' he said, over his shoulder to Matthew, 'never confuse the mountain with the goats.'

'If it were as simple as that,' Matthew muttered.

'So they live in glass palaces!' Peter said confidently. 'That makes them transparent. And it leaves them open to throwing stones.'

'Are you sure you know your way?' Matthew asked.

'Entirely,' Peter said.

They had been kept waiting for three weeks, while Robert Lane was on other business. But now the morning had come, and they had already put in their files.

'That's it,' Peter said, as they reached the end of the bridge and turned into a wide green corridor.

'We come in as official consultants, big deal. We go out as troublemaking amateurs.'

'I wasn't thinking about us,' Matthew said.

They reached Robert Lane's outer office. A man of about Peter's age, in a grey suit, was waiting to take them in. He opened Lane's door and let them precede him. Matthew went in first. Robert Lane rose at once, and came round to shake hands.

'It's really good to see you,' he said, looking up into Matthew's face. He nodded to Peter. The other man took a seat in the corner of the office.

'Is this on or off the record?' Peter asked, looking round at him.

'The term's inapplicable,' Lane said, curtly.

'But you need a third ear?'

'Sit down, Matthew, won't you?' Lane said, easily, and pulled out a chair. He went back round his desk and settled to lighting his pipe. Peter pulled out a chair and sat at the side of the desk, between the two older men.

'I'm sorry about this,' Lane said to Matthew. 'I expect you remember your questions, when you first came to see me.'

'Yes but I had nothing like this in mind.'

'I know, and I'm sorry,' Lane said. 'Of all the people in the world to involve in this kind of . . .'

'Matthew's not involved in it,' Peter interrupted sharply. 'Nobody's involved just by finding things out.'

'I can only assure you, Matthew,' Lane continued, ignoring Peter, 'that whatever else I was aware of, I had no idea about this.'

He gestured loosely towards the files, which lay closed on his desk. Matthew looked away from him, and moved in his chair.

'You're isolating the land deals?' he said, quickly.

'Yes. Isn't that right? Isn't that why you've come to see me?'

'For Christ's sake!' Peter interjected, but Matthew was continuing. 'Nothing can be isolated,' he said, quietly. 'The land deals are a consequence of the nature of the project.'

Lane stared across the desk, then slowly relit his pipe.

'Well I'm sorry to hear you say that, Matthew,' he said softly.

'Did you really think you could fool him?' Peter asked, from the end of the desk.

'Because it isn't really true,' Lane continued quietly. 'There can be arguments, of course, about the financing or even the lobbying. I hope we'll come to that. But the land deals stand out because they involve, on the face of it . . .'

He hesitated. He glanced across at the young man in the corner.

'I mean the question they raise,' he began again, 'is whether there has been improper use of official information. At present we can't say, but we would be failing in our duty if we didn't examine the possibility.'

'Pussyfooting the whole thing,' Peter said, angrily.

'And so I'd better say at once,' Lane continued, touching the files, 'that aspect of the matter is out of my hands. As with anything involving any possible illegality, I've passed it straight on, to the appropriate authority. It will be very closely investigated. At least I can assure you of that.'

'Yes, and it should be,' Matthew said, 'but that's only part of the problem. What matters, fundamentally, is why this project was revived.'

'To clean up wherever they could,' Peter said. 'Buying the land was just an extra.'

Lane turned and looked directly at Peter, for the first time.

'You know that?' he asked, sharply.

'I proved that.'

179

'You proved nothing of the kind. All you proved was an inter-section, a convergence of interests, and that's quite publishable and defensible.'

'Except for the little matter of the land deals.'

'No, the land deals in themselves aren't illegal. The only question, there, is whether official information was improperly used.'

Peter stood up. He threw his briefcase down on the desk.

'I can see the need now for your man in the corner.'

He gestured across to the note-taker, who did not look up.

'He's there to remind you,' Peter said, 'of the limits of the language. In case you were tempted, momentarily, to speak like a man, he's there to remind you to gloze like an official.'

'Sit down, Peter,' Robert Lane said quietly.

'And the next case of improper use of information,' Peter said, staring down at him, 'will be when I take this to the media.'

'You'll do nothing so stupid,' Lane said, not looking at him.

'Why? Because you think you can frighten me? I'm not chasing you now for a degree.'

'Did you ever?' Lane asked, looking sideways at Matthew.

'Yes, I queued for holy orders, at what they call your feet. But it was easier for you then, with the college architecture to soften the process. You may not even know that you've moved, but this now is the hard stuff, in a public world.'

'This is ranting, Peter.'

'Yes, in a ranting world. At the other end of the bus ride.'

Lane spread out his hands on the desk. He looked across, directly, at Matthew.

'This is an old private quarrel. I'm sorry,' he said.

Matthew nodded and looked away from him.

'Yes, perhaps,' he said quietly, 'but still what Peter is saying is the issue before both of us.'

'I told you, Matthew. The illegal stuff, I mean the questionable part of it, the land deals and so on, I've already passed through. It will be thoroughly hunted down.'

'Yes, but what you don't see,' Matthew said, 'is that this is about Manod. It's about a district and its people. It's beyond that about a country.'

'Of course, of course. That's where we all come back to reality.'

'Where we intersect or converge? Isn't that what you said? But I had better tell you plainly that if I had known, at any time,

that it was this kind of project, I should have had nothing to do
with it.'

'Well that's fair,' Lane said.

He picked up his pipe. He did not look again at Peter but he
seemed very conscious of him. Peter slowly sat down.

'And I could have seen your point,' Lane continued. 'But let
me put it my way. I don't know, I really don't know, whether
Manod should be developed, or should be developed in this
way. That was why I asked you to go there and to give me some
advice. But if I had not done so, there would have been no question. Manod would simply have been dead.'

'You mean the project you call Manod, not the actual place.'

'Yes, I'm sorry about the shorthand. You know what I mean.
Because in terms of U.K. resources—in the ordinary way our only
accessible resources—Manod and places like it are simply nowhere
on any list. Yes, they're disadvantaged regions, yes, they have a
case for assistance. But compared with the inner cities and with
the old declining industrial areas they just don't begin to com-
pete. They are marginal problems, in the strictest sense. In public
policy, now, they simply have to be left, while we rebuild the
inner cities and reinvest in manufacturing.'

'I know that,' Matthew said. 'I agree.'

'You shouldn't agree quite so readily. It's perfectly possible
that unless we revive the Manods the problems elsewhere will
remain insoluble.'

'That too,' Matthew said, 'but you were speaking of priorities,
in the short term. A place like Manod can't be destroyed so easily.
Its problems, already, are a century old.'

'All right. I agree. Though if you sat in this place . . .'

He swivelled in his chair. He glanced at Peter and at the man in
the corner, but then turned again to Matthew, leaning forward
across his desk.

'The whole of public policy,' he said, emphatically, 'is an
attempt to reconstitute a culture, a social system, an economic
order, that have in fact reached their end, reached their limits of
viability. And then I sit here and look at this double inevitability:
that this imperial, exporting, divided order is ending, and that all
its residual social forces, all its political formations, will fight to
the end to reconstruct it, to re-establish it, moving deeper all the
time through crisis after crisis in an impossible attempt to regain
a familiar world. So then a double inevitability: that they will fail,
and that they will try nothing else.'

Matthew stared past him through the window. On the skyline of buildings there was a column of black smoke, thickening and spreading as he watched.

'You've excluded revolution,' he heard Peter's sharp voice saying.

'No,' Robert Lane was answering. 'I've not excluded it. The political formations have excluded it.'

'No order dies,' Peter was saying, his voice thin and sharp, 'without generating, inside it, the beginning of the order that is going to replace it.'

The rising smoke was beginning to form a low cloud. Matthew pulled his look back, feeling the enclosure of the office.

'This is the context, Matthew,' Lane said, with his fist on the table. 'That within this deadlock, but almost accidentally, there was this very slight opening, this sketch of a different direction.'

'I see that,' Matthew said.

'And I knew its auspices. Of course, of course, where else would it come from? For the key to the social innovation is the technical innovation. Nobody finances Utopia, but here was a particular convergence: a major social experiment and the need to prove a set of advanced technologies. Were we to pass up that chance because the technologies, inevitably, in a capitalist world, are in capitalist hands? Where else, in that case, would we be able to go? Except back into ourselves: into disdain, into retrospect, into the long complacencies of denunciation?'

He glanced aside at Peter, who sat pale and angry: in effect ignoring Lane but watching Matthew intently.

'These are arguments,' Matthew said. 'There are other arguments. They must all be published. It must be openly decided.'

'Theoretically yes but in fact . . .'

'No. Here in fact. The last respectable reason for secrecy has gone. The land deals have happened. So now it must all be made public. Manod is not an empty space for other people's solutions. Now the people must decide.'

Robert Lane laughed. His normally grey, shrinking eyes, in the overweight face, came alight with the pleasure of a particular intelligence.

'Yes, Matthew, the people! Meaning who exactly, for your neat little vote? The people of Manod, of that valley, of that district, of Powys, of Wales, of Britain, of Western Europe? When you have the kind of decision that will affect them all?'

Peter got up.

'I don't want to be rude,' he began, in a high, strained voice.

'Yes, Peter, you do,' Lane said, quickly.

'Well I don't but I'll still say it: I'm not persuading, like Matthew. Whether all this goes public isn't your decision any longer. It will go public because I shall publish it.'

'Don't try,' Lane said, sharply. 'For your own sake, Peter, don't try.'

Peter stiffened and stared at him.

'That's it, then,' he said, and picked up his case. He looked across at Matthew. Matthew hesitated and then slowly got up. Lane stared from one to the other and then came hurriedly round his desk.

'There's a decisive meeting,' he said, urgently, 'in two days. Here. With the Minister. He wants you both at it.'

'Let him want,' Peter said.

'No,' Matthew said. 'I'll go that far. I'll wait that long.'

The others looked at him. The broken voice was so heavy, the figure so set in its dark stance, that for some moments neither could speak. The face was hard and set and very deeply lined. Under the thinning dark hair he looked, suddenly, a generation older. Far, long: the words seemed implicit in his stance, his voice, his whole being.

'All right then,' Peter said hurriedly. 'For you.'

Robert Lane breathed out deeply. He barely detained them, making the necessary arrangements for the formal meeting.

2. Matthew carried the plastic beakers through the crowded tables to the corner where Peter was sitting. He had insisted on queueing, at the long chrome counter. There were other people at the table. They could just perch on stools, resting the beakers on the table-top which was crowded with what had been left by many earlier customers; empty beakers, paper plates with fragments of food, torn bills, a soaked newspaper. It was difficult to find space for their legs among the crowded furniture and jammed cases. One of the loudspeakers for the recorded music was just above their heads. They had to push their voices to be heard through it.

'I ought to have told you before,' Peter said. 'But I wasn't just threatening. I've already had the offer.'

'What offer exactly?'

'The important offer is for a book on the whole scheme. They'll publish in six months from the time I deliver.'

'You'd use all the papers?'

'Yes. On their lawyers' advice. They think we'd get away with it.'

'We?'

'Well, me. Though their risk's the same. And what they're negotiating now is extracts—some of the really fast stuff—in one of the Sundays. It'll spread really heavy from that, before the book's even out.'

'Burning all your boats?'

'Well, is it? With the official lot, of course. But that's the point now, there's a market. The real contradiction has at last caught up with them.'

'Most of the contradictions have caught up with most of us.'

The other people at the table were leaving. They found a little more space. Matthew stretched out his legs and loosened his collar.

'Are you all right?' Peter asked.

'Yes, just the rush.'

'It's where that bugger's put you. It's all right for me, I can still walk away from it.'

'From the consultancy, of course. So can I. Did I tell you I've accepted this new job in Wales?'

'I knew you would. And that's great, don't you see? We can find these other places where we can really fight then.'

'Do you think I did it for that?'

'Well, and to get back to Wales. And it's more your job, doing the basic research, the basic history.'

'Leaving Manod to be settled by the Anglo-Belgian corporation?'

'After my stuff? Not on your life. They'll just go to the next on their list. The new Manod will be in Calabria.'

'We might regret that.'

'I shan't regret it.'

They finished their coffee. Other people came to their table. Peter, looking across at Matthew, saw that his eyes were closed.

'Are you sure you're all right?'

'Yes. Yes.'

He opened his eyes and looked around. He seemed surprised by the closeness of the people and objects around him.

'There's one more thing,' Peter said. 'If I'm not bothering you?'

'No, go on.'

'I shall do quite well from this stuff. They've paid me a good advance.'

'Yes?'

'I've put it down on a flat. I shall go to Trawsfynydd next week and bring up Beth and the baby.'

Matthew looked across at him.

'Does Beth know?' he asked.

'Yes. I wrote a long letter. And we've talked on the phone.'

'I'm glad,' Matthew said.

'Yes well, I can't explain it. It just all came together. I suppose with this fight on my hands. Because it will be quite a fight.'

'I meant I'm glad for you and Beth.'

'You separate it, do you?'

'Neither way. Just I'm glad.'

'Actually it's my mother as much as anybody I've got to thank for it. She knew what it was. Only she and Beth understood it.'

'Your mother went to Trawsfynydd. I met her.'

'Yes. She hadn't told me. But it was very important for Beth. And meanwhile, all the time, she was arranging this for me.'

'Arranging what?'

'The book. That was her. She made the real contacts.'

Matthew looked down at his hands.

'When will you actually resign?'

'Sorry?'

The low voice had been lost in the rise of the music.

'I asked when you will actually resign.'

'Well I'll come to this meeting. Since you'll still be there. Then I'll do it formally. Since in practice I've done it already.'

Matthew nodded and got up.

'I shan't resign myself. I shall probably finish my year,' he said clearly.

Peter looked disconcerted.

'But I thought . . .'

'Yes. To make it public I'd resign. When it has been fully talked through.'

'But that's an entirely false position. You'll still have months of working for a fraudulent scheme.'

'For a possibility inside it. Until the possibility ends.'

Peter faced him across the table.

'Leaving me to go public and fight it out on my own.'

'Well, you decided that yourself. You didn't ask my opinion.

185

But when you need support I shall give it. I'll confirm all that needs to be confirmed.'

'The facts won't need confirmation. What has to be confirmed is the judgment.'

'Yes. And I said. I haven't yet made it.'

Peter reached down for his briefcase.

'This is just Lane's smokescreen,' he said angrily. 'I knew it would fool you.'

'Not Lane. The proposal itself.'

Peter pushed past the end of the table. They walked out together to the street.

'Yes, Beth told me,' Peter said. 'That evening in Pontafren before the baby was born. The way you had put it to her. A dream of a country. That to give up the dream would be like giving up faith.'

'Yes. Certainly.'

'And what dream do you think it is? This sort of squalid manipulation, the speculators and bureaucrats, using a dream to screw people.'

'Their use. But if there is no other?'

'There are many others. You've lost contact, that's all, with the basic struggle.'

'The basic struggle for what?'

'For control, what else? For controlling our own sort of future.'

'Is it that still?'

'Yes, that or nothing.'

'Then I've not lost touch with it. It's the only thing I'm attempting.'

'By going on working for Lane?'

'By working where I can. By working *for*, always. And by working against only when I finally have to.'

'Well, you have to now.'

They had stopped at a crossing. A taxi swung past them. The rush of air hit their faces. Peter started to cross, as the lights changed, but Matthew did not follow him. As Peter looked back he was standing very stiffly, his eyes unfocused.

'Are you all right?'

'Yes. Yes.'

'I'd better see you back. Where are you going now?'

Matthew moved and smiled.

'It's all right. Don't worry. I'm going to where I lived.'

3. It was the end house, grey, single-fronted, with a wide bay window, where they had lived since they were married. The laburnum by the gate was still grey with last season's pods. Thick clumps of yellow crocus were flowering, under the unpruned roses, which still carried a few pale winter-withered buds.

Susan came to let Matthew in. He had given his key to the Weinbergs, the American friends who had rented their house from October to June. Whenever they were in London Susan and Matthew stayed in the house, in what had been, originally, Jack and Harry's bedroom. Now they had to put the house up for sale, with possession from June. It had been their only home. It made it easier, now, that there were already other people in it.

Tom and Louie Weinberg had been sitting with Susan in the bay-windowed front room. Tom had been correcting proofs at the desk—they still called it the bureau—that had been Harry Price's in Glynmawr.

'You look tired to death,' Louie said, getting up and making room for Matthew to sit by the fire. Tom went to the sideboard to make drinks.

'Not for me,' Matthew said.

'Hey, you've not signed the pledge?'

'It just left me,' Matthew said.

Susan came and sat beside him.

'Was it bad?' she asked, taking his hand.

'Yes, bad enough. Lane's isolated the land deals. And Peter's resigning to write the book of the affair.'

'Leaving you in the middle,' Tom said, bringing a drink to Susan.

'Leaving me nowhere, really.'

'Come on, Matt, you want it to happen. You want that city to be built.'

'Well, I want that country replenished.'

'That country? You mean Wales, or that valley?'

'Well, I could even say Britain, if you pushed me. I want the pattern to break, to some new possibility.'

'But that's what's wearing you out. You can't push a whole system.'

'Neither push it nor settle inside it.'

'I'll get some food on,' Louie said. 'But before I do, Matthew Price, let me tell you something. You look like a man who's been pushing too hard and too long. What you need now is rest, not a night or a week but years, I mean it. So you and Sue go down to Wales, take your new job quietly, leave the fighting to others.'

'Louie's right,' Susan said.

Matthew smiled.

'The prevailing wind from the Atlantic is usually more vigorous than that,' he said, looking at Tom.

'It was,' Tom said. 'It's changing. We're making the effort to settle.'

Matthew laughed.

'You may have room. We haven't. We have to change or die.'

'That's where we all are, Matt. And we're mostly . . .'

'No,' Louie said, interrupting him. 'Because there's a basic difference between people and societies. People really do die, they can't just hold it at metaphors.'

'You still have this illusion,' Tom said, pointing down at Matthew, 'that win a few, lose a few, there's still this close little process, this old English social network, where goodwill and change have some chance of coinciding. So the weight of the social order gets into your bloodstream and reform succeeds or fails in your actual body.'

'No illusion,' Matthew said. 'That always really happens.'

'As effect, right. But not as duty, as vocation: these oversize ambitions that are wearing you down.'

'Ambitions!'

'Sure, ambitions. To be arbiter, now, of that valley and that city. When you've just learned you can't be. When you've learned, as you should have known, that it's all happening out there in the world, through these major agencies.'

'I don't want to be arbiter. But I have to be involved. To be anything less is to deny my whole . . .'

'History? Matthew, you are not history. You're one man working against the grain. All you can do you've done.'

Matthew got up, slowly. Susan and Louie watched him anxiously.

'That's a kindly sentence,' he said to Tom.

'No sentence, Matt. Just the truth.'

4. It was difficult to hear, across the large oval table. The Minister, in the chair, often spoke in asides to his advisers, who sat in order of seniority on his right. Robert Lane, Matthew noticed, was three chairs down.

Matthew had had difficulty in finding a chair for himself. When he had entered the high conference room, past the heavy doors, more than thirty people were already sitting there and most of the vacant chairs were tipped inwards, as reserved, for others still standing and talking in groups. He saw Peter at one end, in a row of men with whom he was busily talking. He at last found a vacant chair, but chairs and papers had to be moved before he could squeeze in. It was very warm, even hot, in the room.

After the informal beginning there was a long and detailed report, from the man on the Minister's right: a very pale, tiny man, who pitched his voice quite extraordinarily low. And he was speaking very rapidly, as if basically only to the Minister and his immediate neighbours. Matthew held his hand to his head, trying to catch all the words. It was a closely detailed summary of the history of the project: ninety per cent of it very familiar but with new names and details coming in from time to time, with no particular signals. Two or three times, now, Matthew had heard what sounded like 'Alf's'. He felt himself getting lost. He stood up. The voice continued.

'You must forgive me,' Matthew said loudly. 'This is really very difficult to hear.'

A dozen heads were lifted and turned to him, in surprise. He had the impression that it was the movement rather than the words that had attracted their attention. The sense of the room was of words flowing without much remark.

The Minister was now looking at him. A man beyond the speaker leaned across and whispered. The Minister looked down at his papers.

'Ah, Dr Owen,' he said, genially.

'Price.'

'Of course. Dr Price. You're having some difficulty?'

'I can't hear all that's said. And there are some quite new details.'

'Well, I'm sorry. This is always a difficult room.'

He looked down again at his papers. The speaker resumed, lifting his voice slightly. Matthew remained standing. A secretary again drew the Minister's attention. Matthew saw Peter, at the end of the table, tip back his chair, smiling broadly.

'Dr Price?' the Minister said questioningly.

'There are already things I have missed.'

'Well, I'm sorry, Dr Price. I'm sure it will all come together.'

'No. There are figures and names . . .'

'I see. Well . . .'

He turned to the speaker, who looked down the long table.

'If Dr Price has some particular question?'

'Among others,' Matthew said, 'what is Alf's.'

'Ah. Yes. Yes of course. Alphs is our shorthand, I'm afraid, for Anglo-Belgian.'

'Your pet-name, in fact,' Peter said, from the far end, tipping his chair forward noisily.

'Order,' the Minister said, without anger.

'I can see that now,' Matthew said, still standing. 'But when that name was first mentioned was there not also a reference to manufacturing capacity? It was that I didn't follow.'

'I'm coming to that full exposition,' said the speaker.

'Dr Price,' said the Minister, and nodded him down. Matthew squeezed back into his chair. As the speaker resumed he noticed several of those round the table looking curiously across at him. One man spoke to his neighbour behind his hand. The quiet voice continued, through these continuing observations. Matthew controlled himself and listened.

It was now almost all new material. The scale of the development had been sharply revised downward.

O.P.P. (Overall Projected Population) was now reset at 42,000. Diffrog, as St Dyfrog came out, was now Alphs' E.C. (Exclusive Capacity). The labour base, in consequence, was now quite differently calculated. Certain marginal and speculative projects could be safely excluded, within a firm projection of sustained viability. On the other hand there was a further associated agricultural project, recently tabled by Alphs, which significantly appreciated the positive forecast. Thus the unanimous conclusion of the specialist panel was favourable.

There was a considerable silence around the large table. Most people seemed to be looking through their papers. It was the slow rhythm of men used to spending their days in meetings: doubtless one much like the other.

'We have no papers on this statement,' Matthew said.

A few heads were raised, curiously.

'Ah yes, Dr Price,' said the Minister. 'They would not have come to you. But copies are being made.'

'It's a radical recasting of the entire project. May I ask some questions about it?'

190

'Yes, of course.'

'We were given the ownership of the factories at St Dyfrog . . .'

'Alphs,' said the Minister.

'Yes. What we were not given was what they would be making.'

'Making? I thought . . .'

He looked down at his papers. His right-hand man intervened.

'Dr Price, you remember, Minister, had some difficulty in hearing. The whole point of the revised project, as it has now come from the Commissioner, is that a city built primarily to demonstrate the new energy and communications technologies will have, as its industrial centre, a significant part of their manufacture. Thus what can be seen on the ground, and working, will be also there as a manufacturing process: for sale and export, evidently.'

'You mean,' Matthew asked, 'teleprocessing equipment, district heating control systems, dispersed production control processes . . .'

'None of this was mentioned,' Peter said, joining in.

'Well the technical material . . .'

'It wasn't just that Matthew Price didn't hear. It wasn't said.'

'I rather doubt,' said the Minister, 'if this particular body is competent to review, or perhaps even to understand, the strictly technical information. On the other hand . . .'

'I'm glad you mentioned competence,' Matthew said, interrupting. 'Perhaps you don't know that Dr Owen and I were appointed as consultants, on this scheme as a whole. For some months we have been trying to review all its aspects. Yet suddenly, at this stage, what is actually being introduced is something quite different—I don't say worse or better, but it is very different.'

'You have my sympathy, Dr Price. It's often the way these things happen.'

Robert Lane came in quickly.

'I would certainly hope, Minister, that Dr Price and Dr Owen will still be asked to give their general opinions, taking account of these new proposals.'

'Well, of course, Robert, they will be most highly valued.'

Robert Lane smiled. The Minister turned a page of his papers, as if to move on.

'Just one other specific question,' Matthew said, raising his voice.

The Minister turned to look at him. His slight smile indicated a precise tension of toleration and fatigue.

'We do have other matters, Dr Price.'

'There was a passing reference to a recently proposed agricultural project. Given the nature of the development we must have details of that.'

'Would it not best come with the other . . . ?' the Minister began.

'I can satisfy Dr Price quite quickly,' said the man on his right. 'It's a new process for improving marginal upland pastures. Apparently the costs of general fertiliser improvement have been prohibitive, but this is a procedure involving the relatively inexpensive application of certain missing trace elements, based on some very recent work, and it appears that the intermediate grazing areas, always a feature of this city, are admirably suited. The demonstration, once again, will be related to in-city production.'

'Dr Price?'

'Yes, thank you. That's interesting. It's very interesting indeed.'

'Except,' Peter said, from the far end of the table, 'that it's all too good to be true.'

'I beg your pardon,' the Minister said, surprised. Peter leaned forward, nervously. He was twisting his papers in his hands.

'You can feed us this technical bullshit but everyone round this table knows what this whole scheme is about. This is a publicly financed set-up for what this particular corporation would be doing in any case. It's not a social development or even, in local terms, an economic development. It's an organized rip-off for an oil company subsidiary and a merchant bank.'

'Dr Owen, please. Order.'

'There's the technical bullshit,' Peter said, 'and then there's the community bullshit. As if any of this was being done for the people now living there or the people who will be brought there. And in fact it's being steered, fast, through a few official committees, while everyone else, including your official consultants, are kept busy looking through quite different proposals.'

'None of this is very helpful, Dr Owen,' the Minister said, quietly.

'I'm not saying it to be helpful. I'm saying it to tell you that you're not fooling anybody. And that you won't get away with it.'

The Minister clasped his hands and leaned forward. He looked along the table at Lane.

'I think, Minister . . .' Robert Lane began, but Peter had moved too quickly. Gathering up his papers and his briefcase he pushed back his chair.

'I'm resigning,' he announced. 'I shall take all this where it ought to be taken: to the public who'll be expected to finance it.'

'Dr Owen, really . . .' the Minister began, but Peter was already walking, rapidly, to the door. Robert Lane jumped up and hurried round the table to try to overtake him. Peter wrenched the door open. He tried to slam it behind him but it moved so slowly, on its heavy springs, that it did not even quite close. Robert Lane pulled it open again, to follow Peter out.

'And now perhaps after that academic interruption . . .' the Minister said easily.

'Where will the people come from?' Matthew asked, firmly. He was sitting very close to the table. He had not looked up as Peter had walked to the door.

'No really, Dr Price, this is a meeting with an agenda. We must take all these questions in a rational sequence.'

'This is the true sequence. You didn't answer Peter Owen. But one of the possible answers is where the people will come from.'

'I really cannot see how that affects it.'

'May I tell you? The feeling in Manod, in that whole district, is against being used from outside. That is also, I needn't say, a very general feeling in Wales. I don't necessarily share Dr Owen's opinions. There were several good things in the original scheme. And on balance there are more in the scheme as now revised. But the crucial factor—you must really appreciate this—is who the people are to be. For this is a country bled dry by prolonged depopulation. Not far away, in the valleys, there is a ravaged and depressed old industrial area. If it can be clearly seen that in these new ways, bringing the two needs together, a different future becomes possible, a future that settles people, that gives them work and brings them home, then through all the dislocation, through all the understandable losses and pains of change, there could still be approval, significant approval: not just the design of a city but the will of its citizens.'

'You are eloquent, Dr Price, but I don't quite clearly follow. Are you saying that this city should be confined to Welsh?'

'I don't mean nationality. I mean that the storms that have blown through that country—storms with their origin elsewhere —should now be carefully and slowly brought under control. In one place at a time, one move at a time, we should act wholly and consistently in the interests of that country, and those interests, primarily, are the actual people now there, caught between rural depopulation and industrial decline, the end of two separated orders, and there in Manod, if we could see it, is a real way beyond them. But only a real way if it belongs to the people on whose land it is being made.'

There was a long silence. Almost everyone around the table was now staring at Matthew.

'Well as to ownership, Alphs . . .' said the man on the Minister's right.

'No, Sir John, one moment,' the Minister interrupted. 'It's not just legal property Dr Price has in mind.'

'That is involved,' Matthew said. 'But these advanced designs are at the moment only technical. Yet there is a unique opportunity, just because they are technically different, to explore new social patterns, new actual social relations. And if Manod could be that . . .'

There was a noise at the door. Robert Lane slipped in and walked round to his place. He was tense and pale.

'Well thank you, Dr Price,' the Minister said, moving adroitly from the break. 'You've reminded us all of the most basic considerations. In fact more than reminded. You've lifted our eyes. You've given us perspective. We are all most grateful.'

He turned a page again. Matthew was not looking at him. After the effort of speaking he felt a long constriction of breath. There was a rising heavy pulse through his neck and shoulders. There were voices somewhere beyond this but he could not distinguish them. He hunched and sat stiffly, clenching his hands on the edge of the table. The heavy pulse was loud and resonant. He could now hear nothing beyond it.

XII

1. SUSAN moved back, quickly, as Harry and Jack neared the bottom of the stairs, carrying the heavy oak wardrobe.

'Pull back on the bloody thing, I'm getting all the weight,' Jack shouted angrily. He was sweating heavily through the shirt stretched tight across his broad shoulders.

'I am pulling, within the limits of gravity,' Harry answered, coolly.

'Now round,' Jack shouted, turning and lifting, and at the same time tossing his head to clear the hair from his eyes.

'Right,' Harry said, as they guided easily from the stairs. They had been carrying furniture and boxes for three hours since breakfast. With Matthew in hospital, and the cottage due to be vacated, they had taken time off work, hired a van, and come down to help Susan. During most of the moving they had been disagreeing, loudly: Jack shouting and Harry being maddeningly precise. Susan smiled to hear them again. It had been like this since they were children and now, as young men, they were as different and as close.

'Put it against the wall by the gate,' she said, following them out with the wardrobe.

'It's for your friends to pick up?' Harry said, walking backwards along the path.

'Yes, Modlen said they'd be up.'

It was a fine spring morning. The grass was bright green along the lane. Small leaves were opening on the high hawthorn hedge. Under the wall from the school the elder and the bramble were in full leaf and there were small yellow-green leaves at the points of the dark green mass of the holly.

'What's this stuff?' Harry asked, looking down at a spread of green shoots inside the gate.

'It's snowberry, I expect,' Susan said. 'He tried to clear it in the autumn but the roots are still there.'

'It looks good,' Harry said.

The big white hired van was now two-thirds full. There was not much more to go. When they had finished loading they were going to drive it down to Dinas, where Susan had bought a house.

The house in London was sold, but the furniture there wouldn't be moved until the Weinbergs went back to Philadelphia. When Matthew came out of hospital he could go straight to Dinas.

'Not touching Manod again at all,' he had said, wryly, to Susan.

'It was only ever temporary, love. And you're not to worry about it.'

'I think about nothing else. I see the cottage and the lane. Stronger images, now, than Glynmawr even.'

'Well Glynmawr's been so changed.'

'And all the rest that Manod means I shall carry about with me anyway.'

'Literally,' Susan said, 'since it almost killed you.'

'No. Not Manod. Nothing new hurt me. It was only the terrible pounding of the old.'

'A pounding in yourself. In your own body. And you'd already fought past your limit.'

'I did nothing at all,' he had concluded bitterly, and turned away, forced into his drugged rest.

'It wasn't too much,' Jack said, jumping up into the van.

'When it's done it never seems much,' Harry said, from the gate.

'There's still the burning,' Jack said, jumping down.

'Yes, indulge your pyromania,' Harry said, smiling. He looked across at Susan. He indicated the wardrobe.

'Why are you giving this then to these people? It's a very good one, isn't it?'

'Yes, it's good. What they call reproduction but the sounder for that.'

'Then why give it them?'

'Because Modlen's been very kind to me. Even today, when you've gone, she'll stay on and help me clean through.'

'You could have paid her.'

'No, love, not here.'

'Still a barter economy?'

'Not that, either. Just the way we help and give things to each other.'

'In the family?'

'In the place.'

She went back into the house. Harry and Jack came in, to collect the rubbish for burning. They started carrying it down the ash path of the back garden.

'He laid this path, did he?' Jack asked.

'Yes, from the fires.'

'As if he was staying here.'

'I think he would have liked to.'

They began heaping the rubbish.

'Keep it well away from the apple,' Harry said. 'It's full of bud, don't you see?'

'Perhaps you'd noticed the wind,' Jack said.

'Of course but it can scorch quite apart from the wind.'

They went on carrying the stuff for burning. One box of Matthew's papers, on the Manod project, had got among the rubbish, but Susan recognized it and carried it away to the car. When she came back Jack was crouching, lighting the fire. Harry was standing by the high hawthorn hedge, watching calmly and intently as the stapled boxes began to catch.

'Whee,' Jack shouted, as a true firebed established itself and the flames suddenly changed in intensity. Harry was still staring into the altering pile.

As the heavy white smoke started rising there was a movement at the gate from the field behind the cottages. Susan, staring past the smoke, saw Gwen Vaughan standing there. She waved and called. Gwen came into the garden.

'Cleaning up, Mrs Price?'

'Just about.'

'Only I saw the fire. I've been dragging one, over the field.'

'What, a fire?'

'Yes, I've got to it at last. That was always a really good field, only Ivor never thought much to it. There's the trees he cut when he was clearing the dingle. I've been dragging them all to burn.'

She looked across at Harry and Jack.

'You don't know my sons, Gwen.'

'Well I've seen them.'

Susan made the introductions. They all shook hands.

'Not a fire like yours will be,' Harry said, smiling.

'Yes well, Ivor said wait saw it up, only it's been there two years. And if I put my ponies in there it'll be some use again. It's the thistle and foxglove I've really got to get down.'

'I noticed the plants,' Susan said. 'It must look lovely when the foxgloves are flowering. A whole field of foxgloves.'

'For a few weeks it's beautiful. Only the more I disturb it the more they'll flower. They come up behind you where you've been working.'

'They can only germinate,' Harry said, 'when the seeds are uncovered, fully exposed to the light.'

'Is that it?' Gwen said.

Her skin was very pale under the cropped black hair. There were fresh red earth stains on her jersey and breeches. Since Ivor had married, and she had moved to Cae Glas, she had come to seem much older: in a way more settled, some of her awkwardness gone and her skin less disfigured, but also harder-looking, more resigned.

'When are you getting your trekkers?' Susan asked.

'For Whitsun, I've booked. Only Dance, as usual, is behind with the conversion. He's put Will Rees on now, as an extra man. Of course he says it'll be ready.'

'Well I hope so,' Susan said.

Jack was circling the bonfire, kicking in the unburned edges.

'And Ivor's up Waunfawr again. He won't leave it alone.'

'I've not seen him or Megan. Since my husband was ill.'

'They're all right,' Gwen said.

She stared at Susan, a very hard stare. Susan looked away.

'And Mr Price is getting better?' Gwen asked.

'Yes, they say so. Though very slowly.'

Gwen stared again, with the same hardness.

'Mrs Price, I was sorry I said all that to him. It was Dance I needed to talk to.'

'I think he understood that.'

'Once I did it come right. Only with people like that I had to look out for myself.'

'It came out very well.'

'Well I saw it did, didn't I? He knew I had trump card.'

Susan nodded. Gwen relaxed her hard stare but there was still, in her features, a quite different expression from when they had come to Manod.

'We shall get on very well down here now,' she said, firmly.

'Well I hope so.'

'I know so. The trekking will go well and I'll say this for Megan, fair play, she'll keep Ivor to it.'

'If the conditions stay right,' Susan said, cautiously.

'It's all better,' Gwen said. 'We've got through it, one way and another.'

There was the sound of a horn from the lane.

'That'll be Modlen,' Susan said.

'Yes. Well you're going today then?'

'When we've cleared up. Yes.'

'Well, I'd better say goodbye then. Though I hate saying goodbye.'

'Goodbye,' Susan said, and on a sudden impulse leaned forward and kissed Gwen's cheek. She was surprised that Gwen held closely to her for some moments, but then they separated and Gwen, quite formally, shook hands. They watched her walk back to the field where she was working and then went through to the lane.

'There you are,' Modlen shouted. 'I told him to wait.' She and Trevor were lifting the oak wardrobe into the back of their truck. Harry and Jack hurried to take Modlen's end.

'Only he's got no patience,' Modlen said, relieved. 'He's like a young dog since we've had that farm.'

The men had put the wardrobe in the truck.

'You shouldn't be lifting, Modlen,' Susan said, smiling.

'Oh this,' Modlen said, putting her hands on her swelling stomach.

'Yes, that,' Susan said, and laughed.

'I'm leaving you up here, am I?' Trevor asked.

'Aye. You want reminding of everything.'

Trevor smiled at Susan.

'I'd stay myself,' he said, 'only I'm all ends up. I've got all the ditches to clear, where the fields was all flooded. Old Preece, I should reckon, hadn't cleared them in years.'

Susan explained to Jack and Harry that Trevor and Modlen were now in Church Farm, at St Dyfrog.

'St Dyfrog? Isn't that where . . . ?' Jack started to ask.

'Yes, where we asked the way,' Harry said quickly. Susan noticed Trevor looking at them. But then Modlen took over.

'I've brought up dinner,' she said, taking a basket from under the wall.

'Modlen, you shouldn't have.'

'Don't worry, I've put his on the timer.'

She turned away from Trevor. And he was impatient to go.

'I'd better say goodbye, Trevor. I may not see you later,' Susan said.

'That's right, Mrs Price. And give our good wishes to your husband.'

They shook hands and Trevor drove off.

'Get a bit of room to move, with the men out of the way,' Modlen said.

'Well Harry and Jack should eat before they drive to Dinas.'

'Don't worry now. I've brought plenty.'

They ate Modlen's food, standing around the open back door. Then Harry and Jack were ready to go.

'You go along with the boys,' Modlen said to Susan. 'I'll finish up here.'

'No, I'll see it clear. And I've got to lock up.'

'I can take the key down to Dance's.'

'Well thanks but I'd rather leave it at the office in Pontafren.'

Modlen looked at Susan.

'You don't want to worry about old Dance,' she said, seriously.

'It isn't that. I'd just prefer not to see him.'

'Or that Juliet,' Modlen said. 'Though she gives you the creeps.'

'It's an illness,' Susan said.

'Well, meanness is an illness with the both of them.'

'I meant, about her food.'

'So did I. But all she does is what they tell us.'

'So does her husband, I'm beginning to think.'

'Him!' Modlen said. 'He's just out for his own.'

'Yes. Still, you and Trevor got your farm from it all. I'm very glad about that.'

'Glad! You should see Trevor. He's like a great boy with it all.'

'Well, I hope it all goes well.'

'He'll make it go well. The both of us will. If they leave us to get on with it.'

'They may,' Susan said.

'Only it's what it wants, round here,' Modlen said. 'A bit of new life put back in it.'

They worked through the cottage, vacuuming and sweeping. Then Modlen insisted on mopping out the kitchen, working backwards to the door.

'Right,' she said at last. 'That'll do till the builders arrive.'

They carried the last things to the car. Susan was driving Modlen back down to St Dyfrog. When they were sitting in the car Susan waited, looking around.

'Sorry to say goodbye to it?' Modlen asked cheerfully.

'Of course. In a way.'

'You'll be better somewhere else. And Mr Price,' Modlen said.

Susan started the car. She drove slowly down past Pentre, where Trevor was turning the tractor in the yard. She turned past the Evening Star and down the long high-banked pitch to the

Dowy. Where the roads joined she slowed, at the steep blind corner.

'You're right to watch out,' Modlen said. 'We call this bit the Wall of Death.'

2. Matthew looked much older, with his glasses and thin hair, his neck bare and drawn above the dark red dressing gown. He was reading so intently that he did not notice his visitor arrive. There was already so much movement around the other beds in the ward.

'Still working then, Matthew?' Robert Lane said, looking down.

Matthew looked up and took off his glasses. Then he pulled himself higher in the bed.

'I'm sorry. I didn't expect . . .'

'I asked Susan if I could come.'

'Well of course.'

'She was doubtful, actually. I think she'd have liked to say no.'

Matthew put down his papers.

'The messenger and the message?' he said, smiling.

'Yes well, I did let you in for all this. And I came to say that I'm sorry.'

'That's extraordinary. I'm not sorry.'

Lane sat on the chair by the bed. He put a punnet of strawberries on the table which was already crowded with bottles, glasses and books.

'I've never in my life felt so guilty,' Lane said, 'as during that last meeting, just before you were taken ill. I'd gone out, you remember, to try to catch Peter. I was still very angry and then I looked across at you. Because Peter was all right, he could simply walk out, make a new career on the scandal.'

'No. That's not fair. He's fighting what he thinks the real cause. And I expect he's right.'

'Right or wrong, he's consistent. That's all I'm really trying to say. But there were you still talking to them, about new kinds of community, new social relations. And Fisher doing his piece about raising our eyes, giving us a new vision.'

'I remember it,' Matthew said, turning deliberately to look at him.

'I don't know how to describe it. I only felt, at first, my own guilt. Because I looked at you sitting there, I didn't then know

201

you were ill, but I saw it, suddenly . . . No, I can't really say it.'

Matthew moved higher in the bed.

'Go on,' he said, harshly.

'Well I saw it, suddenly, as a kind of heroic absurdity. Heroic, certainly, because at all times and in all places you keep saying the same thing, and the right thing. But absurd, also, because of its wild incongruity. Saying it there, to them, and as if you had only to say it. There, within that last, disastrous and quietly spoken carve-up, that final operation of the prevailing forces and the decisive priorities. And within it, taking part in it, you just sat there, stiffly, and you were talking, still, as if it was the beginning of the world.'

Matthew looked away. He stared down at his hands on the hard white hospital sheets.

'You mean, don't you, I was just talking to myself? To and for myself?'

'No, that would be very much easier. Because you are still, don't you see, really talking for most of us?'

'Then there is no problem,' Matthew said, shortly.

'Oh yes,' Lane said, 'there is the problem of the system. And remember it still rules the world.'

Matthew looked away, along the ward. At the other beds there were mostly family visitors. There was a good deal of smiling, through the spurts of conversation, but he had learned, from other days, to know the tiredness from the beds.

'What will happen?' he asked.

'We still can't be sure. It's through the Commission. The Department wants it. And on balance the Government wants it. There's quite a complicated package.'

'And Peter's campaign?'

'Will be a nuisance, certainly. But not more than a nuisance unless they can prove illegality.'

'In the information for the land deals?'

'And in some other transactions. But it could all be settled, well before then.'

Matthew looked again along the ward.

'Is that why you came to see me?' he asked suddenly.

He was astonished at the effect of his question. Lane's face seemed to crumple, the clear pink skin flushing deeply, the over-weight features seeming to blur into nothingness, the shrinking grey eyes badly hurt.

202

'If you think that, Matthew, I must go.'

'I'm sorry. I've got harder. The effect of this is hardening.'

'Well I know.'

'But if you're asking what I shall do I can tell you. I'll put in my formal report, my consultant's report. And I shall at the same time make it available to all the Welsh authorities and organizations. I have several people I'm working with. We shall hold our own public hearings, in Wales.'

Lane didn't answer. He was tapping his lower lip with the middle finger of his right hand. Then he bent his wrist, pointing his hand, palm upward, towards Matthew.

'This is what I'm working on now,' Matthew went on, quickly. 'All the actual Welsh material, all the work and the thinking that is being done in the country but that wasn't in your files.'

'I know some of it,' Lane said.

'I intend to know all of it. And to bring it together. On Manod.'

Robert Lane sighed.

'It will be a lot of work, Matthew. Are you sure you have the strength?'

'For a long fight, yes. Yes, we do.'

'That wasn't what I was asking.'

'No, but it's still the answer.'

Over Lane's shoulder Matthew saw Susan coming into the ward, through the heavy glass doors. He smiled. Lane turned, following his look, and when he saw Susan got up quickly. He met her at the end of the bed and shook hands.

'I'll leave him in your good hands,' he said, warmly. Susan had looked once, intently, at Matthew, but now turned back to his visitor.

'It was kind of you to come, Dr Lane,' she said, without emphasis.

She stood quietly at the end of the bed until he had shaken hands with Matthew. She did not look at him as he left.

3.   Matthew stood looking down at the stone-strewn river, between the chapels in Glynmawr. It was by the old road now. The new straight road for the lorries was thirty yards back, cutting the entrance to the lane which had been curved to make an indirect entry. The old railings by the Honddu had been removed; there was now a chain-link fence, with concrete posts.

—You got a nice book then, I see, Will?

—No.

He could see his father at the bottom of the steep bank, one foot slipped into the river, reaching out for the floating book.

'Like a quite separate life,' he said, turning to Susan.

'Well, it's changed, love.'

'Yes. And that's as much as we can say.'

They had driven down through the village, and had stopped first at the station. The signalbox was still standing, and there was a signalman at its window, but the rest of the station had been flattened, the platforms and waiting rooms ground down into hardcore, an unmarked border to the intercity line. Farther into the village, the straight line of the new motor road had changed the shape of the valley and its settlement. Indeed, where he had looked for the school he had seemed to be somewhere quite different, for the school itself, and the master's cottage beside it, had utterly disappeared, and the high hedges beyond it. He knew where it must have been, at a second look. It was exactly where a pair of new houses now stood. The house nearest the busy road, marked *Show House*, stood on what had formerly been the infants' classroom and the playground. *Laborare est orare. Benedicite, omnia opera.* Glynmawr Non-Provided!

But then they had left the car in the new chapel car park, a corner of the field from Tynewydd that had been divided by the road. They walked up the old road, past the chapels and the shop. The wall from the shop steps was covered with ferns and fine moss. An old sheepdog, with milky eyes, was lying in the middle of the potholed road. He watched them, indifferently, as they passed.

In the next field the old brook had been filled in and the water was flowing down a deep concrete channel under the hedge. The trees by the brook had all gone and there was now a fine open view to the west, to the dark ridge of Brynllwyd, beyond the railway and the tump and the houses and barns in the steeply rising fields.

They stood together, looking up at the fields and the mountain. Matthew pointed out the pine trees that were called the Ship, and the sheepwall beyond it, and the sharp notch in the ridge that was an Iron Age earth-work. He was breathing more easily as he showed her, but she still watched him anxiously.

'Five lines through now,' he said, turning. 'Old road, tramroad, this road, railway, new road.'

'A place they need to pass through,' Susan said, laughing.

They turned and walked back to the car.

'Shall I drive up the lane?' Matthew said.

'Well if you want to, but I can drive.'

'Just this bit,' Matthew said.

He crossed the new road, carefully, and drove round the indirect entry. The lane rose steeply, almost at once. The trees were arched over it, from the high banks, which were green with fern and wild garlic and ivy. Then round the long curve the houses came into sight. Matthew stopped the car. Back to the west they could see now the spurs beyond Brynllwyd, lying open to the distance in their extraordinary colours, ranging from a deep olive-green through shades of mauve and blue to the dark purple, almost black, of the northern scarps.

'Shall we just walk through?'

'Yes, love, as you like.'

They passed the three larger houses. One of them had a sign out offering Bed and Breakfast. Behind them, by the big holly, was the workshop converted to two cottages, Llwyn Celyn, in one of which Matthew had been born. Across the side lane was the larger stone house that his father and mother had moved to, after he had left home. He stood looking from one house to the other. The doors of both were open, on the fine afternoon, but there was nobody about. He walked to the gate of the second house and put his hand, gently, on the gatepost. Then he turned, looking across. The high chimney of the cottage had again been faced with cement. The bedroom window under it was open.

Susan was watching him carefully.

'All right then?' she said.

'Sure. Fine.'

'We'd better get on.'

'Yes.'

He was still staring at the cottage. Under the open window there was a large galvanized water butt. As he stared at it he caught the bitter smell of soaked wood and stagnant water, the sour air breathing from every pore of the wood. When he had leaned over that other butt, as a boy, a pattern of reflections —the jointed pipe, the gutter, the tall chimney—had stirred and dissolved below the dark surface of the water. It had been the month of his going away.

He followed Susan back down the lane. They stood by the car, looking out at the long ribbed spurs of the mountains.

'This is really very like Manod,' Susan said.

'Not the detail.'

'No but the position, the feel, the perspective.'

'Yes, that's what made it so difficult. I mean it disturbed the inquiry. Because when it comes to sustaining or changing, or put it harder, to growth or replacement, I can't only inquire, I'm at once involved and confused.'

'That was why your opinion mattered. And why Lane invited it.'

'Opinion, yes. But I couldn't resolve it. All I've really got to know are the pressures. The conflicting pressures.'

They got into the car. Susan drove slowly down the lane and out to the new straight road.

'You say Tom Meurig's coming tomorrow?'

'Yes, and some of his friends.'

'You must take it very quietly. You can only do just so much.'

They took the Gwenton bypass, looking across at the town, now ringed with new estates. The green dome of the Town Hall still stood prominently at its centre, catching the sun. They turned, across the bridge, for the road to the heads of the valleys. After climbing away from the river they stopped at a layby, under a limestone cliff. They got out and looked back north and west.

They could see far into Wales: to the north Brynllwyd, the Holy Mountain, the Beacon, the high cleft of the Saint's Pass; to northwest the blue hills above the Afren, from east of Nantlais across to Manod; to the west the successive ranges, into a far distance, until the last shapes of the mountains could not be clearly distinguished from clouds.

Where they were standing, looking out, was on a border in the earth and in history: to north and west the great expanses of a pastoral country; to south and east, where the iron and coal had been worked, the crowded valleys, the new industries, now in their turn becoming old. There had been a contrast, once, clearly seen on this border, between an old way of life and a new, as between a father living in his old and known ways and a son living differently, in a new occupation and with a new cast of mind. But what was visible now was that both were old. The pressure for renewal, inside them, had to make its way through a land and through lives that had been deeply shaped, deeply committed, by a present that was always moving, inexorably, into the past. And those moments of the present that could connect to a future were then hard to grasp, hard to hold to, hard to bring together to a rhythm, to a movement, to the necessary shape of a quite different life. What could now be heard, momentarily, as this actual movement, had conditions of time, of growth, quite different from the conditions of any single life, or of any father and son.

'Are you ready to go on?' Susan asked, looking back from the land to the man standing stiffly beside her.

'Yes, love. Yes we must.'